Pastures

By:

John Sterling Bridges

Pastures
By: John Sterling Bridges

Copyright C 2021 by John Sterling Bridges

KDP ISBN 9798594233294

PASTURES

CHAPTER 1

The sun beat down mercilessly on the emerging fruit while deep below the surface the ancient vine's root structure strained to inch it's way deeper into the rocky substrate in a quixotic search for moisture. Ladybugs, released during a club member luncheon the previous weekend, were busy about their business of devouring leafhopper nymphs. Rose bushes planted at the start of each vine row were in a state of wild and abundant bloom. And, the stallion in the neighboring estate's dressage training facility was nickering into the breeze. It was a day like most in the Pastures.

Parker Gillette rounded the turn from the narrow country road into the estate's driveway in his fresh-off-the-showroom-floor Lexus LX 570, and a chirping tire squeal invaded the moment. He came to a skidding stop just outside the gate and hastily punched in the access code. As the giant bronze barrier, with the engraved insignia, "Pastures of Bounty," slowly opened, the impatient son of master vintner Armand Gillette throttled his idling engine. He loved the sound of power, artificial as it was, and dreamed of the real power he would wield as soon as the old man passed.

He fishtailed through the gate before it was completely open and heard his rear bumper thump against it as he sped past. Cursing under his breath, Parker groaned, "Brand new car already has a ding. Stinking gate -- gotta have Pedro fix that piece of junk. I hate this run down old farm." He cursed again and complained to himself as he raced up the winding driveway leading to the main house.

"This old farm," as he referred to it, was, in fact, a state-of-the-art vineyard that occupied much of the Gillette family's 420 acre Carmel Valley estate known as Casa de Abundante which annually produced between 20,000-25,000 cases of some of the finest wine in all of California. The property had been in the family for 82 years.

Although the Gillette surname dated back to the time of the Norman Conquest and the origins of the family's wealth could be traced to eleventh century England, Armand's line had settled in Spain in 1583. Wine had been in their blood and the soil of vineyards under their nails since 1825. Armand was third generation American and had succeeded his father and grandfather in the ownership of the estate and its crown jewel, Casa de Abundante, which translated meant Home of Bounty.

Although Parker was the second son of his generation, he was nonetheless the presumptive heir to take over the family business, the throne as he liked to call it, since his older brother, James, had been killed the year before during a Formula One race in Monaco. The boy's death sent Armand into a terrible depression from which he had yet to emerge. Bitter about fate's plucking of his beloved firstborn, the old patriarch had become an angry and mean-spirited recluse, a self-exiled prisoner in his own castle.

"Where is Pedro?" Parker screamed as he burst into the portico of the grand Spanish revival home.

"I need to see him, and I need to see him right now!"

Receiving no response, other than the whisper of the uncomfortably hot wind, he next threw open the fifteen foot high, hand carved, solid Mahogany door and stormed into the foyer of the house. "I said where is Pedro?" he bellowed, even louder this time, his voice echoing off the walls.

"Hush, you beast. Father is trying to rest. Show some respect for once in your life," scolded Gabriella, Parker's 26-year-old younger sister, in whispered condemnation. "He had a difficult time last night. The doctor just left. Papa desperately needs to sleep."

Parker didn't care much for his sister. She had always seemed to be their father's favorite, even before James died. Maybe it was because she reminded him of their mother Maria, who had passed away years before following a difficult battle with cancer. Whatever the reason, he perceived her as a threat to his ownership and control of the kingdom. He didn't know what his father's will said, but he feared it might disproportionately favor the girl. So, being careful

6

always to play his political cards discreetly, especially when it came to family, he copped an apologetic attitude.

"I'm sorry, Ella. I didn't know. I'm just so frustrated with the lack of maintenance around here. I think maybe we ought to just fire Pedro and be done with it. As far as I'm concerned, he's pretty much good for nothing. Where is Dad?"

"He's upstairs in the parlor. It is cooler there than in his bedroom. Sometimes I wonder why they never installed air conditioning in this place. I know the breeze usually keeps things cool, but on days like today, when it doesn't, it's just plain miserable."

The perspiration anointing Gabriella's face made her look even more celestial than usual. Her smooth, flawless skin, dark brown eyes, high cheekbones and silky black shoulder length hair, which was tied up into a ponytail due to the heat of the day, would make any runway model jealous. Couple her beauty with her intellect, a summa cum laude Stanford graduate, and CPA, it was no wonder Parker was worried and insecure.

The two were interrupted by the sound of footsteps clip-clopping toward them on the terra cotta tile flooring that led to the grand foyer from the dining area.

A demure and professional voice, with a slight Hispanic accent, said, "Mr. Parker, Ms. Ella, would you like for me to fix you a sandwich? We have some tri-tip roast leftover from last night's dinner."

The polite request came from Shelby Garcia, the estate's house manager, and chef. She had been with the Gillettes for nearly 21 years and was practically a member of the family. Her mother had worked in a similar position for Armand's father. Tenure, which usually stemmed from loyalty, discretion, and hard work, was a valued commodity at Casa de Abundante. Most of the estate staff had worked there for more than 15 years.

"Yes, thank you, that would be nice Shelby," Ella answered. "And please also prepare some soup for Papa when he wakes. In addition to rest, the doctor also said it is imperative that he eats. He has lost twenty pounds in the past month and, as we all know, he doesn't have it to lose. He's looking terribly gaunt these days."

"I'll pass, Shelby," Parker said curtly. "I was out late last night with, uh, Cindy something from Pebble Beach, and we just ate breakfast a half hour ago." Then looking at his sister with a sinister smirk and a raised an eyebrow, he added, "Late night, late morning ... if you know what I mean."

"You're pathetic and disgusting, brother. Sometimes I wonder how we could have come from the same parents," Ella chided.

Hearing the biting banter which, sadly, was the norm between the two, Shelby quietly excused herself and disappeared back into the kitchen. With no further word to her brother, Ella abruptly turned and followed her.

Left alone in the cavernous space, Parker stepped back outside to the portico and was momentarily blinded by the sun. The brightness served as a sudden and painful reminder of his hangover and splitting headache. He cursed under his breath and reached into his front pocket for a bottle of pills. After hastily opening it, he raised the orange colored container to his mouth and gulped several of the small white capsules. Wincing at the bitter flavor released as he chewed, he cursed again and returned to his car.

As he turned the car around to leave he thought, *I don't know why I pay this family any mind at all. Under Ella's watchful eye, the old man could hang on for years. What a pain that would be.*

Having forgotten why he raced up to the estate in the first place, Parker pondered his next move while impatiently waiting for the gate to open again. This time he made sure it completed its swing before he drove through.

"Hmm," he muttered favorably, "might as well go to the Club and work out. Maybe Cassie will be there, and I can make some time with her." His mind wandered for a moment, and then a crooked smile emerged as he checked the status of his beard stubble in the rearview mirror, "Yeah ... she is so fine. Parker, you definitely need to make some time with that girl."

The Club, as Parker called it, was officially known as the Cachagua Golf and Country Club. It was the oldest and most prestigious private club in Carmel Valley, and only the elite of the elite were invited to partake in its pleasures. Parker didn't play golf or tennis, but he did enjoy swimming, or at least he pretended to as a justification for lounging poolside and hunting for prey behind his polarized Ray-Ban sunglasses. He was also quite fond of the well-stocked bar in the dark paneled, leather-appointed, men's smoking room where he regularly plied his expertise as a poker player. Texas Hold'em was his game of choice which he won far more often than not.

Because it was Saturday, the Club was more crowded than usual, which was to Parker's liking. To him, it meant more girls at the pool. After a quick twenty minutes in the gym, ten spent doing sit-ups to put a shine on his already rock hard abs and the other ten doing curls with free weights to pump up his biceps and enhance the appearance of his tattoo of the constellation Orion which was strategically inked on his right arm, he walked shirtless out to the pool deck. The pills he had popped were finally taking effect, and his headache was waning while his buzz was building.

He walked by the pool bar and grabbed a two finger Jack Daniels, no ice, before selecting a chaise lounge that provided him with an optimal view of the pool deck area.

Once situated, Parker took a long minute to admire himself. His eight-pack stomach glistened in the direct sun, and his cleanly shaven chest created just the right amount of shadow to accentuate his pecs. The veins in his blood infused arms popped and his lean, muscular thighs and calves rivaled those of Michelangelo's David in the main square of Florence, Italy.

Satisfied with his look at that moment he mused, *I mean, who wouldn't want me? Every girl in her right mind should want me, but only the lucky ones will get me. The hunter Orion would be proud of my physique as would his god Zeus, though Zeus might be jealous that my body rivals his.*

Turning his attention from himself and while safely ensconced behind his dark glasses, he secretly ogled every woman at the pool, but he was looking for one in particular. He was looking for Cassie.

Cassie Weston was a 24-year-old blonde beauty queen from Sedona, Arizona, whose family had moved to Carmel Valley just twenty months earlier. She was a picture of physical perfection at 5' 6" 117 pounds and a literal beauty queen, having been crowned Miss Teenage Arizona when she was 18. Since that time she had been aggressively pursuing a modeling career and was doing quite well for herself. Her most recent accomplishment was to be scheduled for a Sports Illustrated Swimsuit Edition photo shoot in Puerto Vallarta, Mexico. She had no guarantee of actually being featured in the magazine when it was to be published the following February, but to hear her tell it, she was a shoo-in for the cover.

Employing her catwalk saunter, Cassie breezed onto the pool deck fifteen minutes after Parker had arrived. The wait had driven him nearly mad, and unbecoming his cooler-than-ice facade he hopped up out of his lounge chair as soon as he saw her. He waved in her direction, but then caught and berated himself.

Check yourself, dude. You can't look like you want it. You've got to make 'them' want it.

Having effectively self-corrected, Parker dropped his hand wave and instead walked casually in Cassie's direction, feigning conversation with another fellow who happened to walk by. He then stopped at the bar, leaned on the faux tiki hut countertop, and pretended to check his watch, all the while keeping a clandestine eye on the object of his desire -- when she got to within ten feet, Parker made his move.

"Hey, Cass, what's up. You're looking perfect as always. Want a margarita?"

"Sure Parker thanks. I think I will. And, might I say, you're looking pretty good yourself."

And thus, their afternoon conversation, which remained as shallow as the children's wading pool, commenced.

Two hours, several drinks, and a couple of cooling dips in the pool later, Cassie stood to leave. As she slipped her Daisy Duke cut-offs back on, Parker whined, "Hey, what's the matter. Where are you going, babe? I'm not ready to leave just yet. Why don't you stay for another hour and maybe we can drive to Carmel and do some wine tasting. What do you say?"

"Tempting offer," Cassie responded, "but I told my father I'd be home by four. He and mom have invited our new neighbors over for dinner, and they want to introduce me."

"New neighbors -- did someone finally buy the Granger place? I didn't think that run down old farm would ever sell. It's in horrible shape, and they were asking a small fortune."

"Yep -- some family from Napa bought it. Daddy says they're planning to restore the farmhouse and convert the barn into a fancy tasting room or something. Apparently, money wasn't an issue for them. Daddy says their interest was in the dirt, not the buildings. I'll let you know what else I learn from the dinner conversation. Maybe we can get together for tasting tomorrow. I'll call you then -- toodles."

While Parker hated to see her go, he enjoyed watching her leave.

***

"So, what do you think of the place, son?" William Wingate asked his 29-year-old only son, Jacob, as the two stood next to the decaying barn structure and looked out over the tired and weed infested vineyard to the west of it.

"I can definitely see it, dad: Bountiful Pastures - Carmel. It's a brilliant idea, and I think this land is perfect. We've been looking for an opportunity to broaden the appeal of our brand and expand our market. This move can accomplish both. And like I told you, I'll be glad to live here in Carmel Valley for as long as it takes to get this up and running."

"Excellent, Jacob, excellent. I'm so glad you approve. I agree this is a perfect fit for what we have wanted to do. Bountiful Pastures - Napa is comfortably positioned as number two in sales up north, so it's time we expand our horizons to the south. Wine Enthusiast Magazine named Monterey County as one of the best-kept secrets in America, and we are going to capitalize on that by getting in before the industry explodes here as it did back home. Carmel Valley is just like Napa was in the 80s when we first moved there. I know you'll do us proud, son, and you'll have the full backing of the Wingate name and our considerable expertise and resources.

"We already have the rootstock ready to send down and plant. All we have to do is prep the land. Our team has assessed the soil and microclimate, and it is perfect for Chardonnay and Pinot Noir. I think we may try a little Petite Sirah and Merlot as well. But the varietal I'm most excited about is Cabernet Pfeffer. I finally managed to buy some of the Pfeffer vines I had my eye on last month, and I think we'll give them a go down here also. I know Pfeffer is normally used only as a blending wine, but I'm hoping we can create a market for it as a stand-alone varietal."

"It never hurts to try, dad," Jacob replied. "That's what made BP - Napa so profitable … trying new ideas and blends. People are looking for innovation, and we want to be ahead of that curve. Pfeffer is precisely what we need to achieve that. I've read the soil tests, and they suggest the conditions here match up pretty well with a vineyard in San Benito County where that grape is doing great.

"The only big question I have about our expansion plans on this land is water. That old 1919 deed confirms we have the rights to a spring on the neighbor's land to the north, but they've got quite a wine operation going over there themselves. I sure hope we don't have any conflict with them over water rights. I'm going to make it a point to get to know them right away and hopefully put them at ease. I'm going to try to convince them that the Napa motto should apply equally well here, 'if one of us succeeds, we all succeed.'"

Changing the subject, William reminded, "It's just about time for us to leave for dinner with the Westons. They're the family on the south end of the valley, down by the creek. They're not wine people; they're horse people. They also have a daughter about your age. They are fairly new to the valley, too. I think they moved here just a couple of years ago. The father, Charles, is a fine gentleman. I spoke with him several times before we closed escrow. He spoke very highly of Carmel Valley and encouraged our purchase. He and his wife, Ariana, both seem like real salt-of-the-earth type people. I'm looking forward to dinner with them. I'm bringing them a few bottles of our 2012 Cab as a thank you gift."

The two men arrived at the Weston home promptly at 4:30 p.m., per the invitation, and were greeted at the door by both Charles and Ariana Weston. After pleasantries were exchanged in the entryway, the group gradually moved through the expansive living room toward the poolside area and garden in the back.

While walking through the living space, Jacob took note of the architecture and decor. It was definitely in keeping with what his father had said about them being horse people. The hardwood floors looked to have been professionally "distressed" and in front of the giant rock fireplace on the west wall was a spectacular cowhide throw rug. The furniture was a combination of rustic wood and worn leather. In one corner he noticed a sawhorse with a beautiful leather saddle on it and hung from the wall immediately above the unique seat was a Texas-sized set of longhorns. The huge wrap around couch facing the mantle looked comfortable enough to swallow you whole. But it was the art that gave away the wealth of the family. On a grand burl wood table that occupied the center of the room stood a 32-inch tall bronze statue of a bucking bronco. Jacob recognized the piece as one of Remington's most famous, and aptly titled, "Bronco Buster."

When Jacob stopped for a moment to admire the intricacies of the piece, Ariana offered, "You have an excellent eye, Jacob. It is one of the originals cast in 1903 by the Roman Bronze Works Company. It's one of my favorites because Charles bought it for me on our 8th wedding anniversary. The 'bronze' anniversary, you know?"

Jacob had no idea about such anniversary traditions but nodded affirmatively anyway. "And this painting over the fireplace," Jacob said as he moved toward the cavernous opening in the wall, "is that a Russell?"

"Oh, bravo, bravo, you do know your western art don't you! That is 'the' original of that piece. The Director of the Charlie Russell museum in Great Falls, Montana, has invited us to display it in the museum. We are thinking about it because that way so many others will be able to enjoy it, too."

Jacob emitted an audible whistle indicating he was impressed ... not only with the value of the painting but with the apparent wealth of their hosts.

Once outside the elders took seats at an umbrella-shaded table and chatted while enjoying fresh, hand-squeezed lemonade and a tray of various crackers and cheeses. As he sipped on the lemonade, Charles said, "William, you really must have a taste of this cheese. It comes from a small shop in Los Banos in the Central Valley. In my opinion, it is easily the best Peppercorn-Jack in the world. Please help yourself."

Jacob, meanwhile, strolled aimlessly around the backyard continuing his subtle reconnaissance of the property. The pool was, like everything else about the place, large. The underwater surface had been cast to look like a rocky outfall pool beneath a waterfall, and, of course, there was the obligatory waterfall which offered an impressive height of 12 feet. To the left, and just beyond the splash zone of the fall, was a built-in spa area that looked like it could comfortably seat a dozen guests at a time. A more intimate spa for four was cleverly tucked behind the waterfall landing area. A separate dark blue, two-lane, lap pool accented the eastern edge of the fenced portion of the yard. The landscaping was lush and floral. It was evident that Mrs. Weston fancied herself a rosarian as more than 50 different varieties of the thorned beauties graced the half-acre garden.

"I hope the lemonade is to your liking," Charles continued. "The fruit comes from the estate here. We know you are wine folks, but we don't drink alcohol. Of course, most of our guests love wine, which comes as no surprise in Carmel Valley, so rest assured your generous gift of Cabernet will be well enjoyed. And we'll be proud to tell everyone the story of your gift and that you live just down the road here in the Pastures."

CHAPTER 2

When Jacob turned back toward the patio table, his eyes fell on her for the first time. Cassie Weston was approaching from the house wearing a short, yellow, halter-top sundress. Her smart Kentucky Derby style hat, tilted slightly to the left, provided the perfect fashion accent.

All thoughts about Western art collections and the enormity of the Weston's ranch house and the size of the pool and the beauty of the landscaping and the zest of the lemonade immediately disappeared when she entered his vision. To say Jacob was wowed would be a severe understatement. He was, in a word, star-struck, and wholly taken by her outward perfection.

Cassie waved to her parents demurely and then skipped up to her father and gave him a cute peck on the cheek.

"Hi, daddy. I'm so sorry I missed our guests' arrival, but I'm here now and would love to meet our new neighbors."

William extended his hand to the younger Weston. "Hello, you must be Cassie. Your father has told me all about you, and I must say it is a genuine pleasure to meet you, my dear." Hailing Jacob to come join them he continued, "And this is my son, Jacob. Jacob, this is the Weston's daughter, Cassie."

Walking over to the group, Jacob accidentally clipped the corner of a lounge chair and stumbled a bit. Catching himself awkwardly, he extended his hand and said, "Hi, uh, I'm Jacob. Sorry about the not-so-grand arrival. I guess I was a bit distracted and forgot to look where I was going."

Coyly, Cassie took his hand and shook it firmly. Smiling slightly, she asked a question, though she was already well aware of the answer.

"Distracted by what?"

Jacob offered an innocent, sophomoric grin in reply, but said nothing, knowing she already knew.

"Well," Ariana broke in, "let's move to the larger table under the awning. Dinner will be served momentarily."

Not missing a beat, Cassie waited for Jacob to sit and then quickly sat in the seat directly across from him, choosing to rely more on her non-verbal communication skills than her conversational repertoire.

The mealtime banter was fairly generic, as would be expected for an initial meet and greet. Proper first impressions, expressing interest but not opinion, were critical in a setting like this. William was a master in this arena as was Charles. Ariana was the more talkative of the group, so the men allowed her to carry most of the conversational flow.

As the meal drew to closure and the conversation began to wane, Cassie initiated for the first time.

"Jake, I mean, Jacob, by the way, which do you prefer?"

"Yeah, uh, Jacob is fine, sure." Then completing the sentence in his mind, he thought, *actually, whatever you want to call me will be perfectly fine, gorgeous.*

"Have you been down to the stream yet? It's my favorite part of the property," Cassie said.

Without waiting for an answer, Cassie then asked, "Daddy, would you mind if I took Jacob down to see the treehouse by the pond?"

"Not at all, sweetie, you two kids run along and have some fun. We'll probably serve dessert in a half hour or so if you're interested," Charles said.

"Thanks, daddy -- then please excuse us, everyone, I'm going to show Jacob my secret place."

Cassie hopped up from the table and floated over to where Jacob was seated and still trying to take it all in. She then pulled on the back of his chair the way a gentleman might otherwise do for a lady.

"Come with me, Mr. Wingate," Cassie said, pretending to be formal. 'I've got a special surprise to show you."

Though not needing permission, out of respect, Jacob glanced at his father who smiled his approval. The two then exited by way of a gravel path that meandered through the rose garden.

"Looks like the kids are hitting it off already," Charles observed.

"Yes," Ariana followed. "I like your boy, William. He has a good eye for Western art. He knew all about our Remington."

"Thank you," William replied. "You are both most gracious. I can tell we will become good neighbors. You know, he may not show it, but I think Jacob may harbor just a bit of trepidation about settling here in Carmel Valley. Except for his college years away at Princeton, he has always lived with us in Napa. I'm genuinely excited for him to launch off on his own, and knowing he'll have friends like you nearby will put his mother and me at ease a bit."

"Well, you can count on us if any need arises," Charles replied. "It's only been two years since we moved here from Sedona ourselves, so the pains of breaking into a new community are still somewhat fresh for us, too. But, all in all, I think your Jacob will fit in here extremely well. And Cassie has had no trouble assimilating. She already knows many of the young people in the valley and will be an excellent friend for him to have."

Not having a shy bone in her body, as soon as they exited the formal rose garden and were beyond their parents' field of view, Cassie grabbed Jacob's hand and pulled him along as she began to jog down the path that gradually turned from gravel to natural dirt.

"Come on, Jacob, you're going to love this!"

Twenty yards farther and they arrived at the stream which was flowing gently in a southwesterly direction. The bed was only about fifteen feet wide, and the bottom was plainly visible, but the flow was steady. Cassie kicked off her sandals and waded into the mid-calf-deep water.

"Ooh, that always feels so good on a warm day."

Tilting her head ever so slightly to the left and tossing her blonde mane furtively in his direction, she beckoned, with a curled finger, for Jacob to follow. Enjoying the flirtation, Jacob slipped out of his loafers and waded in, giving no mind to his trousers getting wet.

Cassie reiterated, "Isn't the water just heavenly?"

"Absolutely," Jacob said with a broad smile displaying his perfect white teeth. "Now, what was that you said about a treehouse?"

She giggled. "Oh, it's just upstream from here." Reaching her hand toward him, Cassie said, "come on, let's walk in the creek."

The streambed was covered with smooth gray and white cobble that was surprisingly easy to walk on, but being unfamiliar with the place, Jacob kept his head down to focus on each step. He didn't want to stumble again as he had earlier. The clarity of the water was impressive, and Jacob watched curiously as a small brook trout swam by him. He bent over and brought a handful of the streaming water up to his lips and tasted it.

"Cassie, this water is very clean and fresh. Do you happen to know what its source is?" Jacob asked nonchalantly.

"Why, actually I do," Cassie replied. "I asked my father the same question the first time he and I walked along here. We traced the stream all the way up to the source which is a spring located about three miles east of here. It's an impressive spring that puts out water year round, which is saying something around here since it's been so dry for years.

"Look, there it is," she interrupted herself, "my treehouse."

Jacob halted mid-step, and his jaw dropped. There on the north bank of the little creek, tucked into a grove of magnificent coast live oaks, was an utterly fantastic treehouse.

It was like something out of a fairytale. A large swinging bench hung by ropes from a thick lower branch. A sweeping circular staircase made of gnarled wood, complete with railings, meandered up and around the west side of the grand oak's trunk. Jacob's eyes followed the steps as they rose around the trunk and up the tree to three separate platforms on three different levels. Each space, which was large enough for four people and tall enough to stand in, was enclosed by a safety railing also made of the gnarled wood.

As she led the ascent, Cassie pretended to be a sophisticated real estate agent at an open house.

"Welcome to 'Wish Upon a Star,' the most elegant treehouse in all of Carmel Valley. Right this way, Mr. Wingate, and watch your step. This treehouse has three independent suites, each with its own unique character and special view opportunity. Here on the first level, we have a most comfortable parlor with lovely creek views. You'll notice the hickory rocking chairs. They're each over 100 years old. During the late summer and early fall, the sounds of the frogs and crickets at dusk can be quite enchanting. Next, on the second level, we have the beverage room complete with a solar-powered cooler for your favorite beer, wine or soft drink. And then finally, on the third level, we have the sleeping quarters complete with a canopy-covered queen size bed. You'll appreciate the solid wall enclosure on this level, for privacy, of course, and the spectacular views of the Gillette vineyards to the north which produce some of the finest Chardonnay in the County."

"Very impressive," Jacob said. "The treehouse as well as your realtor spiel. So, is the place for sale?" he teased.

"Oh, but of course, Mr. Wingate," Cassie replied with a wink, "All things are for sale … at the right price."

After viewing the expansive vineyards, which Jacob made a special note of, they walked back down to the second level and sat dangling their legs over the edge of the platform while sipping on diet sodas.

"Seriously, Cassie this is really something. Did your family build it? It looks fairly new?" Jacob inquired.

"Yeah, my daddy built it for me even before our main house was finished. He's always spoiling me, you know. But I don't mind; in fact, I love it!" She giggled as she reached back and tied her hair in a quick top-knot.

"Daddy says your family bought the old Granger place. Are you going to move in full time or just use it as a vacation home?" Cassie asked as she commenced her purposed interrogation.

"We closed escrow about a month ago. The place is pretty run down, but I'm planning to renovate and restore the old farmhouse and live there full time. My family is in the wine business. You might be familiar with our label: Bountiful Pastures - Napa. Some people just refer to us as BP."

Feigning innocence, Cassie answered, "I think I may have heard of that. Do you make a Sauvignon Blanc? I'm a Sav Blanc girl, you know."

"Uh, no, we don't currently make that varietal. So you might be thinking of someone else," Jacob replied politely, "but that's okay, I was just wondering.

"Anyway, we are also planning to enhance and expand upon the old Granger vineyard and start up a new label here called Bountiful Pastures - Carmel, kind of spin-off from our Napa brand. I'll be running the operation myself. It's kind of my breakaway project, still associated with the family and the Napa operation, but independent at the same time."

"Wow … that sounds exciting. From what I hear, those old Granger vines haven't been managed very well. Are they still any good?" Cassie asked.

"We think most of the existing vineyard is salvageable, yes, especially the older growth Syrah vines. They should be able to produce quantities of fruit sufficient to sustain our start-up operation, but we're planning to expand fairly rapidly. There are almost 100 acres of prime vineyard land in the back part of the valley that has yet to be planted. We are very optimistic!"

Shifting the conversation to a more personal note, Cassie asked, "So, when will you move in?"

"Actually right now, my father is returning to Napa on Monday, but I'm here to stay. I'm officially your new neighbor."

"Well, that's wonderful news. I'll look forward to getting to know you better, 'neighbor,'" Cassie said as she reached over and with a quick wink, gave Jacob's hand a teasing squeeze.

***

The jukebox from the cowboy bar next door blared the latest outlaw-country tune so loud he had to get up from his desk and close the window to continue his phone conversation.

"Sorry about that," he said to his client. "Happy Hour just started over at the Circle Q."

"Happy Hour? Then what, pray tell, are you still doing on the phone with me, Nate? Boy, you're too young to be wasting Happy Hour on an old horse like me. Listen, I know I've been working you overtime for the past three weeks on this deal. You deserve a night off. So, I'm going to hang up on you now. We can talk again on Monday. Capiche?"

"Yeah, capiche, Mr. Silvano," the lawyer said into the phone. "I'll be here at seven on Monday, so you can call any time after that."

"Good boy, Nate. Now you go find yourself a pretty girl and give her a spin on the dance floor for me, okay? I'll call you around eight."

The phone line went dead, and Nathan Donohue set the receiver back in its cradle. He removed his reading glasses, scrunched his eyes as he pinched the bridge of his nose, and then raised both arms overhead to stretch.

Spin a pretty girl on the dance floor, he thought. *I'd much rather get a decent night's sleep.*

He walked over to the window again and lowered the blind which blocked out most of what was left of the pinkish sunset sky. He locked the front office door and then retired to his private one bedroom residence in the back of the building. Too tired to heat leftovers, he took a quick shower and was lulled to sleep in minutes. The last thing he remembered was the familiar melody of a whiskey lullaby coming from the Circle Q.

Nate greeted Monday morning before dawn. As was his routine, he threw on a sweatshirt and his running shoes and headed out for a five-mile run through the hills just south of the Carmel River. He loved the early morning for many reasons. First, he always beat the heat of the day; second, he didn't have to contend with chatty joggers he might encounter on the trail; and third, he was always back in time to be showered, dressed and at his desk by 7 a.m. Nate did his best thinking in the morning before the phone started ringing and the busyness of the day-to-day got in the way of his passion, the law.

He'd been practicing in Carmel Valley since graduating, Order of the Coif, from law school eight years earlier. Nate grew up in a lawyer's home, so listening to his father's lamentations, he knew all about the difficulties and headaches that came along with law partners. Consequently, he had resolved to be a solo practitioner right out of school. It was tough for the first two years because he had no clients. The reason he didn't have any clients was that he had no experience. Of course, to get experience, you have to have clients. It was a vicious cycle, but he hung in there and finally caught a break in year three of his practice.

His most prominent client, Anthony Silvano, called. Silvano had heard about young Donohue from a friend in Carmel who had good things to say. He was frustrated with the cost and lack of responsiveness he was getting from his heavy-hitting San Francisco law firm, so he decided to give the rookie a try. The project was relatively simple, secure vested rights for use of an old sand mine he had purchased to facilitate his construction business. Nate succeeded in securing not only the rights for the mine but also similar rights to an adjoining parcel which Silvano promptly purchased, a transaction that Donohue was also enlisted to handle. Gradually, as Silvano's business grew, so did Nate's practice. The two became good friends, and Silvano referred many of his business associates and others in the community to Donohue. At one point there was so much work that Nate thought seriously about hiring an associate, but he resisted the temptation, deciding 55 hour work weeks were preferable to having to share office space with someone and, worse yet, be responsible for them. He liked practicing solo just fine.

Donohue's practice gradually evolved to focus primarily on the area of law called land use. He also handled the occasional transaction, but his bread and butter was land use. Dirt and water law is what he affectionately called his niche. Others referred to it as the "black art" of the law because it was so esoteric few truly understood it. There were only a small handful of lawyers on the Monterey Peninsula who specialized in that kind of work and Nate soon gained a name for himself and a reputation for being a hardworking, ethical and successful attorney.

Twenty minutes after sitting down at his desk with his morning coffee and the advance sheets, the phone rang.

"Hello, law offices of Nathan Donohue."

Nate always answered the phone formally because he never knew who might be on the other side and some folks looking for a lawyer appreciated a more professional demeanor than Nate found to be necessary with most of his regular clients.

"Good morning. Is this Mr. Nathan Donohue?" the voice asked.

"Yes, actually it is, my assistant hasn't arrived yet. May I ask who is calling?"

"Sure," the voice replied. "Good morning, Mr. Donohue, my name is Jacob Wingate."

CHAPTER 3

As was his practice, while they were on the phone, but before anything of substance was discussed, Nate quickly typed the name into his conflict check system to be sure the caller was not adverse to any of his existing clients. In a small town, it was essential to ensure you wouldn't inadvertently run into yourself when taking on a new client. Seeing no reference to Wingate in his system, Nate allowed the conversation to progress.

"Good morning. So, Mr. Wingate, what can I help you with?" Nate asked.

"I just moved to Carmel Valley, and I was told you are the man to speak to about land use and water issues. My family just purchased the old Granger farm in the Pastures. Are you familiar with it?" Jacob asked.

"I know the Pastures area, yes, and I've been by the farm you mention. It's the place on the southeast end, isn't it -- the one with the old green barn, right?"

"Yes, that's it. Anyway, my family is in the wine business, and we plan to improve and expand on what's already there. I also want to restore the house and develop a tasting room on the property."

"It is a beautiful piece of ground," Nate commented. "Congratulations on your purchase. But, if the transaction is already closed, what is it that I can assist with?"

Jacob proceeded to explain his plan for the land and the anticipated need for legal advice on several vital issues he presumed might arise. Nate listened intently and typed notes into his computer as they talked.

".... And, then the last item, and maybe the most important has to do with a deed question I have," Jacob said. "There is a mention of water rights to a spring on an adjacent property. As best I can tell, those rights are appurtenant to our land and, based on the language in the deed, they appear to be unfettered. But, I understand water rights in California can be a bit, shall we say, murky sometimes, and I want to be sure I'm on solid footing before I invest in the pumping system and distribution piping I'm planning to install. I think, maybe, the best thing to do would be for us to meet at the property, so I can show you what I'm talking about. You can bring along whatever engagement letter you use, and I'll sign it and formally hire you. Are you available this afternoon?"

"Sure, I can make this afternoon work, and I agree that a site visit would be helpful. In my experience, there are very few things more valuable than actually walking a property when it comes to land use work. How about I meet you out there, at the old farmhouse, around two o'clock?"

"Perfect," Jacob replied. "I'll see you then."

Getting out into the field for work was one of the things Nate liked most about his chosen area of practice. For most lawyers, 'getting out of the office' usually meant going to court or sitting through a deposition in another office. But for Nate, it often meant walking a property and enjoying nature for an afternoon. Of course, practicing in Carmel Valley, on the Monterey Peninsula, and down the central California coast, didn't hurt either.

Nate was familiar with the Pastures area because it was one of his favorite places to bicycle. He had defined a 23-mile loop ride into, around and then back out of the little valley. It was the perfect combination of distance, hills and beautiful landscape. Even though the weather was ideal for such a ride, he decided to drive to the meeting to present his best, professional self at this first encounter. He knew where the Granger farm was because it was at the far eastern end of the valley where he often stopped for a lunch break during his rides. It was a bucolic setting.

Though run down and in need of some serious repair, the farm buildings were nonetheless country-quaint. Stately oak trees surrounded the old house, and a healthy stream ran along the backside of the old barn. A dilapidated corral added to the rustic feel of the place as did the rusting windmill next to it that powered a small well that served the house. Nate pulled up in his Xterra SUV at ten minutes before the hour. Jacob was already there waiting for him.

"Hi, Nathan," Jacob said with an outstretched hand. "I'm impressed you're early. I tend to operate on Lombardi time myself. You know, 'five minutes early is late.' So, ten minutes early is actually ... early. Good for you! Anyway, I'm glad you could make it out. I appreciate it as I'm sure you're busy. Come on into the house. I'll sign your engagement letter and show you some of our preliminary plans for the house, tasting room, and vineyard operations."

After completing the engagement papers, Jacob rolled out the project plans. Though he had referred to them as "preliminary," the drawings he spread out onto the dining room table were anything but. The set consisted of 86 pages of highly technical and detailed plans for the complete restoration of the farmhouse, conversion of the barn to a state-of-the-art tasting room/special-event venue, and a vineyard and winemaking operation. The professional drawings included architectural elevations and renderings, engineered topography, complete water distribution system specifications and hydrological data. These were practically construction-ready drawings, and tens of thousands of dollars had been invested in their preparation. Nate was impressed.

After explaining the project parameters for thirty minutes, Jacob paused and looked at Nate.

"Any questions, Nathan?" he asked.

"Just one … does the deed you mentioned on the phone include any reference to developing the spring or just using it in its natural condition?" Nate asked.

"Good question, and it cuts right to the heart of the matter doesn't it," Jacob said, obviously impressed by his new lawyer. "It does say develop, but old man Granger never did. From what I can see he never did much more than install a single diversion pipe. So, what more we can do under the heading of 'develop' is the million dollar question. Come on let's walk to the spring itself. It's only about a quarter mile from here."

The two men struck out on foot and walked along the fence line that bordered the east boundary of the property. Along the way, Jacob described more about the long-term operational goals of the company and the intent to create a sister label to BP - Napa that would be called Bountiful Pastures - Carmel. Nate was aware of the BP name and was pleased to learn that his new client came from serious money. He always hated having to chase clients for payment of their bills. It was his least favorite part of being a lawyer.

"Do you think you can help us with the new brand label as well?" Jacob asked Nate as they walked.

"It's not really my forte, but I don't see why not. I did something similar for a fellow with a unique running shoe/sandal type invention a few years back. If I need to, I can always associate with a specialized co-counsel, but I doubt we'll need to go there."

Abruptly changing the topic back to the spring, Jacob pointed and said, "There it is, just on the other side of that downed fence."

Nate could hear the water bubbling out of the spring at a healthy rate. He noted the diversion pipe Jacob had mentioned and saw the rest of the water flowing into a naturally defined channel that widened fairly quickly the further it got from the spring.

Stopping to take everything in and process what he was seeing, Nate asked, "Do you know where the water runs to?"

"Yeah, I'm pretty sure it feeds a creek that runs to the west. It passes through a property owned by a family called Weston. Do you know of them?

"Yes. I know them," Nate replied casually. "They're good people. If you're going to start drawing more water from the source, we'll want to take into account whatever use they may be making of it downstream."

"No worries there. I've been to their place, and all they use it for is aesthetics, you know, a babbling brook in the backyard. They're horse people, not grape growers. I'm confident we won't disturb their enjoyment of the stream. There is a lot of water here."

"Yep, seems to be," Nate concurred.

"Follow me, and we'll get a closer look," Jacob said as he carefully stepped over the downed barbed wire fence segment.

Twenty yards farther and they were standing at the point of the pipe diversion immediately adjacent to the main spring.

"So, we think we're going to need to draw about 100-acre feet per year. This gravity-fed pipe only delivers about 20 right now. Thus we plan to install a pump to enhance the flow. Our hydrologist tells us this spring can readily produce the amount of water we need without compromising any of the downstream uses."

Suddenly, the two men froze in place when they heard the distinctive sound of a rifle being cocked. Looking slowly in the direction of the menacing sound, they saw the silhouette of a man on horseback sitting on a rise about forty yards to their north. The gun cock was followed by a shrill whistle intended to get their attention, which it did.

"Hey, you down there -- you're trespassing on private property. I strongly advise you to go back to wherever you came from, and that you do so right now," a deep, growling voice bellowed.

Nate took a step in retreat, but Jacob signaled for him to hold his ground.

"Look, mister, we're not armed, so there's no need for the rifle," Jacob yelled back. "Ride on over here, and I'll explain."

The man prodded his horse which then sauntered down the hill to within twenty feet of the spring. The rifle remained at the ready in his right hand.

"Alright then, explain," the man grunted.

Up close, the man was even more intimidating than first appearances, rifle notwithstanding. Though it was hard to tell while he was seated on the horse, it looked like the man had to be at least 6'6" and maybe 280 pounds. NFL defensive tight end occurred to Nate.

"My name is Jacob Wingate," Jacob calmly began, as if they were meeting in a corporate boardroom. "And this is my ... law ... uh, my friend, Nathan. I own the land just back there. The old Granger Farm."

The defensive end shot back sarcastically, "Well, Mr. Jacob. I don't give a rat's ass who you are or what you own. You are trespassing on my boss's land, and you and your boyfriend here need to leave right now."

"Mister, uh, I didn't catch your name?" Jacob persisted.

"Didn't give it, fool. I'm Romero, and I'm quickly losing my patience," the man said while re-cocking the rifle with a quick snap of his arm.

"Right … well, Mr. Romero, with all due respect, we're not trespassing here. My family owns rights to access and use this spring according to my property deed. I can go fetch it back at the house if you'd like to read it for yourself," Jacob continued.

"Deed, huh? Well, you can take that up with my boss, Mr. Gillette. I suggest you give him a call ...after you get the hell off his land." Firing a warning shot into the air, Romero concluded, "You understand that, city boy?"

The sound of the shot caused both men to recoil involuntarily. Realizing they'd seen what they needed to see, Nate whispered, "Let's go, Jacob, I think this hombre is a bit loco. I've heard of Gillette. I can schedule a meeting."

Sighing heavily, Jacob said, "You're right counselor. I don't want to start a range war, at least not today."

Jacob looked up at Romero and winked provocatively. He then raised his hands in surrender, and the twosome walked back toward the fence. Romero followed close behind them until he was sure they had crossed the fence line. He then saluted them with an extended middle finger and rode off without another word.

"Not the friendliest neighbor in the world, eh?" Nate said, trying to ease his anxiety with a bit of humor. "I guess first impressions are not his strong suit."

"No worries. That guy's just a hired yard dog," Jacob replied. "We have men like that at our Napa vineyard. Just comes with the territory. I'll get things squared away easy enough with the Gillettes. You say you know them? I heard in town that the old man wasn't doing too well."

"I hadn't heard that, but then I don't spend a lot of time in the same social circles that they run in," Nate responded. "Speaking of which, I did hear there is going to be big charity gala in Monterey on Friday night to benefit the local Foster Kids program. It usually draws a pretty impressive who's who list, and I understand the Gillettes are co-sponsoring the event, so I'm sure they will be there. That actually might be a better way to introduce yourself than to have your lawyer call for a formal meeting."

"I like the way you think, Nathan Donohue. Very good."

"You're welcome, Mr. Wingate. And, uh, Nate will be fine."

"Good. I think we're going to make a fine team, Nate ... yes, a very fine team."

***

The gala was being held at the Grand Vista Hotel on Cannery Row in Monterey. The hotel was world renowned and among the most elegant in California. The who's who list Nate had mentioned would be in attendance was even more extensive than Jacob had anticipated, and the valet parking team had their hands full. The cars queuing up to be parked caused Jacob's anticipation to grow. The parking area looked like a scene from the Concours d'Elegance with Porsche, Lamborghini, Ferrari, Mercedes, Bentley, Tesla, and Jaguar all represented. The opportunity to meet so many wealthy people at a single event was incredibly fortuitous.

Nate certainly earned his retainer today, Jacob mused as he stepped out of his car, tossed the key to an awaiting attendant, and headed inside.

The lobby was abuzz with conversation and the collective dazzle cast by the jewels adorning the necks and wrists of the women in the room was almost blinding. Jacob sipped from the glass of champagne he received at the door as he strolled down the impressive hand-carved mahogany staircase to the lower level where a sign indicated dinner was going to be served. The three-piece ensemble playing light jazz music in the wings was a nice touch.

Knowing no one, Jacob perused the crowd looking for a friendly face with whom he might engage in conversation to learn a bit more about the event and, hopefully, about some of the people in the room. While looking for a friendly face, his eyes fell on perfection.

She was standing alone, staring out the large picture window toward the bay. A nearly full moon was rising which cast a golden glow over the otherwise inky black water. Her silhouette in the moon glow was splendid, and as he approached, he found himself mesmerized. Before speaking, Jacob purposed to clear his mind of her distracting beauty.

"Beautiful isn't it ... the moon," he said. "Sometimes I think a moonrise can be even more glorious than a sunrise. A moonrise is a promise of light in the darkness."

"Why that's very poetic," the young woman replied as she turned toward the voice with the poise and grace of a royal debutante.

"Perhaps, but mostly it's just true. When I was a boy my grandfather and I used to camp out in the backyard together when the moon was full, and he would tell me stories about what he referred to as the 'old days.' I have very fond memories of those times."

Realizing he had momentarily forgotten his manners, Jacob interrupted himself, "But forgive me, I failed to introduce myself properly. My name is Jacob Wingate," he said holding out his hand reservedly. "Who might I have the pleasure of talking with?"

Though not in the mood for casual conversation, let alone meeting anyone new, she found the man's polite manner intriguing, and so she responded in kind, "Why, hello, Mr. Wingate. My name is Gabriella Gillette. It's a pleasure to make your acquaintance."

"Gillette? You wouldn't happen to own the vineyard property in the Pastures area of Carmel Valley would you?" Jacob replied casually.

"Why yes. That is my family's estate, Pastures of Bounty. Do you know of it?"

"Wow, sometimes it is such a small world. Yes, I do. In fact, my family purchased the old Granger farm just south of your property, and I just recently moved to town. We plan to renovate the old farmhouse and grow grapes."

"So we're neighbors," Ella said with a hint of pleasure in her voice. "And you're going to restore the farm. I think that is wonderful. I've always loved that old building, and I thought for sure whoever bought the place would tear it down."

"Oh, no never, I love rustic architecture, and although it's run down to be sure, the foundation and bones are solid. I hope to bring the house back to its original glory, with a few modern amenities inside, of course.

"By the way, I hope I'm not intruding," Jacob said. "I don't know many people yet, and when I saw you standing alone, well, I thought perhaps you might know a little something about this event and maybe some of the people here. And besides, the silhouette you cast there, with the moon behind you, well ..."

Jacob caught himself before he got too personal, "I just mean the bay is beautiful tonight."

Ella understood exactly what Jacob was alluding to and smiled at his feeble attempt to cover.

Hmm, cute and polite, I kind of like this guy, she thought.

"Well, I do happen to know about the event," Ella continued. "My family is sponsoring it. We are raising money to support the Foster Kids program in Monterey County. Foster care is a much-needed service in our community, and with all the governmental budget cuts these days, the program is struggling to stay afloat. While the funding is decreasing the need seems to become more and more pronounced every year. My mother grew up in a foster home, so the issue is very near and dear to my heart."

"I guess I stumbled onto the right person then," Jacob followed. "My grandfather, the one I just mentioned camping with, he and my grandmother volunteered as foster care providers a couple of times after they retired. They had some good experiences with the children they tried to help, and also, some not so good."

Their conversation was interrupted by a waiter who invited them to be seated in the grand ballroom.

"Jacob, since you don't know anyone here, would you like to join me at our table? We have an open seat, and that way I can introduce you to my brother, who is also here, and to some of our close friends as well."

"Oh, I wouldn't want to intrude," Jacob said tentatively.

"Don't be silly. Even as important as this event is, it can still get a bit stuffy sometimes, if you know what I mean. I would enjoy your company. Please, join me."

"Well, alright, I'd be honored to join you, Gabriella," he acquiesced.

"Ella," she said, "my friends call me Ella."

CHAPTER 4

After they were seated and Ella had introduced Jacob to the other table guests, the Master of Ceremonies got everyone's attention by clinking his champagne glass. He thanked everyone for coming, lavished generous praise on the event sponsors, and then offered a toast to a successful evening.

While the salad course was being served, Jacob nodded toward the empty chair to Ella's right and asked, "Didn't you say your brother was going to be here? Is that seat for him?"

"Yes, my brother Parker. He's probably at the bar finishing off one more bourbon and schmoozing some politician. I will apologize in advance for him, Jacob. Parker is quite the egomaniac. He actually thinks of himself as some kind of Greek god. He practically worships Orion, you know, the guy in the constellation? He can also be, shall we say, neglectful, when it comes to manners. I'm sure he'll be along before the main course is served. He never misses out on filet mignon."

Jacob enjoyed chatting with Ella's friends at the table and, to a person, they all seemed genuinely interested in his plans for the Granger farm. Napa was a relatively small community, but Jacob was quickly learning that Carmel Valley might be even smaller. It seemed there were seldom more than two or three degrees of separation between any of the people he was meeting, and he made a mental note of it.

Everyone's attention shifted to Parker's arrival as he glad-handed nearly every person at every table on his way over from the bar. As Ella had warned, his manner was abrupt. To the casual observer, however, he might be favorably viewed as abundantly confident and in control. His swagger might have even been impressive if the effects of the liquor had not been so noticeable.

"Hello everyone, sorry I'm a bit tardy, as the event sponsor I had to make my rounds, you know," Parker bragged with a slightly detectable slur as he sat down at the table.

Quickly realizing a stranger in his midst, he stood back up, walked over and stood behind Jacob's chair.

"I don't believe we've met. I'm Parker Gillette. My family is sponsoring this gala. And I'm curious why you are sitting at my head table, yet I don't have a clue who you are? I presume you're with my sister?" he said half-jokingly and half condemningly.

Parker had pinned Jacob in by standing directly behind him, so Jacob couldn't rise for a proper introduction. Parker wanted it that way to remain in complete control of the situation. So, rather than making an awkward scene, Jacob was forced to reach up over his left shoulder to offer his right hand.

"Yes hello, Parker. Ella graciously invited me to join your table. My name is Jacob Wingate. It is a genuine pleasure to meet you."

Upon hearing Jacob's name, Parker's demeanor and tone immediately shifted from professional/political host to agitated/inebriated bully.

"Wingate? Aren't you that fellow we caught trespassing on our property earlier this week?"

Parker said loud enough for everyone at the table to hear.

"On your property, yes, but trespassing, no," Jacob politely but firmly replied. "I met your man, Romero. He does his job well, though he might benefit from a lesson or two in civility. I tried to call you the next day. Did you get my message?"

"No, I didn't get any message. What do you mean you weren't trespassing? You walked right through our fence."

"Well, actually, we have access rights to the spring that is there near the fence line, and I was just checking it out. No harm was done, I assure you. I was hoping we could have lunch together. I'd like to tell you about our plans for the Granger farm. It would be great if we could work together as neighbors, you know."

"No, I don't know," Parker replied belligerently. Then turning to his sister, he said, "Ella, why is this man at our table. He is no friend of ours."

Ella responded defensively. "How in the world can you say that, Parker? You don't even know him.

Goodness, where are your manners? Jacob is a fine gentleman who just moved to the Peninsula, and I thought it would be nice to introduce him to some of our friends, and to you, brother. Please sit down and let's enjoy this beautiful dinner and get to know one another ... please."

Seeing the faces of their other table-mates seemingly siding with Ella, Parker opted to sit down. With Ella sitting between the two men they had minimal further conversation during dinner. As soon as he finished his steak, Parker abruptly excused himself and left the table to continue mingling.

"Jacob, I must apologize for my brother's behavior. He can be quite rude and even a bore at times." Ella whispered.

"No worries. I was on your property, and even though I had every right to be, it would have been better if I'd have called Parker first and properly introduced myself. I was just walking a friend around, you know, showing him the place, and I didn't expect to be met by an armed guard at the spring."

'Yes, Romero," Ella responded with a sigh. "He is my brother's right-hand man. Some might call him my brother's henchman. He can be a bit intimidating, as I'm sure you noticed."

"No matter," Jacob said flippantly, hoping to move away from the confrontation and on to more pleasant conversation. "You expressed interest in the old farmhouse. Would you like to come over and see it sometime? It might be of interest for you to see the current condition, you know, see the 'before' and then compare it to what the place looks like when I'm done restoring it."

"I think that would be fun," Ella replied. "I'm busy this weekend, but maybe sometime next weekend?"

"Great. It's a date. Well, uh, not exactly a date," Jacob fumbled over his choice of words, "it's just, uh, well, I'll call you with a time, and we'll make a plan."

***

On Sunday morning Nate was sitting in the third pew from the front on the right side. He never understood why people always tended to sit in the same seat at church, almost as if their name was on it, but they did, and he thought it funny that he had inadvertently adopted the same practice. The organ began playing the processional as the twelve-person choir filed in, dressed in full regalia. The congregation stood and joined in the opening hymn, the number for which was posted on a wooden plaque that hung on the wall just behind the pulpit.

Valley Presbyterian, which was also known by its recently adopted and more contemporary moniker as The River Church, met in a historic chapel that had previously, for almost 100 years, been home to St. Patrick's Catholic Church. The Catholic parish abandoned the place in the 90s, and the Monterey Peninsula Presbytery bought it. The building was located on a prominent hill just north of the Carmel River in the small hamlet affectionately known to Carmel Valley locals as The Village.

Nate had been attending The River Church since first moving to Carmel Valley and was proud to serve as an usher every other Sunday and to sit on the church's board of directors which met once a quarter. Today was an off-duty day for him as far as ushering was concerned.

After the hymn, the associate pastor informed the congregation of upcoming events and service opportunities and the offering was received. Following the passing of the plate came the time in the service known as "right hand of fellowship time" which was when neighborly greetings were exchanged, and the latest Village gossip was disseminated.

Unlike Nate, not everyone adhered to the same-seat-every-Sunday routine, so he always looked forward to who he might run into during the brief meet and greet time. When Nate turned to shake hands with the congregants behind him, he was pleasantly surprised to see the Weston family. Charles and Ariana Weston were important benefactors to the church and held in high esteem both in religious as well as social circles.

After greeting the two seniors, Nate smiled politely and then tipped his head to acknowledge their daughter Cassie's presence. Because of her beauty, and her reputation, Nate was very cautious around the girl. On the surface, he chalked it up to his proclivity toward shyness, but at a deeper level, he feared the goddess. He had long ago decided she was way out of his league, and he determined that polite avoidance was the most prudent and safest course.

Cassie was having none of his modesty today. Squeezing in front of her mother to edge closer to Nate, she smiled and said, "Hi there, Nate! It's so wonderful to see you this morning!" She then leaned over the pew and gave the somewhat stiff and unresponsive man an awkward hug. Ever the polite gentleman, Nate softened and returned the gesture in kind, gently patting her on the back while thinking about how thankful he was for the intervening pew.

Cassie's interest in Nate was not just casual or flirtatious. She had admired him from a distance for the past year. When, on rare occasion, she would think seriously about the future, her thoughts always gravitated toward Nathan Donohue. Sure Parker was popular and rich and dangerously fun, but while they'd been dating Cassie had begun to recognize an underlying current of anger, jealousy and even insecurity that seemed to haunt him. When she dared look ten years down the road all she saw with Parker was misery, wealthy misery, but misery nonetheless. And she didn't really need wealth. Her family had plenty of that. What she secretly desired was a marriage that would stand the test of time, not unlike that of her parents. In Nate, she saw intelligence, humility, kindness and stability, all the characteristics that Parker so dramatically lacked. The only thing the two men shared in common was their rugged good looks. Finding the balance between enjoying the present and preparing for the future presented a perplexing dilemma for the young beauty the answer to which had thus far eluded her. Due to her less than favorable experience with Parker just the night before, Cassie found herself thinking about the tomorrow part of the equation.

"Nate, would you be available after church to join us for lunch?" she asked.

Ariana, who also had a liking for Nate and deemed him to be among the most eligible candidates for her beautiful and precocious daughter, quickly chimed in, "Oh yes, Nathan, please do. Charles and I would be most blessed to have you out to the ranch house for lunch. Nothing fancy mind you.

We'll just grill some steaks and fix up some corn on the cob. It'll be like an impromptu country picnic, Weston style. Please say, yes."

"Uh, well, Cassie, Mrs. Weston, that's a very nice offer but …"

"But what?" Charles interjected with a grin. "A man's gotta eat, doesn't he? Whatever else you have planned for the day can certainly pause for a simple little lunch, can't it Nathan?"

Seeing he was outnumbered, and not wanting to risk offending Mr. or Mrs. Weston, Nate dropped his resistance. "Yes. Thank you. A country picnic, Weston style, would be wonderful."

Charles and Ariana beamed over their success, and Cassie was clearly pleased with her family's impromptu performance so, grinning from ear to ear, she winked at Nate and sat down.

Resigned to his plight, Nate rationalized to himself as the Pastor began teaching.

Nate old boy, you are about to enter never-never land here. But heck, you do need to eat and whatever excuse you would have made would have been a lie anyway, and that's never good. Truth is always the best policy.

Returning his attention to the sermon, he then heard the Pastor say, "Now, please turn with me in your Bibles to the book of Ephesians, Chapter 4, verse 15. The title of my sermon this morning will be 'Speaking the truth in love.'"

Ha, that's certainly apropos, Nate smiled to himself.

***

Driving back to his house after lunch with the Westons, Nate had to admit the afternoon had actually been enjoyable. Though it turned out to be a far cry from the simple little picnic Ariana had represented at church, the T-Bone steak he ate being large enough to carry him through until tomorrow's dinner, the company and conversation had been pleasant. Cassie had been genuinely friendly and kind and, as always, winsome. For the first time, Nate found himself giving an audience to his instinctual interest in her, and his mind wandered as he drove.

Maybe I've been wrong about Cassie all this time. I mean, maybe her reputation isn't true. Maybe people just say those things about her because they're jealous. I mean, good grief, there is a lot to be jealous of. But, come on Nate, who are you fooling? You don't stand a chance with a girl like her, and you certainly don't have time for a relationship. No, today was fun, but you've got to leave it at that. Besides, between Mr. Silvano's new project and whatever may come of this new Wingate engagement, you're going to be plenty busy at work for the next several months. So, just keep your head down, and don't be stupid.

***

On Monday after the gala, Jacob called and scheduled a lunch with Parker Gillette for Wednesday. He was disappointed in himself for letting the relationship get off on the wrong foot -- first the Romero incident and then the cross words at the dinner event. The last thing he wanted to do was make an enemy in the Pastures -- especially before he even got rolling with his project. So, he was determined to make the lunch a productive one. He decided to take the high road and apologize for the inadvertent trespass and to suggest a notice protocol for his future visits to the spring. He also intended to invite Parker to go duck hunting with him the following weekend. His prize hunting dog, Sierra, had just arrived from the kennel in Napa, having completed a six-month training regimen. He missed his dog terribly and was thankful for the company of his chum again, but he also knew that for the training to take hold he needed to get the dog into the field as soon as possible. Thus, if Parker accepted the invitation, the hunting trip would serve two important purposes, and he would have a gun along just in case Parker brought his man Romero.

The two grape growers' sons met at a restaurant Parker had suggested in the Village called Jenny's. It wasn't much more than a glorified hole in the wall, but it was renowned for its smoked brisket sandwiches which were easily two inches thick and for which folks didn't think twice about driving an hour to enjoy. Parker also happened to own a silent interest in the place that he had acquired by way of a note won at a poker game. He figured he might as well line his own pockets with his own money, unless, of course, Jacob volunteered to pay for the meal, in which case the lining would be all the better.

A chintzy bell clanged as the door swung open and Jacob walked in. Compared to the bright sunshine outside, the interior of the place was dark and even a bit dingy. The vibe was patently country from the twangy music playing through an ancient transistor radio on the counter, to the handwritten menu board behind the register, to the sawdust and peanut shells strewn on the floor. The floor crunched when he walked in. The dozen or so square foursome tables scattered haphazardly around the room were all vintage 1950s, the kind with the two-inch chrome edges, and the bench seats of the five booths lining the left wall were covered in worn red leather. The Fonz from Happy Days could have walked out of the men's room at any minute, and Jacob would not have been surprised.

As soon as his eyes adjusted to the lighting, Jacob spied Parker Gillette facing the door in the back corner booth and sitting across from another man. Gillette caught Jacob's eye and signaled him to join them. When he was within ten feet of the booth, Jacob recognized the other man, even from the back.

Great, he thought to himself, *Romero is here. I wonder if the yard dog brought his rifle along?*

"Hi, Parker, it's good to see you again. Thanks for agreeing to meet with me. Sorry again for getting off on the wrong foot at the dinner. That was totally my bad."

Parker didn't stand but did shake Jacob's extended hand. Romero just looked up and sort of grunted. He then belched loudly as he set a second empty beer bottle down on the table. Parker then scooted to his right toward the wall.

"Here, Jacob, sit. This is my assistant, Romero Calderon. I took the liberty of ordering for us. The meat sandwiches they serve here are famous. You're going to love it," Parker said.

"So I've heard. And thanks for ordering. By the way, lunch is on me, okay? I insist."

That's a good little boy, Parker thought to himself, *now you're beginning to understand who's boss around here. Yes, lunch is on you, punk. And if you're not careful, there will be so much else 'on you' that you'll wish you were back at your fat daddy's mansion in Napa.*

The pre-ordered sandwiches arrived, and the three focused on eating. Romero inhaled his and then barked an order for a third beer. Parker ate with a bit more refinement, but not much more. Jacob praised the flavor of the meat, but could only get half of the behemoth sandwich down before his stomach began to rumble in rebellion.

"So," Jacob began, "I wanted to try to start over regarding our relationship as neighbors. Again, I'm sorry for the other night, and Romero, I want to apologize to you as well. I know you were just doing your job, and I may have acted a bit impertinent. I'll admit the rifle thing caught me a bit off guard and, well, my bravado may have gotten the best of me."

Romero studied Jacob with a strained look on his face as if he wasn't quite following the gist of Jacob's comments.

In response to the stare, Jacob clarified, "What I mean is, I acted like a horse's behind. So, anyway, I'm sorry.

"Look, I admire what you guys are doing on your property in the Pastures. I've tasted your wine, and it is excellent. I don't know if you're familiar with our label, Bountiful Pastures - Napa, but we make a pretty good wine as well. In Napa we have a saying, 'if one vineyard succeeds, every vineyard succeeds,' and that has proven to be true. Napa is the world's most famous destination for wine, even surpassing the Bordeaux region of France, and it's because we all work together, all the vineyards, to cross-market and promote the region. My father and I see the same potential in the Carmel Valley, and we're hoping to combine our strengths with yours and others to establish a reputation that will draw people to the area. It's already happening down south in Paso Robles and Temecula, so there is no reason it can't happen here. We just need to work together."

Jacob paused to take the temperature of his audience and found it to be strangely cool.

Parker broke in, "Yeah, well that's a nice speech, but the fact is our operation is already dominating the market here, and we don't need any help from outsiders. In fact, we are going to be expanding our vineyard during the offseason. We're going to plant an additional 200 acres of vines."

"Wow, that's an aggressive plan," Jacob responded. "We were thinking of planting 100 acres, and I thought that was a lot. Isn't water going to be an issue for you?"

"Nope. We're planning to drop three new wells. According to our hydrologist, there is just enough water in the perched aquifer under our land to irrigate our 200 acres. So we've got no problem there," Parker responded confidently.

"Well, that's interesting to know," Jacob said. "We respect your successes, but I think we can both benefit in a big way if we work together on marketing. Just give it some thought, and maybe we can talk again, huh? There's no rush. We've got time. I'd be very interested in your thoughts and ideas."

"I just gave them to you, 'Jake,' didn't you hear me. Not interested. And by the way, in terms of marketing, you're going to need to come up with a new label name. Bountiful Pastures is way too similar to our name, Pastures of Bounty and we've owned that name for over 70 years. And I've seen your label art, and there is just no way you're going to be able to use that. It looks just like ours. Heck, if I didn't know better, I'd think your daddy stole it from us. And if you try to infringe on our name or our label I'll sue your ass. You understand, Jake. I've got an army of lawyers, and they're all pit bulls. They'll eat you for lunch just like Romero here consumed that sandwich. So, if you want to plant some grapes and make some garage wine in that old barn you bought, be my guest. Just stay the hell out of my way. You say you want to be a good neighbor? Then you just do as I tell you, and everything will be fine. Romero, you got anything to add for the benefit of Mr. Jake here?"

In the same deep, gravelly voice Jacob remembered from the encounter at the spring, Romero's contribution was short and to the point. "You do like the boss says, and you won't need to worry about my thirty-aught-six Winchester."

CHAPTER 5

Ella watched as the doctor drove down the driveway, turned left onto the main road and then disappeared around the bend. She sighed heavily and sat down in the rocking chair perched on the second-floor balcony just outside the library. The distinct smell of the thick lavender hedge that surrounded the portico fountain wafted her way. It calmed her, but also made her sad as she remembered planting the hedge with her mother when she was just 12.

Oh Mama, what am I going to do if Papa goes to join you in heaven? I miss you so very much. I don't know if I'll be able to survive if Papa leaves me, too. I already feel so alone here in this big house. Please pray for me, Mama, and pray for Papa, too. Please send a miracle. The doctor says we need a miracle. I believe in miracles, Mama, I at least want to believe.

"Ms. Ella?"

Though soft, the voice crashed through her thoughts like a freight train, and she nearly jumped up from the chair.

"Ms. Ella? Would you like some dinner?" Shelby asked quietly from the door of the library.

"Yes, Shelby, I'll be right down; thank you."

Ella couldn't decide what was bothering her more, her father's condition, her loneliness, or her brother's constant abuse. All three were pressing down on her at once. She needed help but didn't know where to turn. She ate in the kitchen with Shelby which had become the norm for her. Eating in the big dining room alone was the last thing she wanted.

"Shelby, I need to pray for a miracle for Papa. Do you know of a church that is open on Sunday night that I could go to?"

"The old Catholic chapel in the Village is open on Sunday night," Shelby answered. "I think it is now called The River Church, or something like that. I think their evening service concludes at seven o'clock. I'm sure the chapel building would remain open for a while after that for prayer. Would you like me to come with you?"

"You're so sweet, Shelby, but no, I'd like to go by myself. You can pray for Papa though, that would be very much appreciated. The doctor says he needs a miracle."

***

Despite her belief in God and heaven, it had been a very long time since Ella had been to a church for anything other than a wedding or a funeral. But the need for a miracle was acute, and she felt, though not knowing exactly why, that perhaps somehow God might listen more attentively if she prayed in a church.

She waited in her car across the street until she was sure all of the evening service worshippers had departed. When the last car in the parking lot finally pulled away, Ella got out of hers and walked over to the chapel building. Shelby had been correct in thinking the room would remain open for a time after the service. She slipped in unnoticed and sat in a pew near the back.

The lighting was limited to floor lights along either side of the central aisle, a soft up-light on the cross hanging from the ceiling at the front and candles burning in a candelabra placed atop the organ. Small windows were open on both sides of the front stage area that invited a soothing cross draft to blanket the room.

Because the church had once been Catholic, kneelers were built into the backs of each pew. Ella's upbringing as a little girl had been in the Catholic Church, the family often attending mass at the Carmel Mission, so kneeling felt most appropriate for the seriousness of her need tonight. When she reached down to unfold the padded bar at her feet, it creaked as it opened, and the sound echoed in the empty chamber. After carefully positioning herself in a humbled manner, Ella began praying for the miracle her father needed.

Outside, a pair of curious eyes watched as Ella prayed. The man circled the chapel building twice to view the interior from as many angles as possible to ensure the girl inside was alone. He then paused and looked furtively around the outside garden area as well to confirm the two were indeed alone. Having adequately assured himself of privacy, the man quietly approached the chapel door and entered, being careful not to allow the door to make any noise.

He stood silently in the foyer and listened. He could hear the muffled sound of earnest prayer, but could not make out any of the words. He hesitated, feeling a sudden pang of guilt for eavesdropping and then turned to leave. As he did his jacket sleeve brushed against a stack of church bulletins sitting atop the table next to the door, and they spilled onto the floor. He froze, hoping the sound would not be detected, but it was.

Startled by the sound, Ella stopped praying and whispered aloud, "Hello is someone there?"

Realizing he would now have to either run or confess his presence, the man stepped out from his hiding place in the foyer and into the back of the chapel.

"Hello, Ella. I'm very sorry to bother you."

"Jacob!" Ella exclaimed in a slightly louder whisper. "What on earth? Why are you here?"

Jacob shrugged, walked over and sat down next to the girl, folded his hands and placed them on his lap. He sighed, "Again, I'm so sorry to have disturbed you. I know how important private prayer time is. Actually, that is why I am here as well, but when I saw you, I just couldn't decide what to do. I need to pray, but I didn't want to interrupt your personal time. But then I thought how nice it would be to talk with a friend. But then I decided no, I should leave you alone. Well, when I finally decided to leave and turned to go, I clumsily bumped into some papers by the door. Kind of embarrassing, I know. I'm really sorry."

"Jacob, you needn't be sorry. God can hear more than one prayer at a time. We can pray together. I hear there is power in numbers when it comes to praying. I am here to pray for my Papa. He is very ill, and the doctors say he needs a miracle. I believe in them, miracles that is. I think he is suffering from a broken heart from my oldest brother's death a while back. But God can mend broken hearts, don't you think?"

"I do," Jacob replied. "I am here for a similar reason. My grandmother, who was married to my grandfather -- remember the one I camped with in the backyard? Anyway, she is dying. She has lived a good life. She is 93 years old and, frankly, she says she's ready to go to heaven to be with my grandfather. So, I guess, in a way, my prayer is kind of selfish, because I'm praying for her continued health when she says she wants to go." Jacob lowered his head, "Is that a wrong thing to pray for, Ella?"

Ella reached over and took hold of Jacobs folded hands. Their eyes met, and the glow cast by the floor lights caused hers to sparkle. Jacob saw a compassion in her look that he had never before experienced and it moved him.

"No, Jacob. It is not a wrong thing to pray for someone you love. God knows our hearts and our motives. You need not worry about that. I suppose if he had his way my father would also choose to die, yet I pray for a miracle for him. So, in truth, we are praying for the same thing -- you for your grandmother, and I for Papa. Come let us lay our burdens and requests before the Lord."

Side by side the two prayed silently for their respective family members. Then, with neither knowing what the other was thinking, they both prayed a similar prayer that God would allow their friendship to grow and possibly even to bloom.

***

The following morning Jacob was up at dawn to take Sierra for a walk. The purebred Brittany spaniel was the pride of the third generation litter of hunting dogs born into the Wingate family. Jacob's father had become enamored with dog breeding after a visit he made, at the invitation of a fellow Napa vintner, to Westminster during the AKC National Championships. The intense training required for the Brittany to be helpful during bird hunting became one of the elder Wingate's passions. Sierra had been a Christmas gift to Jacob two years earlier. Like the classic dog love affairs, Marti and Shiloh, Timmy and Lassie, Terhune and Lad, Jacob and his pup became inseparable. Having left Sierra with a professional trainer for dog "boot camp," which had been a necessary evil from Jacob's perspective, he was thrilled to have his best friend back by his side.

The two walked along the creek bed all the way to the Weston's property. At various points along the way Jacob stopped and commanded Sierra to wait while he walked on ahead. The time intervals between the wait and come commands varied, and he also practiced hiding out of sight of the dog. Each successful exercise brought rousing praise from Jacob to Sierra as well as a tasty treat morsel. When they arrived at the Weston treehouse, the two sat next to the creek and talked.

"Sierra, I missed you something fierce. I'm so glad you're finally back home with me, girl. I think you're really going to like Carmel Valley. It's beautiful here, and the birds are everywhere. I can't wait to take you out into the field. We are going to have so much fun together."

Sierra sat and listened attentively, responding with tail wags to words she recognized such as her name, girl, and birds. Humans always imagine their pets can understand far more than they do, but it really doesn't matter. Love for a dog is as blind as it gets.

Later that morning, Jacob met with his new lawyer to discuss the lunch conversation he had with Gillette. He was a bit surprised at the simple office set up Nate maintained, at least compared to the high rise offices their Napa family attorneys in San Francisco had. But something about the efficiency and focus it enabled was attractive to Jacob. So far, everything he had observed about his new local attorney affirmed his selection.

After listening intently to Jacob's account of the meeting, Nate asked, "So, he actually threatened you like that? That's pretty bold."

"Yep, he used those exact words. I walked away understanding that my new neighbor has absolutely no interest whatsoever in being neighborly, so I guess that means we're going to have to fight fire with fire. I want to sue him before he can sue me," Jacob stated resolutely.

"Well," Nate pondered for a quick moment. "We can't sue him for the threat, but we could bring an action to restrain and enjoin his new wells. We can assert, by his own hydrologist's report, that if he drills new wells to irrigate his acreage, he will deprive your spring of its source. Assuming they are hydrologically connected, which is a reasonable assumption, Gillette would thereby interfere with your water rights regardless of whether you pump more water out of the spring or not."

"Exactly what I was thinking," Jacob responded. "I think I'd also like to sue him on the name and label issues. I don't think it is right that someone can legally object to our new winery's name by laying claim to the word 'pasture' or the notion of 'bounty.' I don't think those terms should be subject to copyright or trademark protection. Besides, I don't see that much similarity in our label art, but if that's a problem I can always change that easy enough. The name is the big thing, though. Our entire business model is based on expanding our already established Bountiful Pastures name. Using the BP moniker is critical to the success of our Carmel vision."

"I can see that, and yes we can bring an action on that issue as well," Nate continued. "Combining the two matters will tend to complicate things a bit, but not so much that we can't manage it. And at the preliminary injunction stage, we don't have to prove our case. We just have to show the equities of maintaining temporary status quo favor us and a likelihood of prevailing on the merits at trial. So, I assume you want this done sooner than later, correct?"

"Yes. I'd like to file and serve a lawsuit by the end of the week if that is doable. I'm sure you've got other pressing matters, but I'd appreciate it if you could make this a priority. I can even pay you an extra fee if you'd like."

"No, that won't be necessary, Jacob, I won't need an extraordinary fee. But if that Romero fellow starts harassing me, I might ask for hazard pay," Nate joked.

***

The lawsuit was filed and served that Friday and the matter was set for hearing on the temporary restraining order two weeks later. Parker Gillette was furious when he learned that Jacob had taken such an aggressive posture and was quick to disparage him to Ella. In turn, Ella sought to defend her new friend.

"Well, Parker, I'll admit I am a bit surprised by the lawsuit, but I'm sure that you must have done, or said something, to provoke it. I don't think Jacob is at all mean-spirited, and he would only be acting in defense of his property," Ella said during lunch at Casa de Abundante.

"If suing your neighbor isn't mean-spirited then I don't know what is," Parker complained, raising his voice. "This guy is a bad actor and needs to be dealt with. He picked the wrong person to come after; I'll tell you that. I'm going to make sure he regrets the day he decided to challenge Parker Gillette!"

"Parker, calm down, please, and lower your voice, or you'll wake Papa. What did you say to Jacob when you two met for lunch? Maybe he misunderstood something. Maybe this lawsuit is all just a mistake. Maybe you should call him and see if some understanding can be reached."

"Ella, you are so incredibly naive. I simply told Wingate we were going to use our water to irrigate our land and now, according to the lawsuit, he thinks it's his water. And I told him he'd have to change the name of his vineyard and wine because we already own the Pastures of Bounty name. These are simple facts that any 'neighbor' would understand … but no, not this bozo. No, he just waltzes in with his boy lawyer, some no-name, two-bit ambulance chaser with a one-room shanty office in the Village, and acts like he owns the whole stinking valley. What a pair they are --

93

Tweedledee and Tweedledum, or maybe more like dumb and dumber -- whatever. I'm going to make them both pay. The Gillette family owns this valley, and I'll be tarred and feathered before I'm going to step aside to anyone, especially this punk."

Seeing that her protest was only making her brother angrier, Ella decided to stop pursuing the conversation. After they finished lunch, she stepped away to the library and placed a call to Jacob.

"Jacob, hi, this is Ella Gillette ... I'm well, thank you ... Yes, I enjoyed seeing you at the church as well. Praying together was nice ... Yes I'd love to get together again sometime ... this Saturday night? Why, sure, I guess so ... Yes, I like wine, and I'd love to meet you for a tasting at the Left Bank in Carmel ... Yes, 6 p.m. would be perfect. Now, what I called about, I just wanted to let you know that Parker is extremely upset about the lawsuit you filed last Friday. I'm sure you have your reasons, but I would like to understand them for myself, since my family is involved, after all. And I also want to warn you to watch out around Parker. He can be very volatile, and I wouldn't want to see anyone get hurt. Especially not you Jacob … Yes, you're welcome, and thanks, I'll look forward to your explanation and the wine tasting. Bye."

***

Jacob picked Ella up a few minutes before six on Saturday. As they pulled away from the gate, he turned left.

"Jacob, I thought we were going to Carmel?" Ella asked, confused by the left turn.

"We are, but remember I mentioned about showing you the farmhouse before I restore it? Well, some of the remodel work is going to start next week, so this is your last chance to see the 'before' condition. It'll only take a few minutes. I'd also like to introduce you to someone special to me."

The driveway approach to the farm was dramatically understated compared to the entrance to Casa de Abundante. There was no gate to speak of, just an old wooden entry arbor with a street number carved into it. The driveway was a well-worn, narrow, and rutted dirt path.

Jacob drove carefully to avoid as many potholes as he could. The old green barn was to the right and just in front of the house.

"Welcome to the future home of Pastures of Bounty - Carmel," Jacob announced proudly as they came to a stop near the front door. "It's not much to write home about today, but in 12 months you'll hardly recognize the place."

Jacob ran around to open the door for Ella and then he took her by the arm as they walked up the five rickety steps to the wraparound veranda.

"Watch your step," he joked, "I wouldn't want you falling through any of these rotted boards."

Ella gasped favorably as they walked through the front door. Although old and run down, the house was very spacious, and it's size seemed accentuated by the fact that the furnishings were extremely sparse. A large picture window at the back of the house was visible from the front door and provided a spectacular view of a natural oak forest coupled with a few outbuildings.

"We've obviously got a lot of work to do," Jacob said apologetically, "but we're committed to faithfully restoring the place to look like it did when it was first built. The Grangers even gave us some old photos that we're using to guide the project. Come on; I want to introduce you to my friend, Sierra."

The only thing remotely new looking on the property was a dog run that had been constructed behind the barn. As soon as the two walked out the back door, Sierra began barking a greeting.

"You have a dog?" Ella asked. "I love dogs, even though we never had one, I always wanted one."

Jacob opened the gate to the run, and Sierra bounded over to them. "Sit, girl," the man commanded.

Despite her exuberance, the dog immediately obeyed and waited for further instructions.

"Sierra just finished formal training in Napa. I'm told she graduated at the top of her class," Jacob beamed. "She is my very good chum, and I'm thrilled to have her back with me.

"So, Sierra, meet my new friend, Ella," he said to the dog.

As if on cue, the pup turned her attention to the girl and lifted a paw to shake hands.

"Well," Ella responded to the dog with a smile, "it is very nice to meet you, Sierra. I can see you're quite fond of your master, as I think I may become as well."

***

The Left Bank tasting room was located in the downtown area of Carmel. Jacob had learned about it from one of the guests at the Gillettes' table at the Gala and had been anxious to try it out. He had an affinity for French wines ever since he learned about the famous, "Judgment of Paris" in 1976. His father told him the story about the historic blind wine tasting competition in Paris that pitted the best varietals of France against those of Napa. The publicity stunt, organized by a Brit of all people, stunned the world when Napa wines took first place for both red and white varietals. True to the motto that when one does well all do well, the notoriety of the win thrust

Napa onto the world's wine stage and the previously innocuous little valley in northern California never looked back.

As they entered, Jacob was pleasantly surprised by the feel of the tasting room. The sign outside had been fashioned out of old gnarled vine stocks, and the Dutch door at the entry emitted a kind of country feel, even though the place was in the midst of downtown. A large window seat occupied the west wall, and the window was open, allowing a cool breeze to flow through. The tasting bar was made of dark green quartz stone, and the furniture was warm and comfortable. It was somewhat similar to the oversized leather stylings he had admired at the Westons' ranch house. The bar host was very welcoming as Jacob walked in.

"Hello, and welcome to Left Bank. My name is Todd Scott, and I'll be pouring for you this evening. I can't say that I recognize you. Are you visiting Carmel on vacation?"

Scott's assumption was premised on his extensive experience in the local wine business. Well over half of the visitors to Left Bank were, indeed, on holiday from somewhere else. As they conversed,

Jacob made mental notes of as many details about the room as he could, knowing that it wouldn't be long before he would be deciding on a theme and ambiance for his own future tasting room. He had purposed not to emulate the Napa experience, but rather to try to define something different, something more Carmel Valley. Scott was extremely knowledgeable about wine and Carmel and was an excellent conversationalist. He was one of those people who you took an instant liking to and who made you feel special from the moment you walked in the door.

Impressed, Jacob thought to himself, *I may have to hire this guy to run my tasting room.*

Jacob noticed a table in the back was available, so he escorted Ella toward it. He had taken the liberty of calling ahead and ordering a flight of wines to taste and a cheese plate for them to share.

"Jacob, I'm so glad we were able to get together here. I've been wanting to spend more time getting to know you, and this is, well, just perfect. Thank you for inviting me, and thanks again for showing me the farmhouse; I'm excited about your project," Ella said.

"It's kind of funny, but for all the years I've lived here, I've never actually been to this tasting room. One of my girlfriends always raves about the wine here. The name of the place, Left Bank, is interesting. Might you know what it means?" Ella asked.

Jacob smiled at Ella, and to himself, at the prospect of getting to talk about one of his favorite places in the world, Bordeaux.

"Yes, actually I do," Jacob began. "The Left Bank refers to the Garonne River in the Bordeaux region of France. The river flows from the Pyrenees mountains in Spain north through France. So the left bank is the west side of the river. You're probably familiar with Bordeaux blend wines. Well, wineries on the left bank use primarily Cabernet Sauvignon as the base varictal whereas the right bank wineries focus more on Merlot. The differences in flavor can be quite pronounced, but both are very good. Interestingly, when we make Bordeaux blends here in California, we tend to use all five of the classic blending varietals which, in addition to Cab and Merlot, also include Malbec, Cab Franc, and Petit Verdot grapes. I hate to be a California wine snob, but honestly, I think our approach to these blends is much more interesting and robust than that of our French cousins. The flight I ordered for us this afternoon includes three different Bordeaux blends; one is in the classic left bank style, one is traditional right bank and the third reflects more of the California variation on the theme. I'll be interested to know which you like best."

"I guess I shouldn't be surprised given what your family does, but your knowledge of French wines is pretty impressive," Ella commented. "Even though wine is my family's business as well, to be honest, I never paid too much attention to the details. I just enjoy the flavors. I always left the business and winemaking worries to Papa, and now I guess, to my brother."

"How is your father?" Jacob asked.

"Not much change, really," Ella said with resignation. "I am still praying for the miracle. Yesterday the doctor offered some good news that Papa has gained three pounds and his blood pressure was a bit stronger, so there seems to be some reason for hope. Thank you for asking, Jacob. I appreciate your care and your prayers. But, now back to your story about France."

"Well, that's about it, as far as the left bank is concerned. I take it you haven't been to Bordeaux, but have you been anywhere else in France?"

"Oh, yes, I love Paris," Ella beamed. "My favorite thing to do in the city is float along the river Seine. It is a very romantic thing to do, especially at night. But, as much as I love Paris, my absolute favorite place in all of Europe is a small town in northern France called Giverny."

"Seriously," Jacob said excitedly, "Giverny? Do you mean where Monet's home is? Why, that is my favorite place in France as well. I mean, the garden there, it's just spectacular. Of course, the famous lily pond and bridge, but just as impressive is the rose garden next to the house. I love how it is allowed to grow somewhat wild. So many European gardens are manicured and formal, but Monet's garden is not so meticulously kept. I love wandering through and getting lost in the natural beauty of it all."

"Jacob Wingate, you never cease to amaze me. Are you a lover of gardens as well? We do seem to have quite a bit in common, don't we, my new friend?"

CHAPTER 6

While they enjoyed the wine, Jacob answered all of Ella's questions about his lunch meeting with Parker and why he decided he had to file the lawsuit. It was as she had suspected, and she assured him that she didn't think ill of him because of it. Together they talked about ways the conflict might be amicably resolved as both desired for that to occur.

"... but, when it comes to Parker, sadly it's almost always his way or the highway," Ella said quietly. "I just hope the matter can be resolved quickly so perhaps healing can begin. And Jacob, I know I already said it, but my brother can be irrational and compulsive and, I fear, even dangerous, so please, please be careful around him. If you have to revisit the spring, I think it would be prudent to call for a sheriff standby, just in case."

"I appreciate your concern, Ella. I really do. But I don't plan to go back to the spring until after we get a preliminary ruling from the court. I hope that Parker will come to his senses once the judge has spoken and that things will gradually calm down after that. I'm sure we can find a way to cooperate to share the water in a manner that can work for both of our properties. The Westons' home is also downstream and benefits from the spring, so their needs will also have to be taken into account."

"You know the Westons?" Ella asked.

"Yes, to a degree. I met them when my father was here. They seem like nice people. They have a lovely home."

"Did you meet their daughter, Cassie? You know, she dates Parker now and then."

"Really? Yes, I did meet her. She seemed nice enough -- maybe a bit flamboyant, to use a word, but certainly friendly. I'm surprised though that she would date your brother. They seem kind of like oil and water, wouldn't you say?"

"It is a bit strange," Ella continued, "but Parker seems to have some kind of magnetism when it comes to women. Maybe it's his bad boy demeanor or his money or his looks, I don't know, but I just don't get it. Most of his girls tend to be the floosy type, you know, one night stands. But Cassie Weston is the exception. She is pretty sophisticated, and I don't think she would be one to be impressed with Parker's money given her family's resources. So, maybe there is a side of my brother that I just can't see. I'm hopeful that is the case. I want to believe the best about people, but I struggle when it comes to my brother."

"Hmm, well the court hearing is next Friday, so we'll just hope for the best," Jacob said, trying to bring the subject to a close. "Do you have dinner plans? There is a new restaurant within walking distance of here. They specialize in small bites, Mediterranean mostly. I tried it a few nights ago. It has a fun atmosphere, and they have live music or, if you prefer, we can order something to go and picnic on the beach. What do you say?"

"That would be nice, Jacob. Yes, I'd love to. I think the beach option sounds best. But no more discussion about business tonight; let's just enjoy getting to know each other."

***

The restraining orders were set for hearing at 9 a.m. in Superior Court Department 7. The Honorable Judge Thomas McGeorge was presiding and called the attorneys forward. Parker Gillette and Jacob Wingate remained behind the bar in the gallery to watch their chosen gladiators engage.

The bailiff, a large, self-important man who had apparently not stepped foot in a gym for over a decade, stood, shushed the spectators, and advised everyone to silence their cell phones or have them confiscated. When he was satisfied that he had brought all present into submission, he proudly patted his sidearm, adjusted his size 48-waist trousers, nodded to the judge and returned to his appointed wooden chair near the side door.

The judge rapped his gavel and announced, "The matter of Wingate vs. Gillette is now called. I have reviewed the papers submitted by each side and am ready to hear oral argument. Attorney for the plaintiff, Mr. Donohue, please proceed."

Nate had learned it was seldom productive to merely reiterate the arguments contained in the written briefs. His approach was instead to highlight two or three key points and then try to engage the judge in conversation to draw out those issues he thought most salient. True to form, Judge McGeorge wasted no time cutting to the chase.

"Mr. Donohue, I'm sure you are aware that under California law an overlying landowner has rights to the groundwater beneath his property. In this case, you seem to be claiming an equal right to water flowing to your client's land from a spring on Mr. Gillette's ranch. Why should I not conclude that Gillette's right is superior to yours because he is the overlying owner and your client is merely an adjoining beneficiary?"

"Thank you, your honor — excellent question sir, and one that goes to the heart of our matter. The answer is found in the case cited in our moving papers called Peters v. Truman. As in that case, here Mr. Wingate has a contractual right to the spring water which was affirmatively granted to his predecessor in interest by Mr. Gillette's grandfather. As such, Gillette chose, of his own volition, to subordinate a portion of his overlying rights to his neighbor. In fact, the contract evidencing that grant reflects that consideration in the amount of $10,000 was paid. This case is a matter of contract rights, your honor, not common law water rights. Moreover, our request for relief is not to necessarily establish superiority of right at this time but rather to simply ask for equal footing concerning the water. If you will, the opportunity to share in the water … the water we paid for and which is an appurtenant property right to the Wingate land. Mr. Gillette has said he intends to use all the groundwater underlying his land to irrigate his vines which means, as a practical matter, there will be no water left for Mr. Wingate to use. That would amount to a breach of contract, and it is that anticipatory breach we are asking your honor to enjoin. Without court-ordered restraint, while a trial is pending, Mr. Wingate's existing vines will suffer significant harm whereas if the status quo is maintained until trial, Mr. Gillette loses nothing and will only suffer the inconvenience of having to wait to plant his expanded vineyard."

Jacob felt himself physically relax as he watched Nate argue before the court. His attorney's knowledge of the law and demeanor were superb, and it appeared the judge was being persuaded. He glanced over at Parker who was nervously scribbling notes on a pad.

"Thank you, Mr. Donohue. Do you have anything to add to your written arguments on the issue of the name and label injunction you are concurrently seeking?"

"No your honor, we will submit that question on our papers unless you have any particular aspects you would like me to discuss."

"No, thank you, I think you briefed the matter thoroughly, and I understand your arguments."

The judge continued, "So, Mr. Moncrief, do you care to rebut what Mr. Donohue has argued either in his written materials or during his oral argument here this morning?"

Moncrief was the senior partner of the 57 lawyer San Jose law firm called Moncrief, Wilson, and Hayes. They were heavy hitters in the arenas of California water law and trademark disputes. The silver headed statesman stood with great panache and rather than answer the judge's direct question, he began delivery of a polished and obviously rehearsed oratory. Two minutes into his speech, McGeorge cut him off.

111

"Mr. Moncrief, I am well aware of the cases cited in your brief and California common law, so you need not belabor those holdings. Do you have anything 'new' to add? I'm particularly interested in Mr. Donohue's characterization of the water debate sounding in contract. Do you have any rebuttal on that point, because, to be candid, I am inclined to rule in Mr. Donohue's favor on that point."

Moncrief stammered and looked to the two young associates seated at the table with him, but neither had anything to offer beyond chagrined expressions and shrugs.

Parker could not contain himself and abruptly stood and blurted out from the gallery, "Your honor, may I have a minute with my attorney?"

"Mr. Gillette, please sit down sir, you are out of order," McGeorge responded, clearly annoyed by the interruption.

"But, judge, this is obviously a water rights case and ..."

"Mr. Moncrief, please control your client, or I will have to ask the bailiff to escort him out of the courtroom," the judge said in an angry tone.

The portly bailiff sprung to his feet ready for action. After threatening everyone's phones, his day was usually occupied with employing various techniques to keep from falling off his chair while snoozing. A request from the judge to forcibly remove someone from chambers was cause for some serious celebration and would make fodder for storytelling at the local watering hole for at least a week.

"But, judge," Gillette's protest continued, "it's not fair to prohibit me from testifying, I have a right to confront my adversary in open court, I demand ...."

The impetuous demander after twice being told to be quiet was more than McGeorge was willing to endure. He brought his gavel down with a loud crack on his desk and, visibly angry, he barked to the anxious officer, "Bailiff, please remove Mr. Gillette ... now!" Like a defensive lineman awaiting the snap of the ball by the center, the bailiff practically flew through the small swinging door that separated the gallery from the lawyers' table. He hovered over Gillette and glared at the man as if he had just been convicted of a heinous felony.

"You heard the judge, sir; he said now."

Realizing any further protest would almost certainly doom the case, Moncrief looked over his shoulder at his client and nodded that he should leave. Parker was furious and for a moment considered taking the bailiff on, but then at the last second, decided he'd rather not spend the rest of the day in jail. So, creating as much disruptive noise as he could muster without speaking, he stormed out of the courtroom.

Smiling to himself for successfully displaying his judicial power to all those present, McGeorge then asked, "Very well, Mr. Moncrief, do you have anything further to add?"

"Yes, your honor -- first, my apologies for my client's outburst. Second, on the trademark issues, I would ask the court to consider the same status quo argument Mr. Donohue mentioned regarding the water. Namely, the only inconvenience his client would suffer if the restraining order is denied is having to wait until trial to begin labeling his wine, and by the admission in his brief, that wine won't be ready for bottling until long after the trial. That is all, your honor."

"Thank you, gentlemen, you may step back. I agree with both attorneys regarding status quo, and therefore with regard to the temporary restraining orders, I rule in favor of Mr. Wingate on the water question and hereby order Mr. Gillette to cease from drilling any new wells at this time. I rule in favor of Mr. Gillette with regard to the trademark issues of name and label art. I will issue a ruling on the formal injunctions within the next few weeks. That will be all. Madame clerk, please prepare and circulate an order. Thank you. Next case."

As the attorneys filed out of the room, Parker was waiting on a hard wooden bench in the hall outside. Jacob made a move to speak with him, thinking he might smooth things over with his neighbor, but Nate gently grabbed his arm.

"Not right now, Jacob. I think we should let him cool off a bit. Maybe the split decision will mollify him to some degree. But right now, I think we should just leave. I'll touch base with Moncrief this afternoon, come on."

In a coffee shop next to the courthouse, Jacob and Nate talked about the outcome of the hearing.

"Nate, you were fantastic in there. Your contract theory was pure genius. Waiting on the name issue is not all that critical for me for the reasons the judge articulated, so I consider this morning a win, for sure. Parker knows we mean business and maybe now he will mellow out a bit. I can plant our new vines and irrigate them, which is what was most important for me time wise. Look, now, I want to take a conciliatory approach from here. I really don't want the war between us to escalate if I can avoid it."

"I understand and agree," Nate replied. "I'm always looking for solutions rather than war. I like a good fight as much as the next lawyer, but it's not about me. What matters is accomplishing your objectives in the most efficient and cost-effective way possible. We will, of course, continue to move forward with the litigation and discovery will ensue, but I will be sure to do so in a cooperative way. We'll just hope that Gillette and

Moncrief will do the same. You know, it takes two to waltz just like it does to tango."

***

Parker's blood boiled all the way back to the estate. He stormed into the house and slammed as many doors as he could on the way to his private office in the east wing of the mansion. He cursed under his breath while he poured himself a double whiskey and slumped into the oversized chair at his desk. He reached for his cell phone and punched speed dial number one. Romero came on the line instantly.

"Yes, boss. How did it go?"

"I need you to get up to the house right away. I'm in my office. We need to talk about that loser Donohue. He's got to pay for humiliating me in court."

Romero hopped into his Jeep Cherokee and drove back to the house. On the way he thought to himself, *This is good. The boss is going to give me some rein to go after this boy. It's been a while*

117

since I got paid to hurt someone. This is like Christmas come early.

Parker was on his third glass of whiskey when Romero rumbled into the room.

"Close the door and come sit down," Parker said in a seething tone. "So, we won half the argument today, but we lost on the water issue. The judge's ruling is going to set me back on planting out the 200 acres for a full year. That stinking young buck lawyer was so arrogant with all his legalese. I want to make him hurt before we start taking depositions on the lawsuit. You know, so maybe he'll think twice about getting all cocky with me again. And I want to send a message to Wingate, too. Both of those guys need to be shown who's boss around here."

"Any limits on how far I can go, boss?" Romero asked expectantly.

"I think my sister has taken a liking to Wingate. I have no idea what she sees in that Napa boy, but I need to be careful when it comes to him. If she ever traced an injury to him back to me, there would be hell to pay around here -- so nothing directly physical for him. But the lawyer, Donohue, I'll leave him to you. Just don't kill him. That could get messy. And be smart, I obviously can't have any of this linked back to me."

***

After church on Sunday, as everyone was filing out of the chapel and thanking the pastor for the message, Cassie approached Nate out on the lawn.

"I heard you won a big case in court, congratulations. I'll bet Jacob is just pleased as punch. He's such a nice fellow. I think his plans for the Granger farm are wonderful, and if I heard right, part of what he is fighting for has to do with the creek that runs through our property, so I guess his success will stand to help us, too. Is that right?"

Nate couldn't help but enjoy the attention he was receiving from this beautiful girl. Since their luncheon at the ranch house a few weeks before, Cassie had become much more friendly and had actually reached out to Nate on several occasions. It almost seemed as if she was seeking out opportunities to run into him in the Village. It was kind of flattering, and he found himself wondering if she might be interested in going out on a formal date.

"Thanks, Cassie," Nate said, "I can't really speak to the details, of course, but generally speaking you are correct that the injunction the court granted will indirectly benefit your parents' property by maintaining the spring flow to the creek."

"Nate, would you be interested in coming out to our home again and this time maybe taking a walk along the creek?" Cassie asked. "There is a special place I'd like to show in the back corner of our property that I know you'll like. Maybe we could take along a little picnic. It's a perfect day for a picnic, don't you think?"

"Yeah, sure, that sounds nice. You know, I was thinking about asking you to dinner some time. I haven't been to the Cantina for a while. I hear that the band playing this weekend is pretty good. Maybe after our little hike along the creek, we could zip over to the Cantina for a quick bite?"

"Nate, yes, absolutely yes, that would be perfect. Why don't you come over to our place around three o'clock? It's a short walk to the spot I want to show you, and then we can make it to the Cantina in time for happy hour. I'll see you then."

CHAPTER 7

The walk Cassie took Nate on was very similar to the one she had enjoyed with Jacob a month earlier. For this occasion, however, she didn't put on her alluring flirtatious facade because she knew Nate wasn't attracted to that. Instead, she dressed down a notch, more comfortable and less concerned about being perfect. One of the things she liked most about Nate was that she didn't feel the need to impress or attract; she could just be her true self.

The whole beauty queen thing had been fun, especially in the beginning when she was in her early teens. It provided an opportunity to meet interesting people and visit fun places. But as she aged up and began having some successes the game started to change on her. Her parents never really forced her in any particular direction, and Ariana was not one of those Hollywood-doting-type mothers trying to live her fantasies out through her daughter, but the whole tenor of the pageant environment just caught Cassie up in its grip, and she found herself conforming. She never really liked it, but didn't quite know how to escape it.

By the time she won Miss Teenage Arizona, she was firmly caught in the tentacles of the lifestyle. She skipped college to pursue modeling, and the work and money flowed. To all her friends, she had struck it big and was the luckiest girl alive. Not knowing how to cope with the whole fame and fortune thing, she gave into it and, like an addiction, it started to control her. She knew it was hollow and that beauty was fleeting, but she couldn't help herself. Like an alcoholic in denial, she told herself she was in complete control and could stop whenever she felt like it. But, once she realized that wasn't true, she started looking for a way out.

Dating Parker had not helped the situation because his narcissism insidiously fed her selfish side. It was like one step forward and then two, sometimes three steps, back. She loved it and hated it at the same time. The one mistake her parents did make was to give her too much autonomy too soon. She needed someone to teach and encourage her to say no, someone to help guide her choices, but no one in her life had the presence of mind, courage, or fortitude to help her in that way. Her attraction to Nate was, at least in part, that he didn't feed her vanity, and was even seemingly repulsed by her pursuit of it. He looked for and saw the good in her, the deep down Cassie that she so desperately wanted to resurrect.

When they arrived at the treehouse, Cassie told Nate the story of how it had been a gift from her father and how much she adored her parents.

"Your folks are really special," Nate agreed. "This treehouse may be a bit over the top, but it is certainly unique."

Cassie loved how unimpressed Nate was by "things." He was much more about the person than the things they possessed, or sometimes, that possessed them. He was also honest, almost to the point of being brutal about it, but that too was a refreshing change to the girl around whom everyone always said she, and her life, and everything about her existence, was perfect. She had never met anyone quite like Nate, and she was coming to believe he was worth pursuing no matter what the cost.

"Do you want to climb up to the top?" she asked innocently. "The view from up there is pretty nice."

"Sure," Nate replied innocently. "This treehouse reminds me of the old Disney movie, "The Swiss Family Robinson." Did you ever see the replica of their treehouse at Disneyland? It's not there anymore, but when I was a kid, I remember it was one of my favorites. It wasn't even a ride; it was just a giant treehouse you could climb up into and play around. I spent hours in it imagining I was marooned on some secret island. My siblings always moaned about how much time I spent in that tree because they wanted to ride the rides. But for me, using my imagination was always more fun than the rides."

At the top platform, they looked out to the Gillette vineyard to the north and the Wingate property to the east. A breeze had picked up, and both felt a chill. Cassie instantly realized that the bed on the third level might be misinterpreted, but didn't quite know how gracefully to explain her lack of intent. Whether he perceived anything inappropriate, Nate played it down and, after scouting the view, calmly suggested they descend back down to the creek.

He is such a gentleman, Cassie thought to herself, as the two sat chatting and soaking their feet in the cool refreshment offered by the water. Their conversation flowed almost as naturally and freely as the creek did.

*****

The Cantina was one of the hippest places in Carmel. It was located on the edge of the sand and even had a few small tables with umbrella covers sitting on the beach. An expansive redwood deck providing unobstructed views of the Carmel lagoon and Point Lobos Reserve to the south was the center of activity. The fare was, of course, Tex-Mex, and the margaritas were legendary. The band Nate had mentioned was just starting their first set, and only two couples were on the dance floor when they arrived. They snacked on chips and salsa while awaiting delivery of the drinks they had ordered. The fifth song played was a slow country ballad that each of them was familiar with.

"Would you like to dance?" Nate asked.

"Sure," Cassie answered as she scooted back from the table. She had hoped an opportunity to dance would arise. Not only would it give her an appropriate chance to get closer to Nate, but one of her talents, in her early pageant days, had been modern dance, so she was very accomplished on the dance floor. She took it slow nonetheless, again recognizing that with Nate, less was more. And, once again she found herself reveling in the fact that she didn't need to strive to impress this man who was so grounded and real.

Over the course of dinner, Nate learned a great deal about Cassie's past, her life in Arizona and the struggles associated with the career path she had chosen. In turn, Nate told his story, and about the fiancé that he lost during his time in law school. Both had relational wounds that were in need of healing. Nate drove Cassie back to her house just after 9 p.m. The air was still, and the crickets were singing joyous harmonies that filled the early summer evening.

"Nate, thank you for a wonderful afternoon and evening," Cassie said. "I don't think I've shared some of the things I told you about tonight with anyone else before. I feel free and comfortable around you. Thanks for being, well, for just being you. I really appreciate your friendship."

"Well, to be honest," Nate responded humbly, "I have to admit I avoided you for a long time. You are a beautiful girl, and I was ... well, I was intimidated. But getting to know you these past few weeks, you are so different than what I expected. I'm learning that you are a lovely person inside, too. You are approachable and sweet and vulnerable and genuine and kind and ...."

Cassie stopped him mid-sentence with a kiss. Though surprised, Nate found himself welcoming the gesture, and he kissed her back. He then separated from her enough so their eyes could meet. When he smiled at her, her heart melted.

***

Romero relished the thought of showing Jacob Wingate a little discipline, though he received little from his parents growing up. His father left the family scene when he was five years old, and a twenty-year prison sentence for manslaughter kept them apart after that. His mother did what she could to fend for Romero and his three siblings, but as soon as he was able, Romero was forced to quit school and work to help support the family. He quickly tired of minimum wage jobs and because of his size became an enforcer for a local gang leader at the age of 16. Testimony to his gang days was inked on his left forearm. In an ornate Celtic font the tattoo was an obscure acronym: KOBK -- kill or be killed. His work as an enforcer came to an end when, at the age of 22, he was convicted for assaulting a police officer. While on probation, after spending three years in the nearby Soledad prison, he took a job as a laborer in the Gillette vineyard. Parker quickly recognized the big man had potential beyond picking and processing grapes, and after ten years with the operation, he had been promoted to the rank of ranch foreman.

Romero had been casing the old Granger property for the past week and a half. To avoid detection he gained access by way of the same downed fence segment that Jacob had used to visit the spring. He rode up to the spring on horseback and then hiked by foot along the creek until he reached the back of the farmhouse. His charge had been to punish Wingate without physically hurting him which presented a bit of a quandary for Romero.

Wingate's existence in the Pastures was fairly simple, and short of burning the house down,

Romero was at a loss to determine a good way to punish the man ... until, on day eight of his surveillance, it came to him. The only other resident at the house, so to speak, was Wingate's dog. The two seemed to be pretty close, and Wingate made it a point to walk the dog every morning and then to train him at night. It was a handsome hunting dog and, Romero presumed, probably worth quite a bit of money. Romero decided the dog would make a perfect target, and Romero hated dogs. As the plan took shape in his mind, he looked down at the ugly two-inch scar left by the ragged incisor of a pit bull that had attacked him as a boy and smiled at the notion of exacting a measure of vengeance against the species while doing his boss's bidding at the same time. It would be a "twofer."

On Thursday Jacob drove off to town just before the noon hour and Romero's opportunity to implement his plan finally arrived. Once the car was out of sight and earshot, the former gang enforcer walked toward the dog run from his position in the trees next to the creek. The dog started barking an alert to his master, but his master was gone. Romero banged on the dog run fence to taunt the animal who became more and

131

more agitated. The man then growled at the dog and kicked dirt on him. But for the fact that Romero stood on two feet instead of four, you would have thought that two vicious dogs were fighting to the death. Once he finished his taunt and concluded he had established sufficient superiority over the caged canine, Romero reached into his backpack and tossed a piece of raw steak over the fence and into the dog run.

"There you go, you cur. Enjoy your last supper," the man growled.

Romero watched with prurient interest as the dog woofed down the steak and then almost immediately began to gasp and choke. The man sat down next to the fence and, as if watching an exhibition at the Roman Coliseum, cheered as the dog suffered in anguish before his eyes. Mercifully, the poison was relatively fast acting, and within less than two minutes the animal was dead. Romero sat for several minutes after the dog stopped breathing and grinned with satisfaction. Then, pretending he was Caesar, he held his right hand high into the air and with great fanfare dramatically pointed his thumb down toward the ground and pronounced aloud, "Death!" Before he left, Romero taped to the fence a type-written, pre-prepared, three-word note that read, "You've been warned."

***

Jacob answered his cell phone on the third ring. It was Ella.

"Jacob, oh Jacob, good news, the best news really, Papa seems to be getting better. The doctors just left and told me they believe he is going to recover. My prayers for a miracle have been answered."

"Ella, that is great news," Jacob replied. "I couldn't be happier for you. You know, I haven't met your father yet and would very much like to … that is, when you think he is strong enough to receive visitors. I'd like to wish him well and express to him my interest in his daughter."

Ella paused on the phone for a long moment wondering if she had heard Jacob correctly. "Excuse me, what was that last part, I think our connection might be weak," Ella asked.

"I said, I'd like to tell him that I'm interested in you, Ella. Look, we've been seeing each other for several weeks now, and I'd like to date you on a more regular basis. I assume, based on our talk the other night that you're okay with that idea, right?"

"Well, of course, I am Jacob, it's just that, well, it's just, I don't know what to say. I'm so excited to hear that your heart is in the same place as mine. And to know you want to talk with my father about our relationship is just so, just so right and honorable and perfect. Yes! We must make arrangements for you to meet him as soon as possible."

"Good," Jacob said with a sigh of relief, "for a minute there I thought maybe I'd misread your feelings. Ella, I care for you and would like very much to pursue a relationship. Let me know when your father is up to it, and I'll drop everything and come right over.

"By the way, have you mentioned anything about 'us' to your brother yet? I can't imagine he'll be too happy about the idea."

"No, I haven't," Ella said sheepishly. "I probably should, but, to be honest, I'm a bit afraid of how he might react. Parker is so mercurial, you know? Maybe, when you come over to talk with my father, assuming we receive his blessing, we can talk to Parker together then."

"I'm fine with that idea," Jacob said. "I'm sorry you have to be fearful of your own brother, but I do understand. He can be rather impulsive. But rest assured, I won't let him do anything foolish. You'll be safe, of that I am sure."

***

As was his routine when he finished work for the day, Nate lowered the blind on the front window to his office, locked the front door, and retired to his residence in the back. It had been a long and tiring day of grinding through a several-hundred-page due diligence binder related to a property Mr. Silvano was looking to purchase down in Big Sur. It seemed the deeper into the document history he dove more questions were raised than answered. He was not all that surprised though because coastal properties were often the most difficult to assess regarding permit compliance, especially in

Big Sur where the culture was premised on the idea that when it comes to governmental permitting it is usually better to ask for forgiveness than permission.

After changing clothes, Nate poured himself a glass of day-old Cabernet and sat down to a Greek salad and an oven roasted chicken breast he had picked up at the deli during lunch. When he finished eating he relaxed in his recliner and dialed Cassie's number.

"Hi, Cassie … this is Nate. I thought I'd just call to say hello and ask how your day went."

"Nate, your call is perfectly timed. I just got the best news. The date for my Sports Illustrated shoot has finally been set, and I expect to get word any day about my travel arrangements. I'm so excited!"

Hearing a silent pause on the other end of the line, Cassie continued, "Nate, did you hear my news? The SI shoot date is set!"

"Yes, Cass, I heard you. I'm sorry, but you know how I feel about that whole gig. We've talked about it and, well, I know you're excited, but I have to be honest, and I'm still not convinced it's the best thing. I mean, having a million men ogling you in a magazine ... call me old-fashioned, but I don't like it. I know it's not my place to say anything, but, well, if we're going to see each other, I just feel like I need to be honest with you ... even if it might hurt."

Cassie had anticipated Nate might feel this way and that is why she hadn't called him about the news. But, when he called her, she couldn't help but share her excitement with the new man in her life. The second he paused in response she knew she'd made a mistake telling him and was already regretting it.

"Come on, Nate. I know what you said earlier, but this is a big deal for me. This is my career. It might not be the most traditional job, but it's what I do. I'm using the gifts I was born with, and I can make a lot of money if things go well. I can't just throw it all away now. Can't you understand?"

"Oh, I understand alright, but this is about priorities, Cassie. And if your priority is fame and fortune and your choice of paths to achieve that is to pose for a magazine while wearing little to nothing, well, I don't know. Like I said, maybe I'm old-fashioned or even prudish, but I can't support it, at least not for me. When we've talked, I thought I understood that you weren't all that happy with the direction you were headed. You led me to believe you were looking for some kind of change. That being the case, I thought maybe, just maybe, someone like me might fit into your life. And for the past few weeks, it has kind of felt that way, but now, I guess I'm not so sure, and I wouldn't want to stand in your way.

"Look, we haven't really known each other very long, and so I guess it isn't fair for me to suggest you change paths. I understand that. I like you, Cassie. But, at the same time, I don't really see us going anywhere if you continue with the modeling thing, at least in the direction you're headed with it right now.

"I think, rather than get into an argument about it, maybe we should just take a break from seeing each other. You do what you need to do regarding the photo shoot, and I'll focus on my work. Things are going to heat up pretty soon for me anyway in the Gillette case. Maybe after things settle down for both of us, we can reevaluate where we are. I'm sorry, Cassie, but I don't see any alternative at this point. My mind isn't going to change about the kind of girl I'm looking for."

"Fine, Nate!" Cassie erupted. "I may not be all mom and apple pie enough for you. I get it. And you're right; I think we do need a break. I can't just abandon everything I've been working toward for eight years because of some guy I've dated a half dozen times. I don't know what I was thinking. I'm not your type, and you're certainly not mine. I guess I just needed a little quiet time and you gave me plenty of that. Well, I'm rested now, thank you very much, and it's time for me to get back in the saddle ... back to realizing my potential."

Her anger and hurt and frustration grew as she spoke.

"In fact, rather than taking a break, let's just break it off altogether. If you miss me, you can join those other million men admiring me in Sports Illustrated come February. Goodbye, Nate."

CHAPTER 8

After the argument with Cassie, Nate had a difficult time sleeping, so the phone call that came in at just after midnight was almost a welcome reprieve.

"Nate, this is Jacob. Is there any way you can come out to the property right now, tonight. Something terrible has happened, and I don't want to disturb anything until you have a chance to see it. I know it's late, it's way late, but this is extremely important. Nate, I may be in danger."

Nate threw on his clothes and splashed his face with cold water trying to shake the grogginess out of his head caused by the three more glasses of wine he had consumed after the conversation with Cassie. He was at Jacob's house in ten minutes.

"Jacob, what is it, man? What happened?" Nate asked anxiously.

"I was out late at dinner with a prospective wine distributor, and when I got home about thirty minutes ago, after changing clothes I went out back to say hi to Sierra. Someone killed her," Jacob said sadly. "Come with me back to her run. I haven't touched anything. There's a note."

Jacob had not gotten around to installing any lighting in the back of the house, so it was pitch black. The heat of the day was still lingering in the air, and the ordinarily calming sound of crickets was strangely eerie. Jacob handed Nate a flashlight as the two made their way over to the enclosed dog run.

"See, here's the note I mentioned," Jacob said, his breathing rapid and uneven.

Nate shined his light in the same place Jacob was shining his, and together they read the warning. Neither said anything. Jacob then lowered his head and tapped Nate on the shoulder.

"My Sierra is over here," he said sadly as he walked ten paces to the left.

After taking pictures of the scene with their cell phones, the two went inside and sat down at the dining room table.

"So, what are you thinking, Jacob? Who do you think could have done this?" Nate asked.

"Well, I think it's pretty obvious, don't you? It had to be Gillette, or more likely that half-crazed henchman of his, Romero. But how are we going to prove it?"

"You may be right about that; it sure makes sense," Nate concurred. "I knew they were volatile, but I didn't think they would actually get violent. This is a pretty drastic move. Do you think we should get a restraining order, you know, to at least keep them off your property?"

"I want to do any and everything I can to get these guys," Jacob said. "I've been trying to be civil, mostly because of Ella, but there's no turning back now. This is all out war. There can't be a happy ending to this story. Parker Gillette and I can never be neighbors. It's either him or me. Do you think we should call the sheriff?"

"Yes but not until after I can get my investigator out here. I know the deputies try, but half the time they can spoil more evidence than they actually collect. I can have my guy over here at nine o'clock tomorrow morning. We can call the sheriff at 10. Are you good with that?"

"Yes, totally, Nate -- I have every confidence in you. I really want to get these guys though, and I think the best way may be to embarrass them in public, so I think we should also call the local newspaper and make some headlines with this. Maybe flood social media, too. That is, as soon as we have solid evidence."

"Maybe," Nate hesitated, "but let's talk about it before you do anything. Online warfare can be dangerous."

***

Several days later Ella called Jacob to report that her father was continuing to improve and that she had spoken with him about his request to meet him. They agreed to meet together with him at the estate at 4 p.m. the next day. Jacob decided not to mention the Sierra incident to Ella because he didn't want to upset her nor draw her further into the escalating feud between himself and her brother. She would learn soon enough when they had the necessary proof to go public.

Jacob had driven by the great bronze gate guarding the formidable mansion many times as it was located on one of only two roads leading from the Pastures to town. He was accustomed to ostentatious vineyard homes, and this place, he thought, would fit quite comfortably up north in Napa. Ella left the gate open, so Jacob was able to drive right up to the house.

"I'm so glad you could make it!" Ella said skipping through the portico to greet Jacob. They embraced for a quick moment and then Jacob gave her a tender kiss on the cheek.

"I'm so glad, too. Meeting your father is very important to me. I trust he is still feeling up to it?"

"He has spoken of nothing else all day," Ella answered. "Come, follow me. I'll give you a quick tour of the house, and then we'll meet Papa. He's upstairs in his study."

The Casa was impeccably decorated in early 20th century Spanish motif. As Ella walked him around, Jacob imagined himself in the court of some wealthy prince, or maybe even a king. Ella was proud of their home, but not in an arrogant way. She took pains to describe the architecture and a bit about some of her favorite pieces of art. Jacob enjoyed every minute of the tour.

"... and those two spears above the mantle are from the running of the bulls in Pamplona. My other brother dared fate there three years ago."

"Other brother?" Jacob asked.

"Yes, sorry I haven't mentioned James before. He died in Monaco a year ago, but the pain is still very fresh, so I tend to avoid the subject. I believe his death may be what has caused Papa's health to fail ... a broken heart, you know?"

"I'm so sorry, Ella. Losing a loved one can be crushing. I still miss my grandfather terribly, and he's been gone for almost five years now. I'll be sure not to mention anything about it around your father."

When they finally arrived at the study which was located just off the master bedroom suite, Ella stopped and took Jacob's hands in hers.

"Jacob, just a word to the wise about my father, his way is very old school. His language and manners are, well, romanticized. He speaks like he is an ancient philosopher or poet. I think, in his old age, he has taken to imagining himself as a 19th-century Spanish aristocrat or perhaps even Don Quixote. So, anyway, please try not to be distracted by his panache and just filter through his poetic way to find his meaning. It's very endearing to me, but others find it a bit distracting."

Ella then knocked gently on the door and entered the room.

"Papa, how are you feeling?" she asked as she approached and kissed him on the cheek. "This is my friend, Jacob Wingate -- the one I wanted you to meet."

Armand was significantly better than he had been just two weeks earlier. He seemed alert and engaged. But for his weakened physical condition, no one would have suspected he had been at death's door so recently. The old man cleared his throat and extended his hand.

"Mr. Wingate. It is my pleasure, sir. My dear Gabriella tells me many good things about you. I trust perhaps at least half of them are true."

The old man chuckled at his own joke which brought on a short coughing spasm.

"What do you think of our Casa de Abundante, eh?"

"It is spectacular Armand, truly one of a kind. And the art is magnificent. I was especially drawn to the Benlliure sculpture in the library. Is that an original?"

"Ella, I see your man has an eye for artistic beauty as well as the physical beauty you possess. This speaks well of him, appreciating beauty in all its forms, that is. But to answer your question, Jacob, no, the piece you saw is an excellent reproduction, we have loaned the original to the Museo Nacional del Prado in Madrid. They are most grateful to watch over it, and I rest easier knowing our treasure is safe there.

"So, Ella tells me you have something you would like to ask me, eh?" Armand said with a smile and a wink toward his daughter.

"Yes, sir. Well, I have been seeing Ella for almost a month now, and we have gone on a few casual dates together. You mentioned her physical beauty which, of course, is undeniable, but Mr. Gillette, I am most attracted to Ella's inner beauty. She is a wonderful, kind and loving person. And she can be very funny as well," Jacob smiled broadly, "we have shared many good laughs together.

"So, sir, my question, really more a request actually, is that we would like your blessing to see one another on a more serious level. Years ago one might have considered what I am referring to as courting, but in today's vernacular it would, I suppose, simply be called serious dating.

"I would not presume to move in that direction without your approval, and so, that is my request for now. Where things might lead in the future is unknown to me, but to find out we must take a step at a time down the path."

"Well said, young man well said. Life is a journey and the path a mystery, but to live life and experience all it has to offer one must indeed walk the path a step at a time. The fates can be kind or cruel but must nevertheless be met along the way. Do not fear them. Walk on, yes walk on. Walk on together, and if love is your destiny then blessed you shall be.

"The kind fates introduced me to love during my walk with Ella's mother, Susanna. She was as beautiful to the eye as Ella, but as you say, also beautiful in the heart. My dear Gabriella is my joy you know, and her heart I will guard to my last breath. So be careful with it Jacob, treat it as the treasure of inestimable value that it is.

"I have also met the cruel fates, and they are the worst kind," Armand continued. "They rob and steal our joy and our hope. But, you must not allow them to prevail over you. They nearly destroyed me when they took my boy, James. Always remember, no matter how dark and hopeless the shadows along the path may seem when you're in the depths of the valley, light ever remains on the other side. For the shadows only exist because of the light. If you walk steadily through the shadowland, you will eventually emerge back into the light. So, yes, walk on, walk on indeed."

Then turning to Ella, Armand said smiling, "I like your man, Ella. I sense in him a spirit of goodness and wisdom. You have my blessing child to walk the path together, and I will pray joy for you both as you do."

"Thank you, Papa. Thank you. Thank you for your blessing and your wisdom and your prayers. I am so grateful that you kept walking yourself and can once again begin to feel the light of life's joy. I love you, Papa."

The father and daughter embraced for a brief moment as Jacob looked on. He felt as if he should perhaps step away to give them privacy but then thought better of it wanting to experience the depth of their love, to maybe understand it and perhaps someday be able to emulate what he was seeing. This step down their path together was indeed one to be captured and remembered forever.

Outside in the portico, Jacob and Ella sat on a bench holding hands and talking as the fountain rained gently into its giant pool.

"Ella," Jacob finally said, "I loved your father's 'way', as you said. His formality and romantic nature were infectious. I liked it. Perhaps we should all return to the 19th century. All things considered, I think our meeting went well, don't you?"

"Very well," Ella responded. "I have not heard Papa speak with so much hope since before James died. I think perhaps he sees some of James in you. Anyway, I am pleased, Jacob. And wherever our path may lead, I know we will find joy in the journey, and I'm looking forward to that."

"As am I, Ella."

The two embraced and then kissed as a pair of evil eyes surveilled their moment from the library window above.

This is not good, definitely not good. This puppy love infatuation must be snuffed out before it can bloom or I will lose everything, Parker mused to himself. He then picked up his phone and hit speed dial number one.

"Romero, meet me in the vineyard at the well pump house in ten minutes. I have a job for you."

***

Cassie had been an emotional wreck since her break up with Nate the week before, but the excitement of the upcoming photo shoot kept her going. Her parents weren't helping things either as they seemed to side with Nate. They never said anything affirmatively to discourage her modeling pursuits, but when she told them the reason she wasn't seeing Nate any longer they both confessed that they had, for a long while, harbored reservations about her career path. Everyone, it seemed, except Parker and her friends at the Club, seemed to be turning against her. Her musings were interrupted when the phone rang.

"Hello. Yes, this is Cassie Weston .... Oh, hi, yes, Sports Illustrated, what can I do for you. I'm so excited about the Mexico trip. Is there a change in schedule? ... What? ... Canceled? ... The whole shoot? When will it be rescheduled? ... Not canceled? Wait, I'm confused … I'm canceled? … What? No, there must be some mistake. I've been scheduled for months. I have a contract with the company … The contract gives the company the right to bow out? … But why? Did I do something wrong? Did I miss a deadline or something? Can I talk to someone in charge about this? This is really important to me, you know … Well, okay. But tell your boss I'm going to have my lawyer look into it, and I'll be getting back to you."

She plopped down on the couch and tossed her phone to the side.

How can this be? My whole career rides on this shoot. What in the world am I going to do now? There must be a way around this, but who is going to be willing to help me? Certainly not my folks or Nate. Who else has a lawyer? Parker! Parker has a lawyer, and he has always been encouraging of my career, I'll give him a call.

She dialed Parker's number, and he picked up on the second ring.

"Hey there Cassie, long time no hear from. What's my favorite blonde been up to? Hey, when is your

Mexico trip or have you already gone? Is that why I haven't heard from you?"

"Parker," Cassie began weeping into the phone, "that's why I'm calling. No, I haven't been to Mexico yet. The shoot was scheduled for next week, but the company just called me and said I've been dropped from the model list. I have a contract, Parker. They can't just drop me like that at the last minute, can they?"

"Babe, I'm so sorry to hear that. And, I don't know about the contract thing, but I'll be glad to have my lawyers take a look at it if you want. Listen, I am tied up tonight, but let's get together tomorrow night and talk about it. Why don't you come over to the house, around, seven and then we'll drive down the coast and find a quiet place for dinner where we can talk this through. Okay?"

"Yeah, okay. Thanks, Parker. I miss you, and I need you now more than ever. I'll see you tomorrow night. Bye."

Even before she hung up the phone Parker's mind was swirling with the possibilities.

This is almost too good to be true, he mused. *The timing couldn't be better. I get some time alone with the beauty queen, and then she'll be the perfect foil for my plan. The fates are indeed smiling on me tonight.*

He then picked his phone back up and pressed speed dial number one.

***

Jacob glanced down at his phone when it rang but didn't recognize the number, so he let it go to voicemail.

Later, while preparing to turn in and checking his emails and text messages, he saw the banner notice reminding him of the voicemail. He opened the function and held the phone up to his ear.

A mysterious voice he didn't recognize said, "If you want information about your dog's killer, meet me at the Circle Q tomorrow night at 11 p.m. I'll be wearing a red bandana."

The cryptic message clicked off. Jacob hit replay and listened to it again, and then again. He thought about calling Nate, but it was late, and besides, he convinced himself, he didn't need his lawyer along. This was his fight, and if someone had information about his pup, he could get it himself. Deep down, he also had to admit the intrigue of it all was rather enticing.

***

During their dinner on the expansive private balcony overlooking the Pacific that Parker had rented for the evening, Cassie spilled her heart out about her profound disappointment over the canceled Sports Illustrated opportunity. Parker dutifully listened and made sure her wine glass was kept full. With dessert, he offered her a unique 30-year-old Port he had brought along. He told her it was from Spain and was one of the best from his private collection. After finishing off nearly three bottles of wine between them, Cassie had little ability to resist the after-dinner offering.

"Ugh!" she said scrunching her nose after tasting the dark, thick nectar. "That's got a strange aftertaste to it."

"Yes, age will do that to a Port sometimes. But this is an extraordinary bottle. It comes from a small village called Caldes de Malavella. They have famous thermal springs there where you can soak away all your worries and troubles. I thought it appropriate for you tonight, Cass. We want to put your problems behind you so you can enjoy life in the here and now."

"Malavella," she slurred, "Malavella sounds like a very nice place."

"And they dance there, too," Parker tempted. "The dancing is unrivaled in all of Spain. And the women, they are the most beautiful in the world -- but none are as beautiful as you. Dance for me, Cassie. Show me your beauty in motion."

The drug Parker had slipped into her glass of Port was taking effect even faster than he had anticipated. The wine in her system was probably helping it along. Cassie's mind was spinning as the balcony lights strung above them seemed to dance in mid-air. Parker brought up some sensual Spanish music on his phone and set it on the table to play. Cassie felt a wave of warmth and desire flow through her as the music melted away whatever natural reluctance she might have otherwise had. She stood up from the table and began swaying to the sounds of desire that were filling her head.

"Dance my beauty ... dance," Parker cooed to his prey.

CHAPTER 9

Jacob sat alone at the bar looking at his watch. It was 11:15 and still no sign of the red bandanna. He ordered a third gin and tonic and decided he'd wait another fifteen minutes before giving up and going home. Because it was a weeknight, there was no live band, and the musical repertoire of the jukebox was stale. Even though smoking was technically not allowed, the owner had apparently decided the rule didn't apply to marijuana. The odor emanating from the back table practically choked the whole bar, and if a sheriff's deputy had wandered in, he would probably have arrested everyone in the place. Cowboy bar was an apt description of the Circle Q, with a touch of Santa Cruz mixed in.

Jacob felt his focus begin to drift but chalked it up to the third shot of alcohol combined with the second-hand effects from the back table aroma. The music seemed to invade his mind more profusely, but he found himself unable to remember the lyrics of the well-known tunes. He asked the bartender to open a window because he was sweating and beginning to feel a bit nauseous.

Man, this gin carries quite a wallop, Jacob thought to himself, *I wish I'd stopped at two.*

Slowly Jacob began to slump in his seat, and the bartender came around and helped him move to the booth by the front door. He propped him up and leaned his head against the wall to make it look like he was just drunk and asleep. The bartender then put a half-empty bottle of Jack Daniels on the table beside him before returning to his duties behind the bar.

Romero entered the room at 11:30. Seeing Jacob incapacitated in the booth, he walked over to the bar and ordered a shot of tequila. He paid the bartender in cash for the drink and gave him a $1,000.00 tip.

"Thanks, I owe you one," Romero said, "and I'll bring you a fresh supply of GHB, next week. If anyone asks, he's my cousin from Oregon who can't hold his liquor worth squat."

The big man laughed at his own joke as he turned from the bar. He helped Jacob to his feet and ushered the stumbling figure out to his awaiting pickup in the dirt parking lot. His rig spit gravel which pitted the front window of the bar as he sped away toward the appointed coastal rendezvous spot.

The two arrived 30 minutes later. Because of the late hour, the restaurant parking lot was nearly abandoned, just as Parker had planned, so no witnesses. Jacob was almost comatose, so Romero had to hoist him up on his shoulder to carry him inside. The big man plodded up the rickety staircase, leaning heavily on the banister as he climbed. When he got to the door leading out to the back balcony, he stopped and waited for the signal.

Parker had been watching and waiting for his man to arrive and as soon as he saw him, he waved to him to enter and deposit Jacob onto the couch by the door. The plan was to loosen Jacob's clothing to make it look like he was involved in the act of passion. Romero did so quickly and then stepped out of the room to await further instruction, though he wished he could stay and watch.

Cassie was so far under the influence that she didn't notice the new arrival to the balcony as she continued her dancing for Parker. With the table now set, Parker played his next card.

"Oh... Cassie... you are so, so, alluring. Hey girl, for fun let's turn this dance session into a photo shoot. What do you say? Show me how you were going to impress those big wigs at Sports Illustrated. Show me how you were going to get yourself onto that cover."

Cassie liked the game and immediately began to play along.

"They like to see a lot of skin," she slurred, "you know, like this."

She slowly began unbuttoning her blouse and proceeded to perform a bit of an impromptu striptease. Parker was practically salivating. She slipped off her shirt and then her jeans. Clothed only in her undergarments she teased, "How do you like my bikini, mister?"

Parker picked up his phone and started taking pictures. He pretended to be a European fashion photographer and moved back and forth and left and right snapping photos from different angles as he coaxed the girl to move more sensually.

"Nice, Cassie, you make my camera happy, go girl."

Smiling and giggling, she blew a kiss at the camera and then stumbled a bit over her own feet. When Parker could see she was almost ready to drop into unconsciousness, he set his phone down and gently guided her over toward the couch.

"This man is the vice president of Sports Illustrated," Parker lied. "He will decide who gets the cover. Tell him how much you want it. Whisper in his ear, I'm sure he'll listen."

The light was dim, and Cassie was so far gone she didn't have a clue who the man on the couch was, or frankly, where she was. In her mind, she was on a beach somewhere in Mexico becoming famous. She sat down beside Jacob and began cooing into his ear. Her hand reached into his partially unbuttoned shirt, and she started rubbing his chest.

Parker's voice continued to lead her deeper and deeper into his evil labyrinth by encouraging her to persuade the SI executive of her willingness to do whatever it took to become the cover model.

"Go on, tease him a little, Cass. He likes it," Parker taunted, as he retrieved his phone from the table.

Moments later both of the victims were out cold on the couch. Satisfied he had what he needed, Parker dispatched Romero to take them both home.

"Be quick about it," Parker ordered. "And don't you dare touch either of them, you hear me! If you do, I'll know, and you'll find yourself right back in Soledad. Don't doubt me, man. You know I have the power to make that happen. Just get the job done, and be sure no one sees you. I'll meet you in the morning, down at the barn, and we'll talk about next steps."

***

The phone woke Jacob from a dead sleep the following morning.

"Yeah..." Jacob muttered, half unconscious.

"Whoa, friend, you don't sound so good. Are you sick or something?" Nate responded immediately.

"Or something, yes," Jacob answered groggily. "I don't know what hit me last night, but I feel like it might have been a bus. Seriously, I can't remember ever feeling this lousy before. Maybe I'm coming down with the flu or something ... uh, wait a minute, I think I'm going to be sick."

Nate heard the phone drop to the floor, footsteps running away and then a horrible retch. He waited, and then another series of retches met his ear. Finally, Jacob returned to the call.

"Ugh, are you still there? Sorry about that, Nate. As I said, I'm in pretty rough shape over here."

"Well listen, I've got big news, and in your condition, it might be better if I came over there to talk. Are you good with that?" Nate suggested.

"Sure, I'm certainly not going anywhere."

Finding the door unlocked, which he thought a bit odd after the warning his client had received the week before, Nate let himself into the house. Finding Jacob head down in the commode again, he slipped into the kitchen and hunted around for soda crackers and 7-Up. Returning to the bedroom, he offered his home remedy to his client.

"I'm sure food is the last thing on your mind, but you need to keep something in your stomach, and more importantly, you need to stay hydrated, so here you are, the full extent of my medical expertise, soda and crackers."

"Thanks, man, just put them there on the bed stand," Jacob managed, "so what's your big news?"

"My investigator finished up his analysis and delivered his report to me. He got a 93% match on a fingerprint from the warning letter. It's not absolute proof, but darn close."

"Okay, so who is it? The suspense is killing me."

"Your first suspicion – it was Gillette's man, Romero Calderon."

Jacob nodded and then smiled to himself.

"Now we can file a formal report with the Sheriff, so they can go arrest the guy," Nate said matter-of-factly.

"About that," Jacob interrupted. "I've decided to use this information in another way. I want to keep it private for now and use it as leverage in the water dispute. I think I can talk turkey with Parker now, and with this proof that he killed Sierra, or at least ordered her killed, I think I can convince him to be reasonable."

With a heavy dose of skepticism, Nate replied, "And, what if he doesn't?"

"Then I'll leak it to the local press and splash it all over the Internet. His business reputation, what little he may have, will be ruined. He would never risk that, so I'm pretty sure he'll cooperate."

"Jacob, you know I advise against this sort of tactic. It's tantamount to extortion. That's his game, not yours. And once you start down that path, there's often no return, and both parties usually get sullied if not completely embarrassed. Don't do it, man."

"Thanks for the advice, Counselor. I wouldn't expect anything less from you, but my mind is made up. Only a nuke is going to get Gillette's attention, and I'm going to serve this one up on a platter. Thanks for the report. Just leave a copy on the table on your way out. I'll call you later. Now if you'll excuse me, I need to revisit the bathroom."

Nate left to the sound of more vomiting and thought to himself, *dang that's one ugly flu, I'm going to stop by the pharmacy this afternoon to get a flu shot.*

***

On the opposite end of the Pastures, Cassie was awakening. Her head was splitting, and her mouth was dry as a bone. Try as she might she couldn't recall much of anything following the dinner with Parker and had no idea how she had gotten home.

Seeing her finally rustling in the bed, Cassie's mother poked her head into the room.

"Cassie, are you alright? It's almost noon, dear. You haven't slept in this late since high school. There's a flu bug going around. Does your stomach feel okay?

"Thanks, Mom, my stomach is fine. I just have a headache. I guess I just needed to catch up on my beauty sleep. You know, for Mexico."

"Yes, Mexico, of course, dear ... well, come on down when you're ready, and I'll fix you something for breakfast, or, uh, lunch, or whatever you want. Father and I are going to town to meet some friends around two, so it should be plenty quiet around here if you need more rest. Love you."

Her parents' love was so extraordinary; she wondered why she hadn't just listened to them about the SI gig. The only people in her life who seemed to care about her were all in agreement. Only Parker took her side in the debate. Parker? She tried again to remember details of the evening with him.

Dinner. Big Sur. On a balcony. Wine, lots of wine. Something about a spa or bath? Dessert. Little hanging light bulbs. Port. Yeah, that strange tasting Port. But what then? Charades? Did we play charades or something?

She realized she had neglected to change before crawling into bed as her clothes were still on, but suddenly she felt uncomfortable like the clothes didn't fit right and were tugging at her. She sat up on the bed and stared down at her shirt.

"What the?" She uttered out loud. "These buttons are all buttoned wrong. No wonder it feels like this blouse is choking me. But how ...?"

She stopped mid-sentence as a partial memory flashed in her mind.

Dancing ... and ... a striptease ... Parker! Why that no good loser took advantage of me last night.

Her furor continued to rise as she tried to remember more, but couldn't. *Well, I hope he enjoyed my little dance,* she argued to herself, *because I will never, ever darken his door again. But what now.* She sighed heavily; *you're going to have to confess being fired by Sports Illustrated to the folks and probably to Nate, too. I can only hope and pray they'll forgive my stupidity.*

***

Jacob was feeling half human again by mid-afternoon and decided to call Parker Gillette. Gillette's assistant answered and took a message. Three minutes later Parker returned the call.

"Wingate ... Parker Gillette here. I understand you just called. What do you want?"

"Hello Parker. I have some information I think you'll find very interesting, and I'd like to share it with you, in person," Jacob said.

"If it's about the lawsuit, have your lawyer call mine. I don't want to waste any time talking to you directly."

"Well, this isn't exactly about the lawsuit, though I suppose it could become related," Jacob hinted. "I think you're going to want to see this, at least before anyone else does."

Because he was well accustomed to his own voice, Parker knew the sound of a snake when he heard one, and he recognized a familiar hiss on the other end of the line. He wasn't worried though, because of his successful adventure in cinematography the night before. He was, however, intrigued by this sudden change of tactic by Wingate, from Mr. Nice Guy to gutter fighter. So, he invited him over for a drink at five.

"Thanks, I'll be there," Jacob responded, "but I think I'll probably pass on the drink. I haven't been feeling too sharp today."

"I'll be in the library," Parker said.

Hanging up the phone Gillette smiled a half-cocked crooked grin, *I'll bet you haven't felt well today Mr. Napa boy. Ha, but you haven't felt anything yet. Just wait until I get through with you. You'll be running home to your mama, and she won't even take you in.*

***

Ella was surprised when Shelby told her that Jacob had pulled up to the gate. She ran down the stairs to meet him in the foyer as he walked in.

"Jacob! This is certainly a nice surprise -- but what … no flowers?" Ella teased.

"Hi, Ella, yeah, sorry no flowers this time … I must be slipping. Please don't tell Armand," Jacob tried to laugh off his error. "The reason I didn't call is that, well, I'm here to see Parker, about some business."

Ella's intuitive antennae went up immediately and began signaling a warning.

"Jacob, you know better than to trust my brother. Whatever he is proposing is not going to be good for you. You really must not let yourself be drawn into his lair. I know you want to make things right with our family, and I respect and admire that, but I am convinced that just isn't possible with Parker involved. I actually think he may be plotting against Papa and me to seize control of the estate. I can't point to anything in particular; it's just this feeling I'm getting. Parker has done nothing but complain about Papa since his health started coming back. The other night he and Papa had words, harsh words, and Parker stormed out of the study, slammed the door and cursed a mean streak all the way down the hall. The next thing I know that dreadful man, Romero, was meeting with Parker in the library. I tell you he is up to something terrible, Jacob. Please, just walk away.

I will tell him you got a sudden emergency phone call or something, but please don't meet with him."

Ella's report was troubling. Jacob knew Parker hated him, but to think he might be plotting against his own family was a new low, even for Parker.

"Ella, I appreciate your concern, and I want to talk with you about this threat you perceive, but, well, I asked for this meeting, so Parker is not baiting me into anything here. Please trust me; I know what I'm doing.

"Look, our meeting shouldn't take more than a few minutes. How about you and I go out for dinner afterwards. Your choice -- I don't care where we go, as long as I'm with you."

Ella smiled at the kind words, reluctantly consented, and hurried off to get ready. Jacob made his way up the stairs and found Parker seated in the library on a chair next to the window. He didn't rise to greet Jacob, but instead just grunted and waved him over.

"Okay, so what is so important that you drive all the way over here to show me, eh? Did you discover some other mystery deed giving you more rights in my land?" Parker moaned disgustedly.

"No, nothing like that. Did you hear my dog was killed at my home a week or so ago?" Jacob began.

"Nope. I heard nothing of the sort. Did you report it to the sheriff? Sorry for your loss. I had a dog once when I was a boy. He was a good friend."

"You can save your false sympathies for someone else, but don't waste them on me, you lying sack of ...." Jacob caught himself before cursing.

"I've got proof that your man, Calderon, killed my dog -- poisoned her. I have no doubt he enjoyed watching her suffer. He was a fool though because he left a calling card -- a note taped to my fence threatening me. Well, you should buy your man some gloves for Christmas because he has a very recognizable fingerprint which we lifted from the note. I've got him, and consequently you, dead to rights on this." Jacob paused to gauge the reaction and was surprised when he saw none.

"You don't say," Parker finally replied calmly. "Well, I don't care if you have a video of him doing whatever you think he did. It doesn't matter to me because you'll never make it stick. You haven't gone to the sheriff yet because you know he won't even make an arrest based on whatever flimsy evidence you had patched together by some amateur Sherlock Holmes. What did you hope to gain by marching in here with this wild-eyed accusation anyway, Napa boy?"

"I figured you'd get smart, Gillette, and maybe we could settle our differences, if I conveniently lost the evidence and found it in my heart to forgive your henchman. I'm thinking something along the lines of an agreement by which we share the water, so both of our vineyards can expand. I'll even change the art on my label if you back off the name dispute, which, by the way, is a bogus claim to begin with."

Jacob still didn't get a rise out of Parker who just sat there stoically smiling. He then started laughing. A soft chuckle at first, but then he burst out into a loud, boisterous, bellowing laugh that was so hearty that when he tipped back in his chair, it almost fell over.

"Napa boy, you are crazy, you know that? You come in here all self-important and puffed up with some little ginned up report and allege I had something to do with killing your animal and then have the gall to threaten me to my face. You just committed extortion man, do you know that. You are far dumber than I gave you credit for. But look," Parker sneered, "I'm a reasonable person, so how about I make you a counteroffer."

CHAPTER 10

"A counteroffer ... what are you talking about? I'm offering to forego ruining you in the press in return for a little fairness. There's nothing to counter with. It's take it or leave it because I'll beat you in court anyway," Jacob blustered.

"Well, let me just put it to you this way, Wingate. If you go to the press or breathe a word of your supposed evidence outside this room, you will rue the day. Trust me on this; you will wish you never bought land in the Pastures. You will wish you never met me, or my sister. You will regret everything you ever did to cross me. I will destroy you – do you hear me. So, that is my counter offer, I will spare your miserable existence."

"You have nothing on me, Parker. Maybe in your twisted mind, you think you can make something up, but you have nothing, and you know it. So, let's leave it like this, I'll race you to the press, and then we'll see who is going to ruin whom. You are really a piece of work; you know that? Oh and by the way, if you do anything to hurt Ella, it will be the last thing you ever do. You got that. You leave her out of whatever plan you think you're hatching. I swear, I'll see you rot in jail if any harm comes to Ella. Now, I'll be leaving. I'd advise you to tell Calderon to run, very far away, and that you prep your lawyer to defend you on criminal charges."

***

The following morning Nate called Jacob around ten.

"Jacob, we won. The court ruling on the temporary injunctions just came out, and we won, on all counts!"

"Even on the name and label issues?" Jacob followed.

"Yep, we won everything. We still have to prevail at trial, but in issuing the injunctions, the judge has already concluded we are likely to win on the merits. Man oh man is Gillette going to blow a gasket. I wouldn't be surprised if he even fired that pompous lawyer of his. This is huge Jacob, congratulations."

***

Moncrief called Parker just before noon to report on the judge's decisions. As Nate had predicted, Gillette exploded in anger, though he didn't fire his lawyer on the spot. After hanging up, and while he was still fuming, he closed his office door and inserted the thumb drive into his computer. He then took a deep breath and sat back to admire his work.

"Ooh ... I can't wait to show you what I have to offer. Kiss me ... I'll never tell ... " the female voice on the film coaxed. The audio then went quiet, but the video continued for another several minutes.

Parker rocked back in his chair and blew an imaginary kiss toward the computer monitor.

You may have won the battle, Wingate, but I'm going to win the war and destroy you in the process, he smiled to himself.

Gillette then picked up the phone and hit speed dial one.

"Yeah, boss," the deep voice on the other end said.

"Romero, it's time to drop the bomb. I need you to contact your internet people about releasing the video. I'll have it edited to what I want by tomorrow morning. Come by the house and pick it up at eight. I want this online by noon tomorrow. Can you do that?"

"Yeah, boss, no problem. Can I have a copy, too?"

"No, you fool! We can't risk any whiff of this getting back to us. We have to make sure it is uploaded in such a way that no one can trace it to me or you or even to the Carmel area. This has to be completely untraceable and no one connected to me, including you, can say a word, let alone possess a copy. You got that?"

"Yes, boss."

"And one other thing ... it's definitely time to teach that Donohue boy-lawyer a lesson. I assume you've just been waiting for the right moment. Well, that moment is now. You have free rein as long as nothing is connectable to me. Have fun with him. I'll look forward to reading about it in the paper."

***

Cassie was sunning next to the pool at the Club when it went live on the Internet. Her headache was long gone, and she was feeling better physically and thinking through how to apologize to Nate. She had already made amends with her parents who were, as always, gracious to her. Their capacity to forgive never ceased to amaze her. She was also contemplating her future. If she wasn't going to become famous by way of Sports Illustrated and was having second thoughts about a modeling career in general, what direction should she pursue? It wasn't too late to go to college, but that seemed like an awfully difficult path -- four years of studying for some vanilla degree that might get her an entry level job at some company doing who knows what. No, that didn't make sense and certainly didn't sound like much fun. Maybe she could learn the horse business and work for her father? Perhaps she could open up a fitness and yoga studio? Maybe she could sell clothing and cosmetic products online? She was frustrated and felt alone and rudderless.

"Hey, Cassie," a close friend named Becca called out. "Girl, I can't believe you did that. I mean, like, wow! That was a bold move. Did your agent suggest that or did you come up with it on your own? Between this and your cover on Sports Illustrated in February, you are going to become a national celebrity. If you ever need an assistant, you know, someone to travel with you and manage your calendar and correspondence, keep me in mind. I'd love to work for you and travel the world."

"Becca, what are you talking about?" Cassie asked, removing her sunglasses and propping them on the top of her head. "You may not have heard, not many people have, but my SI photo shoot got canceled the other day. I'm rethinking the whole modeling career path. It should actually be me asking you about a possible job in the future. Speaking of which, how is your job at that accounting firm going? Oh, and what were you referring to when you said 'wow?'"

"You are funny, Cass. I'm referring to your Internet video, silly. It just came up an hour ago. It's very hot, Cassie, almost too hot for my blood. But I must confess, I watched the whole thing, more than once. I mean, girl you were, well, let's just say you were 'very' provocative."

Cassie sat up straight in her chair with a look of stunned disbelief. She quickly glanced around and saw another friend across the pool. When she made eye contact, her friend flashed her a big smile and a double thumbs up. She then expanded the scope of her glance, and it appeared as if everyone was either watching something on their phones or whispering and pointing her way. Fear began to rise, and she felt a tear forming.

"Becca, I'm not sure if I know exactly what it is you're talking about. I didn't do anything for the Internet. I don't know anything about a video. But looking around, it seems like maybe everyone else does. Could you come with me to the locker room and show me this thing?"

As the two girls walked away from the pool, Cassie heard a cat-call whistle and cringed.

Oh, my God … I hope this isn't what I think it might be. Would Parker stoop so low as to make a video of me and post it on the Internet? He couldn't possibly be that cruel. Why would he do that anyway? He likes me. Doesn't he? No, that can't be it. Calm down, girl. Let's just wait and see what Becca has to show you. This must all be some mistake.

Cassie felt herself quickening her pace to escape the pool area as another whistle was blown her way, and then a male voice called out, "Kiss me … I'll never tell."

Once in the locker room, Cassie closed and locked the door. "Okay, show it to me," she requested of Becca.

"Cass, you're scaring me. You mean you don't know anything about this? But, how can that be? You're the star of the thing."

"What thing!" Cassie screamed. "Just show me the darn video."

It was a short clip, only about fifty seconds, so it loaded almost instantly. Cassie took the phone from Becca's hand and flipped it sideways, so the video image filled the entire screen. What she watched confirmed her worst nightmare. It was the restaurant balcony alright; she recognized the little white hanging lights and the couch. What she didn't recognize was the girl in the tape. It certainly looked like her and sounded like her, but she had no recollection. As the scene unfolded, tears of shock and shame and embarrassment began to stream down her cheeks. Her life was ruined. How could Parker, or anyone for that matter, ever do such an evil thing? She hit the replay button and watched it again. Having previously been so fixated on the images of herself flashing on the screen, she suddenly realized there was another person with her on the couch, the object of her enticement. He was lying next to her, disheveled, but still partially clothed. She touched the pause button at the bottom of the screen and then enlarged the image with her fingers to zoom in on the face of the man.

"No!" she gasped. "No! Not Jacob Wingate. Oh, my God! Nate is going to kill me. My parents are going to kill me."

She handed the phone back to her friend and slumped to the floor, crying. Becca sat down next to her and put her arm around her.

"Cass, you really didn't know about this?"

"No," Cassie whimpered. "I just can't believe this. No! I was drunk and probably drugged. I had no idea. I don't remember doing any of that. I can't believe this! I was there, at that place, wherever it is, having dinner with Parker Gillette. He must have pulled out his phone and recorded me. I have no idea how that guy got there. This is all a terrible mistake, but now the whole world has seen it. What am I going to do?"

***

Nate was knee deep in legal research when his phone rang. His assistant, Lisa, picked it up in the front room and then buzzed Nate.

"A reporter from the Village Gazette is on line one, shall I take a message?"

Hmm, Nate thought for a second, *this could be an interesting opportunity.*

"No, Lisa, please ask him to hold for a minute and then ring him through."

Boy, those guys at the Gazette never miss a beat, Nate thought to himself. *It seems like they are on top of everything. Maybe that's why they have such a broad-based readership? So, they must have heard about the Judge's ruling in our favor yesterday and want a quote for their article. Okay, I'll give them one, this time. Even though I don't usually like to play things out in the press, I'm sure Jacob will appreciate a humble victory quote. And who knows, with the right tone, maybe we can bring Gillette around to being reasonable. It's worth a shot anyway.*

The phone rang again, and Nate picked up ready to talk about the case.

"Hello. Oh, hi, Greg ... Yes, Jacob Wingate is my client ... sure I'll be glad to answer a few questions, I assume you're calling to talk about the ruling from the Superior Court yesterday, right? ... What? ... What salacious Internet video? ... No, I don't know anything about it, why would I? ... What was that you said? ... Jacob, Jacob Wingate in a video? ... Well, I wouldn't know anything about that, and I'm sure you must be mistaken … No, I don't have any comment, of course, I don't have any comment on something I know nothing about … Sure, I'll call you back if I want to offer a statement before you print your article. When's your deadline? … Okay, got it. So you're not calling about the Judge's ruling in our favor yesterday regarding Wingate v. Gillette? … Okay, but you may want to go down to the courthouse and read about it, it's pretty big news in the Pastures … thanks … bye."

Nate set the phone down and buried his head in his hands.

This is precisely what I feared might happen if Jacob went after Parker in the media. Oh, my God … a video? How in the world could this have happened? Now we're going to be on the defensive when we should be riding a wave of momentum. This could haunt the case for months and may taint the jury pool. Unbelievable!

Nate picked his phone up again.

"Hey, Lisa, will you see if you can find a video that just went live on the Internet. I'm not sure what it would be called or how you might track it down. All I know is the reporter said it was salacious and involves our client, Mr. Wingate. You certainly don't have to watch it, just forward the link to me, will you?"

"Oh, I know exactly how to pull it up," Lisa responded without hesitation. "It'll just take a second to send you the link. My girlfriend showed it to me during lunch. It's got like 10,000 views already and is looking like it will go viral, at least locally. I didn't recognize the guy in the clip, but everyone knows the girl. Not all that surprising that she'd do something like that though. It's that model girl, Cassie Weston."

Nate sat, shell-shocked, for several minutes and the mild headache he was feeling from missing his morning coffee started pounding for attention.

Wingate and Cassie? What in the world. How? Why?

He picked up the phone but then put it back down again. He closed his eyes tightly trying to focus on what might have happened. Finally, he turned to his computer and clicked on the link Lisa had forwarded to him. His jaw dropped as his eyes widened in utter disbelief.

"Jacob, this is Nate," the lawyer spoke into the phone. "I just got a call from the Gazette. Uh, we have a serious problem. Have you been on the Internet today?"

Jacob was sitting in the living room of his parent's house in Napa. He had flown up in a private jet early that morning for a business meeting with his father and their corporate lawyers to strategize the rollout of the new brand in Carmel Valley since the judge had ruled that they could.

"No, not today ... I'm up here in Napa working with my father and the attorneys on the plan to introduce Bountiful Pastures - Carmel to the wine world. With the judge's ruling behind us, it looks like all systems are a go for the launch. We've got a ton of work to do, so I'll probably be up here for several days, if not a week. What problem are you referring to? Whatever it is, I'm sure it can wait. We are on a huge roll right now, and there is nothing that can stop us, thanks to your good work, Counselor."

Nate paused and took a deep breath, "Jacob, are you somewhere we can talk privately or are you in a meeting right now?"

"Yeah, I'm good. We got started around seven and worked through lunch, so everyone is on a break right now. Your timing is good. What's the big deal, Nate? What's this problem all of a sudden?"

"Jacob, I think you should hang up and then search on your phone or computer for the phrase 'Yowsa - Hot time in Carmel.' After you've watched the video call me right back, okay?"

"Sure, buddy, I'll call you back in just a minute."

The search engine found the phrase immediately. The link display said it had 10,412 hits. He clicked and watched the grainy, dim-lit video clip in horror.

"Oh, my God!" he blurted out loud to himself, "how?"

He immediately picked up the phone and called Nate back.

"What is this, Nate, some horrible joke? Where did this come from? Did you see the number of people who have watched it? I swear I didn't do this. I have no idea ...."

"Calm down, Jacob. I assumed you knew nothing about this. Do you remember how lousy you were feeling yesterday morning?"

"Of course I do, I thought I was going to puke my guts out. I almost went to the emergency room, but before I could muster the strength to drive myself, it passed, and just like that I started feeling better. My stomach muscles are still sore from all the heaving, but otherwise, it looks like I'm going to survive. But, why do you ask? What does that have to do with this video?"

"Listen, I think you might have been drugged. You've heard of the date rape drug GHB, right?"

"Yeah, I've read about it in the newspaper."

"The side effects after ingestion are similar to what you were suffering yesterday morning. You appear to be completely out of it in that video, almost unconscious, so maybe that's what happened. Traces of the drug usually dissipate within 24 hours of ingestion, but it's possible they might still be able to find something in your system if you hurry down to a lab and have some tests run. Tell them exactly what you're looking for, so maybe they can put some focus markers out to look for it. Even if they don't find anything, the drug is at least a plausible explanation, and we're going to need one of those, for sure."

"You think I was drugged? I mean, who would do that, and why?" Jacob asked.

"Do you really need to ask? Come on, think about it, man. You threatened Gillette, right? And then he learned about the court ruling against him. I told you media wars could get ugly fast, and I wouldn't put anything past Parker Gillette."

"Wow, I think you may be right, Nate," Jacob said, starting to catch on. "I'll get down to the hospital here right away and get those tests done. What else should we be doing?"

Nate paused and thought for a moment. "Actually, I think it is a good thing you're up in Napa. You have a legitimate reason to be away and this way the local media won't be able to hound you for a comment or story. If they call me again, I'll fend them off. Hopefully, this will blow over in a few days, but if not, we'll have to come out with a formal statement of some kind. In the meantime, you should keep your head down. Maybe hole up at your parents' house and try not to go out anywhere, and don't talk to anyone about this. Anything you say might just inflame things and make it worse."

After hanging up the phone, Jacob closed his eyes to think. A minute later he opened them and picked the phone back up.

Shelby answered the phone and called out to the garden, "Ms. Ella, the phone, it's for you. It's Mr. Jacob."

Ella came running into the kitchen and grabbed the phone from Shelby without even taking her gardening gloves off.

"Hello," she said breathing heavily, "Jacob, I thought you were up in Napa?"

"I am. Ella, are you in a place where we can talk for a few minutes?"

"Well, let me take these gloves off -- I was out in the garden -- and I'll go into the library. It will be quieter there so we can talk, hold on just a minute."

Jacob waited patiently on the other end of the line thinking about what he was going to say. *How do you tell the girl you are falling for that your half-naked image has been splashed all over the Internet in a seedy video making it look like you are having relations with a buxom blonde on a couch? There is just no good way to sugar coat this.*

"Okay, I'm back. Go ahead, Jacob," Ella said.

"Ella, what I'm about to tell you is not going to sound good, and I apologize in advance, but I need to ask you to please not hang up until I'm finished. Please promise me that. I need you to hear the whole story. Can you do that?"

"Yes, of course, Jacob, but you're scaring me. What news could be so horrible that I would hang up on you?"

"The other night ... I got this mysterious phone call. The voice said he had some information about who killed Sierra."

"What! Someone killed your dog. Oh, Jacob, I'm so sorry. You never told me?" Ella responded.

"Yeah, I was going to, and I'll explain that later. So, anyway, I went to meet this mystery person at a bar. He never showed up and the next thing I know I'm at home sick in bed with what I thought was the flu." Jacob paused and took a deep breath before continuing.

"Well, it turns out it wasn't the flu after all. We think I may have been drugged at the bar."

Ella interrupted, "Oh dear! My poor Jacob, are you alright? Was the drug poison? Are you going to recover?"

"I'm fine now, physically at least. Please, let me continue. Just a few minutes ago, I got a call from my lawyer, Nate Donohue. He told me to look something up on the Internet. Ella, while I was drugged, someone laid me out on a couch and took some of my clothes off and made it look like I was making out with some woman who was also, shall I say, scantily clad. It looks like some two-bit R-rated movie. It's just awful. But I tell you I was completely unaware of what was going on. I was drugged, or something, but I don't have a clue what happened or how I got there or any memory at all of the couch scene ... nothing. It's just all a blank in my mind. Ella, you must believe me; I would never do anything like this, never."

"Who was the girl?" Ella asked coldly.

"Well, that's the other weird thing. It was actually a friend of mine, Cassie Weston."

CHAPTER 11

As soon as their call finished, Ella went to her computer and searched for the video. She too found it almost immediately as it seemed to be everywhere on the Internet. The view counter was up to 14,143 hits. She watched with disgust what Jacob had described to her on the phone. The man she had befriended and sought her father's blessing to date was there lying in the arms of and being fondled by another woman, an almost naked woman. As he had described, Jacob didn't seem to be moving in the video and appeared to be unconscious, but that detail would likely not be noticed by the vast majority of viewers. She watched the clip twice before slamming the laptop shut in anger.

Ella walked down to the kitchen to retrieve her gardening gloves but was intercepted by Shelby.

"Ms. Ella, is everything okay? You look upset," Shelby gently probed.

"No, everything's not okay. Everything is terrible. Oh, Shelby ...." Ella said before breaking into tears.

Shelby quickly grabbed two chairs from the table and brought them over to where Ella was standing. The older woman eased the girl down onto one of the seats and then sat next to her in the other.

"Tell me, Ms. Ella, what is it? What can I do to help?"

"Oh, Shelby ... it's the most awful thing. I'm even embarrassed to share it with you. But, well, Jacob was videotaped in a very compromising position with another girl, and it's being played all over the Internet. And worse yet, the girl is Cassie Weston, Parker's floozy. I just can't tell you how hurt I am. I mean, Shelby, I think I was falling in love with Jacob, but now ... now, how can I pursue a relationship with him? He says he was drugged or something and can't remember making out with Weston, but, come on, really, no one would forget kissing that woman. I just don't know."

Shelby gently put her arm around the sobbing girl and offered, "Ms. Ella, maybe it is all a mistake, or maybe Mr. Jacob is telling the truth. We shouldn't rush to judgment. We should wait and see where this goes. I'm sure he feels the same way about you; in fact, I know it. I have seen it in his eyes, Ms. Ella. He loves you. Have faith little one, have faith."

***

Following his conversation with Jacob, Nate had trouble focusing on anything else, so he decided to clear his head by going for a bike ride. It had been a few weeks since he'd ridden, and he figured it would be good to get out and work his legs a bit. He sent Lisa home early and locked up the office just after 4 p.m. He was changed and on his bike by 4:30.

He left by way of the separate back entrance to his living unit and headed west along the winding Carmel Valley Road. Nate turned north at Laureles Grade and was feeling strong as his legs burned while climbing the steep three-mile hill to the summit. On the other side of the Grade, he meandered through a high-end residential area and then finally to the Pastures.

By the time he reached the small valley where the vineyards that were occupying so much of his time were located, his heart rate had calmed from the climb, and he found a comfortable rhythm. It felt good to be out on the bike again, especially in his favorite area to ride. Although the roads in the Pastures were narrow, barely wide enough for two cars to pass each other safely, traffic was practically non-existent. If he saw a dozen cars in the small valley that afternoon, it would be a lot.

He rode past the Gillette estate and its giant bronze gate as he headed east. In addition to the vineyards, horse pastures and fields of wildflowers dotted the landscape. When he rounded the back end of the valley, he saw the Wingate property and imagined in his mind's eye the old house and barn restored as his client was intending and the vineyards refreshed. Jacob's plans would convert the now dilapidated farm property into the crown jewel of the Pastures. On his way back, riding toward the west, the sun was lowering in the sky and the early evening colors were beginning to appear around the edges of the clouds. He took in a deep breath and reveled in the tranquility of the Pastures and the good health he enjoyed.

Though he was trying to escape work, Nate couldn't help but think about the events of the past few days. Eventually, his mind drifted to Cassie, and a pang of sadness began to dampen his otherwise exuberant time in the bike saddle. He couldn't shake the image of the girl he had, only a week before, thought he might pursue a serious relationship with, lying on that couch and seducing his client. How could she ever have agreed to make such a despicable video, much less collaborate with the likes of Parker Gillette in doing so? It was all so disappointing, so depressing. How could he have been taken in by her story about wanting to change course in her life? Had it all been a ruse? Maybe it was an elaborate scheme to learn inside information about Wingate and the case? He would put nothing past Parker Gillette in that regard, but Cassie? It just didn't seem like her, at least not the girl he thought he was getting to know. But the facts were irrefutable; the Internet video didn't lie. She was obviously complicit in a scheme to take down his client and friend Jacob Wingate. He shook his head in disbelief and sad resignation.

As he reached to pull a water bottle from the down-tube bracket on the bike, Nate heard the distinct sound of a racing car engine behind him. Startled by the audible invasion into his otherwise placid ride, he glanced over his left shoulder. Out of the corner of his eye, he saw a dark-colored oversized pickup speeding in his direction. The road was so narrow that there was no shoulder to speak of, but he veered over as far to the right side as he could. Just beyond the road edge was a relatively steep seven-foot drop off into a drainage swale that was mostly dry. He squeezed the handlebars tightly to withstand the whoosh of wind he anticipated would hit him as the truck barreled by.

Instead of wind, Nate was shocked to feel the side mirror of the pickup smack against his left shoulder. The force of the blow caused him to careen out of control and off the side of the road. As soon as his front tire fell off the pavement and onto the soft sandy slope of the swale, it froze, as if he had hit quicksand, and his forward momentum propelled him up and over the front handlebars. Because his shoes were clipped into the pedals, he remained seated while soaring, upside down, 30 feet off the side of the road and down into the bottom of the swale.

As he thus flew through the air, his mind somehow operated to alter the scene into slow motion. For a split second, upside down, he saw the pickup continue its pass by and noted the color was dark blue. He then saw the edge of the road underneath and then behind and then gradually above him. He felt almost weightless as he fell through the air down into the swale. As he realized the ground was closing in, he instinctively grabbed tightly onto the brake levers, which were meaningless while flying, to brace for impact. The split second before he hit the ground somehow Nate was reminded of a skydiving class he took once and the importance of tucking and rolling in the event of a hard landing. Of course, he'd never practiced such a move landing upside down on his head while strapped onto a flying bicycle. But his instinct at the moment caused him to tuck his chin to his chest so that when he hit he landed on the back side of his helmet and the brunt of the impact was absorbed by his shoulders and upper back rather than his head and neck.

As he hit the ground, his torso continued the somersault, and his bike eventually came full circle and crashed in front of him. The force of hitting immovable earth overcame the toe clips securing his cycling shoes, and the bike was violently ripped from his body and cast aside. After that, he flailed and bounced, like an abandoned rag doll tossed from a moving vehicle, along the bottom of the swale until he gradually came to a halt in a crumpled and bloody heap.

The force of the landing on his back caused his diaphragm to spasm pushing all the air out of Nate's lungs. He gasped and choked as he drastically sucked for air, but found none. He was suffocating as the dirt and mud at the bottom of the swale filled his mouth, eyes, and nose. He felt an electric buzz shoot down his spine, and his left shoulder popped loudly. He blacked out, but only for a few moments, though he wished it had been longer to mask the incredible pain he was feeling in every cell of his mangled body. When he regained consciousness, he was finally able to inhale oxygen into his deprived lungs, and he did so with a loud gasp as if returning to the surface after being trapped underwater for several minutes.

Once he had partial wits about him, Nate tried to take inventory of his injuries. The electric shock caused him concern about his spinal cord, but he took solace in the fact that he was able to move and feel his extremities. His shoulder was dislocated, and the pain from it was intense. Blood was pooling on the ground near his face, and he realized it was pouring out of both his nose and mouth. The smell of it mixing with the earth caused his head to spin, and as he tried to turn away a wave of nausea overwhelmed him, and he vomited into the growing red pool. Likely internal injuries he decided just before vomiting a second time. His next determination was a concussion. The last thing he remembered, before again losing consciousness, was the stark reality that he had told no one of his riding plans, and it would be dark in less than half an hour.

***

After slipping unnoticed out of the Club locker room with the help of her friend, Becca, Cassie drove aimlessly around the Peninsula all afternoon. At one point she parked in a vacant lookout area at Point Lobos to restart, and ultimately finish her cry.

She ventured home just before 5 p.m. and was relieved to find her parents were still out and about. She decided to park her car at the end of a seldom-used fire road on the west end of the property, so as not to be seen, and she then walked easterly along the stream toward the treehouse. When she was well past the main house, she stopped for a moment to soak her feet in the water. As was always the case, the water felt refreshing on her skin as it rushed by her bare feet, but it did little to soothe the ache in her heart. She knew she needed a cleansing far deeper than mere water could ever reach. When she finally arrived at the treehouse, she grabbed a cold drink and then climbed to the top bedroom level. She fell in a heap on the mattress and wept, thinking about the last time she had been there with Nate, and then about the time before that with Jacob, both of whose lives, along with her own, she was sure she had ruined.

When the sun was entirely gone, she realized that due to lack of any meaningful moonlight and the consequent blackness of the night, wandering home, though possible, would be unwise. And she was in no mood to deal with the inevitable confrontation she would have to have with her parents, so she decided to spend the night in the tree. Laying alone in the blackness, she replayed the sordid scene from the night before over and over in her mind. Every time her memory stopped at the dance. Frustrated, she turned her thoughts to what she might do tomorrow. No scenario played well in her mind, and once again she began to cry.

The thought of Nate's certain heartbreak overwhelmed her, and without thinking it through, in a sudden desperate frenzy she pulled out her cell phone and dialed his number. It rang five times before going to voicemail. Oddly, the sound of his voice on the electronic message provided the only moment of peace she felt all day.

***

The buzz of the phone ringing wrestled Nate's mind back to semi-consciousness.

"Phone," he whispered to himself as he slowly opened his eyes. Then, without lifting his head, he rolled his eyes around to survey the immediate area and saw a soft glow just out of reach to his left.

"Phone," he uttered once more before falling back into the deep and dangerous stupor the concussion had induced.

***

"Where's Ella tonight? It's not like her to miss dinner," Parker asked Shelby as he finished the last bite of steak and pushed his plate away.

"Oh, she is very upset, Mr. Parker, so she asked me to bring dinner to her room."

"Upset?" Parker said, feigning ignorant concern, "What about?"

"Something about her boyfriend, Mr. Jacob," Shelby replied. "It was confusing what she told me. She said something about a film on the Internet. She has been in her room most of the afternoon. She said not to expect her again until morning."

Perfect, Parker thought, *and so tonight's the night. Sister is self-exiled, and there will be no one else in the house to worry about.*

"Shelby, I think I'm going to go to bed early tonight as well. Why don't you take the night off and go visit your daughter and grandson in Salinas."

"That is very kind of you, Mr. Parker, thank you so much. They will both be thrilled because tonight is my grandson's band performance at school."

"That's nice, Shelby. You have a good time. You can even come in late tomorrow if you'd like. We'll be fine for breakfast. Maybe see you around ten, okay?"

"Yes, yes, thank you, Mr. Parker!"

Shelby gathered her things quickly and slipped out the back door before Parker could change his mind.

Now that she's out of the house, there is nothing in my way. At last the opportunity to take my rightful place as owner of Casa de Abundante and the vineyards has arrived.

Parker quietly snuck upstairs to his room and retrieved the large syringe he had hidden a month before in the back of his armoire. For a while, it looked like he wouldn't have to use it, but over the past two weeks Armand was getting stronger rather than weaker, and that was going to frustrate his plans. So, he decided he'd just have to help nature along a bit.

With the syringe in his back pocket, Parker stopped outside Ella's door. He listened carefully for several minutes. When all he heard was the steady breathing of a deep sleeping person, and was finally satisfied it was safe, he moved down the hall to his father's room.

Again he listened closely from outside and was pleased to hear the steady drone of his father's snoring. He slowly opened the heavy oak door and stepped inside. He stood motionless for a minute, allowing his eyes to adjust to the darkness and to steel his nerve. Because of the moonless night, the only illumination in the room came from the red and green lights of the vital sign monitors. Fortunately for Parker, the intravenous cart was positioned right next to them.

Arriving at his father's bedside, Parker stopped and stared at the old man. His resolve was firm but his hand, for some reason, was timid. His mind flashed back to the stream fed by the spring.

***

It was early November. Harvest was finished, and the workers were busy crushing the grapes and preparing the juices for fermentation. It was always his favorite time of year because the tension level at the estate was substantially less than in the months leading up to and during the harvest. It was also a favorite because holiday decorations gradually began to appear.

First, Thanksgiving arrived with its orange and gold and brown colors. The horn of plenty overflowed, and the autumn leaves started changing color. The crispness in the air and occasional morning frost stung ears and noses. The pumpkin carvings surrounded the portico, and the slimy inner seeds from the gourds were washed and then roasted in salt and spices.

Later, Christmas would arrive with all its fest, hope and glory. He and his brother and father would make their annual man-pilgrimage up to Jack's Peak to select, cut, and haul down from the mountain the grandest of all Christmas trees - two of them: one for the portico and one for the inner foyer. One year, with the help of some neighbors, they brought home two twenty-footers. They always practiced Christmas carols with Mama accompanying the family on the baby grand piano. They practiced parts. Father always sang bass. He and James shared duties with the tenor line. Mama sang a beautiful alto and Gabriella sang an angelic soprano. One year they were asked to share a song at the Christmas Eve candlelight service at the Carmel Mission; father was never so proud.

Parker swallowed hard and tried to push the memories away, but they kept coming: floating down the Carmel River in May, after the dangerous peak flows, but while the current was still strong enough to provide a good ride; fishing for steelhead near the mouth of the river and then later wading in the lagoon; hiking and camping -- just the boys -- up on Chew's Ridge; renting a huge private boat and taking the family and the ranch staff whale watching on the bay; and hunting wild boar in the backcountry of the Ventana Wilderness. The list went on and on, and the barrage of memories began to soften Parker.

He walked across the room and sat in a chair near the huge picture window facing north. With no moon, the stars shone much brighter than usual, and though not visible in the summer sky, Parker was reminded of his favorite constellation, Orion, definable by its famous belt of three perfectly aligned stars, and he imagined it visible on the western horizon. He fixed his mind's gaze on the mythic huntsman who had been set in the heavens by Zeus himself. In a way, he fancied himself a modern-day Zeus.

What would Zeus do? Parker mused as his will to complete the task seemed to wane.

Gradually the past was supplanted by the present and its myriad disappointments and frustrations, the most recent being the arrival of Jacob Wingate to the Pastures. His anger was rekindled, and the embers that had been consuming him for the past month quickly burst back into flame.

Then he allowed the future to enter - thoughts of ownership and control of the Pastures of Bounty, of rising to celebrity status in the world of California wine, and luxuriating in the riches that would provide for every whim and every toy he could imagine, including vacation homes in Spain and Kauai and, perhaps, even a castle in Ireland or a chateau in Burgundy.

But, before any of that deserved future, or his rightful ascension to the throne could come to pass, father, or Papa, as Gabriella always insisted on calling him, had to take his place in the heavens.

Yes, it was time for him to assume the mantle. To be a king, like Zeus, a god-king. To rise to his predestined position of rule, he must act like a king. He must assume the responsibilities of the throne to partake of its glories. As his predecessor Zeus had done to Orion, it was now his time to usher Armand to his destiny, to his place in the stars alongside the great huntsman.

Parker slowly rose to his feet and returned, resolute, to his father's side. Pulling the empty syringe from his pocket, he slowly withdrew the plunger and inhaled deeply as the barrel filled with air. He did not miss the irony of using air, that which gives and sustains life, to now extinguish it.

He carefully inserted the needle into the intravenous tube connected to his father's arm and slowly pushed the plunger down deep into the barrel. He watched intently as the giant air bubble made its way through the tube and then gradually disappeared into his father's body.

"Goodbye, father -- may you enjoy the company of Orion."

CHAPTER 12

The following morning Ella awoke early. After peeking into his room to confirm her father was still asleep, she slipped out the back door by the kitchen and headed out for a walk in the vineyard. The sun was on the verge of lifting over the hills to the east, and its illumine cast a dramatic pink and red sky above. The air was still, and the songbirds were beginning their choruses. The earth was moist from the morning dew, and she inhaled deeply to capture the musky smell of the fruit ripening on the vines. As she walked, she thought about Jacob and his profession of innocence regarding the video. She replayed their conversation in her mind, but this time, rather than listen to the words he spoke, she focused on the tone and emotion of his voice. He was afraid, but not for having done anything wrong. He was afraid that what had happened, something over which he had no control, would ruin their relationship. In the depths of his voice, she heard love.

As she walked, Ella prayed for wisdom regarding her relationship with Jacob. She also prayed for her father's recovery, and while in the midst of the vineyard she, of course, prayed for the upcoming harvest. Her step lightened as she walked, and the sun gradually began to warm the field. She felt renewed and invigorated as she approached the edge of the vine row where she paused to enjoy the fragrance of a pure white rose growing there.

In a vineyard, 180 miles to the north, the same sun and sky were greeting Jacob; only the rose he smelled was ruby red.

***

When Cassie rolled over, the blanket that was loosely covering her rolled with her and exposed her backside to the coolness of the morning. Her slumber thus interrupted; she slowly opened her eyes to greet the new day. She was groggy due to the lateness of the hour when she had finally succumbed to sleep. But her perspective was fresh, and her resolve to confess everything she could to those she loved was firm. Sitting up, she peered out to the vineyard and marveled at the pink hue bathing the vines. She whispered an imperceptible thank you heavenward and picked up her phone. She dialed Nate's number.

As she had unknowingly done the night before, her call buzzed the phone lying in the grass four feet to Nate's left, and once again it stirred him to a state of partial consciousness.

"Phone," he again uttered, but this time he endured the pain necessary to reach for and answer the device.

"Hello," he said in a crippled tone.

"Nate? Nate, is that you? You sound far away. Nate, this is, this is Cassie -- can we talk?"

"Cassie, yes this is me, I need help," he spoke weakly into the phone. Pushing the speaker button, he then laid the phone on the ground and rolled over onto his back. Breathing heavily, he continued, "I was hit by a car while riding my bike yesterday in the Pastures. I'm about two miles from your house. I can't get up on my own. I need help."

"Oh my God, Nate! Don't move; I'll be right there," Cassie said excitedly. "I'll bring my father to help."

"Thanks, coming from your place I'll be on the left side of the road. I'm down in a drainage swale so you'll have to look for me. Pretty sure I'm going to need to go to the hospital."

"Oh, Nate. I'm so sorry. Should we call an ambulance?"

"Let's see how mobile I am when you get here. I survived the night, so I should be able to handle a ride to the hospital.

"Cassie, thank you for calling -- your call may have saved my life."

Cassie started to break down on the phone. Through her tears, she said, "Nate, I am so sorry for the way I acted, and I'm sorry for so many other things I need to tell you about," her voice trailed off in sorrow.

"We'll have plenty of time to talk, Cassie. Don't worry. I'll see you soon."

Cassie hurried down from her loft in the tree and ran back to the main house. Her mother was in the garden enjoying a cup of English breakfast tea and a croissant. When she saw her daughter running and waving wildly, Ariana stood to greet her.

"Cassie, we missed you last night. Is everything okay, dear?"

Cassie fell into her mother's open arms and began weeping. "Momma, I'm so sorry for everything, so, so sorry. But right now I need to find Daddy. Nate's been hit by a car and is lying injured in a ditch. We need to get him to the hospital."

Together the women ran into the house to get Charles, and the three then immediately got into the family SUV and headed east toward where Nate said he was lying. Fortunately, the bike had flown up onto the far bank of the swale, and they were able to see it from the road. They came to a screeching stop in the middle of the pavement and hopped out of the vehicle. Cassie saw him first and ran down the hill. In her haste, she lost her balance and fell to her knees scraping them on the rocks and gravel. Her adrenaline washed away any momentary pain, and she regrouped and made it over to Nate. Cupping his head in her hands, she reached down and kissed him gently.

"Nate, Daddy and Momma are both here to help us. Can you sit up?"

The foursome gradually made it back up to the awaiting car. Nate nearly bit through his lip trying to keep from yelling out in pain as they folded him into the back seat of the SUV. Thirty minutes later they unfolded him onto a gurney at the emergency room entrance.

***

When Ella returned to the house she re-entered through the back door she had departed from. The kitchen was strangely quiet, and she called out for Shelby. Receiving no response she walked through the ground floor rooms of the Casa looking for her friend, but every room was empty.

Curious, she thought to herself, *I wonder if she is ill.*

Returning to the kitchen, Ella checked for voice messages on the phone, but there were none. Confused, but deciding Shelby would eventually arrive, Ella proceeded to fix breakfast for herself. She didn't cook very often, so in a way, she looked upon the situation as a kind of treat. She opened the refrigerator and stared at the bounty inside, wondering what to prepare. She decided to make a scramble with eggs, cheese, and bacon. As an afterthought, she threw in two more eggs and some diced mushrooms because Papa loved mushrooms.

She prepared both plates of food and placed them, along with two small glasses of fresh orange juice, on a tray and walked upstairs. Setting the tray down on a small table in the hallway outside her father's suite, she knocked gently on the door. Hearing no response, she turned the knob and whispered her arrival.

"Papa, good morning." She then retrieved the tray and stepped into the room. While walking toward the bed, she began speaking, "Rise and shine sleepy head. I made us breakfast," she said proudly. "Shelby is running late this morning, and I was up at dawn," she continued, as she set the tray down on the nightstand. "Oh Papa, the sunrise was magnificent this morning, and the vineyard is teaming with life."

Realizing her father had not yet responded, Ella moved in closer, "Time to wake up Papa, here let me help adjust your pillows."

As she leaned in to kiss her father on the forehead, she noticed the pallor on his face and his complete lack of movement.

"Papa?" she said more loudly and with concern. "Papa?"

Ella placed her ear next to the old man's mouth to listen for breath but neither felt nor heard any.

"Papa!" she cried out.

She checked for a pulse in his neck and again felt nothing.

Her eyes immediately welled and began spilling large tears. She looked down at her beloved father, and weeping laid her head down on his unmoving chest. Slowly, through the fog of her grief and the blur of her tears, the reality set in that she was alone in the room.

***

The emergency room team quickly took Nate's vitals and, with the assistance of the Westons, filled in as many details as they could muster about the accident. The team whisked Nate away and down the hall toward the diagnostic center for X-rays, an MRI, and a CT Scan. Cassie felt helpless and hopeless as she watched him being wheeled away. Her father put his arm around her and hugged her close.

"He'll be alright, honey. Don't you worry."

As the three sat in the waiting room, two punk teenagers walked in. They both wore ball caps twisted to the side and pants that looked like they would fall to the floor any minute. As they chattered, it seemed every third word was a profanity of some sort. The one with brown hair sported a tattoo of a skateboard on his forearm. The one with the blonde hair wore a makeshift sling around a mangled wrist. They were, no doubt, aspiring X-Game professionals destined never to make it to the big show.

"Dude, you're 180 pop-shuvit was so awesome ... until you crashed and burned. What a loser," the brown hair teased his friend with a guttural laugh.

"Yeah, I may have bit it, but at least I had the guts to try it, dude. You just sat there and videotaped 'me,' the great 'me,' on your phone. The You Tube is going to be awesome. I bet I get more views than the time I flew off that cliff on my mountain bike and busted up something awful."

The two sat on the opposite side of the waiting room from the Westons as their annoying banter droned on. When the blonde looked up at Cassie, she smirked and shook her head in disdain. Then the blonde nudged his counterpart, and the two started giggling. The brown hair pulled his phone out and appeared to search for something. When he found it, they both watched it intently and then looked back up and stared at Cassie. They then watched the phone again and then stared back up at Cassie. The blonde then waited for her to make eye contact with him again and when she did he licked his lips and blew her an imaginary kiss.

Oh, no, not the video, Cassie thought, as she realized what the two gang bangers were looking at. She felt herself begin to get red in the face from a combination of embarrassment and anger. All she could think about was running. But run to where? She leaned over and whispered to her mother that she would prefer to wait in the hospital cafeteria and suggested they all get some coffee. Her parents were quick to agree, and she was glad to escape the leering eyes of the skateboarders. As they walked away, she heard a cat call from behind her.

"Those boys were terribly rude," Ariana said as they sat down at the small sterile table to wait for their drinks. "Why do you think they were giving you such a hard time, Cassie?"

While she could have easily chalked it up to stupid teenage boy hormones, Cassie decided there was no time like the present to confront her demon and confess to her parents like she had intended to do before her morning plan had changed so dramatically with the call to Nate.

"Mom, Dad," Cassie began, "those boys were just being jerk teenagers, but there is something that has happened that I need to share with you. It is very embarrassing, and I feel terribly guilty about it, though in truth I'm not entirely sure how it happened or why. I need to tell you and ask for your forgiveness. I need to ask a lot of people for forgiveness. I think this may be just the wake-up call I've needed to reevaluate the direction I've been headed."

Her parents sat quietly and waited for their only daughter to continue. Both knew that now was not the time to interrogate.

"The other night I found out that the Sports Illustrated photo shoot, that I was so sure would be my big career break, got canceled. I was devastated, and I didn't know who to turn to, so I called Parker Gillette."

As soon as they heard Parker's name, both of her parents sat up straight and adjusted their chairs knowing the news was bound to be worse than they thought.

"I went over to Parker's, and he tried to encourage me. He said he'd have his lawyers look into it, the SI contract that is. He seemed to want to help and was acting all kind and everything. He took me out to dinner at this little out of the way place down near Big Sur. We had a few drinks, well, maybe more than a few, and I got a little drunk. Then, well, I think he might have slipped me a drug of some kind because I started acting all weird and honestly don't remember much more from there."

Cassie paused and took a deep breath before continuing.

"And then, I did some things that were pretty bad. Somehow I, or someone, took most of my clothes off and ...," her voice faltered before she could continue. "I ended up on a couch with a guy, and someone videotaped it. It looked awful, like we were, you know, but we weren't, I mean, we didn't, I'm sure of that. But, the next morning someone posted the video on the Internet, and the thing went viral. The last time I looked there had been something like 50,000 views."

Ariana audibly gasped but held her tongue while Charles peered deeply into his daughter's moist eyes with the understanding and compassion only an unconditional love could produce.

"But, as bad as all of this was, is, for me, the worst part of it is the man I was laying on the couch with. I don't think he was even conscious. I mean when you look at the video he is just laying there. I don't think he moved a muscle. But his clothes were partially off, too, and to the casual observer, it would sure look like he was enjoying himself. But, well, the man ... he was our new neighbor, that really nice fellow, Jacob Wingate."

Ariana lost it at that point and stood from her chair.

"Oh my God, Cassie ... how could you ... I mean, implicating that nice boy. What in the world are his parents going to think of us? I just can't believe this!"

"Dear," Charles said calmly, "aren't you hearing Cassie? She thinks they were both drugged. This was a setup of some kind by someone nefarious. Cassie may be at fault for allowing herself to be vulnerable and in a position to be taken advantage of, but I can understand how, under the circumstances, that could have happened. So please, Ariana, please sit back down and let's talk this through some more."

Hearing the wisdom of her husband's words, and realizing her reaction had been an emotional response to the pain of knowing someone would treat their daughter in such a despicable way,

Ariana sat back down. Reaching into her purse, she got a handkerchief and dabbed at her eyes.

Charles continued, "So you were with Parker Gillette. Do you think he had something to do with this? Have you confronted him?"

"I don't know, Daddy. I can't believe he would stoop so low, and I don't know why he would want to hurt me. I know he doesn't like Jacob, and the two of them are suing each other over the spring, but this seems like it would be a pretty desperate move. But then, I mean, who else would do it? And if it wasn't Parker then why didn't he try to stop it? But how do we prove something like that? When I tried to track the Internet post back to its origin, I got nowhere. It's like it came from the dark web or something. Maybe someone with better computer skills could find out?"

***

As soon as the lab opened at 9 a.m., Jacob called about his test results. The technician he spoke to said there was a minor trace of something that might have been GHB in his system, but because

237

of the time that had passed, they couldn't be 100% sure.

When Jacob had earlier shared the terrible news with his father, together they had concluded Jacob was a victim of foul play. William had called in his San Francisco law firm, and they put their best investigator on the case. So far, however, he had come up with nothing. The Internet post had been done professionally, and in such a way, the investigator said, even the FBI would have a hard time tracing it. So they had no way of connecting the incident to anyone, let alone Parker Gillette.

"I'm just sure it was him, Dad," Jacob offered in frustration. "I mean, I don't know that many people in Carmel Valley, and I certainly don't have any other enemies down there. The girl, Cassie, is a mystery though. She seemed so nice, and her parents were very gracious when we met them. In fact, my lawyer down there, Nate Donohue, has even dated her a time or two. They broke up recently, but Nate's a pretty good judge of character, so it's tough to understand her role in all of this. Maybe I should call her directly and ask what she knows. I suppose the worst thing that could happen now is she would hang up on me."

As they were speaking, Jacob's phone began to buzz. He looked at the caller ID and saw it was Ella.

"Dad, I need to take this. Would you excuse me for a minute?"

Jacob stepped out of the room and into the dining area.

"Hello, Ella," Jacob waited for several seconds before hearing a faint sniffle on the other end. "Ella, is that you, are you alright?"

"Jacob, yes, it is me; I have some terrible news."

"Oh no … I guess when it rains it pours. What has happened? You sound pretty upset."

Ella choked back her tears as her voice cracked. "Jacob, Papa passed away last night."

"Oh, Ella ... I'm so very sorry to hear that. I thought he was improving? Did something happen?"

"He was improving," Ella replied. "It was so strange. He was in excellent spirits when I last saw him yesterday afternoon, but when I brought him breakfast this morning, he was gone. He died in his sleep. At least he went peacefully. I know he was old and his time was near, but I'm still so terribly sad." She broke down crying again.

"Ella, is there anything I can do? I hate being away at a time like this."

"I've spoken with Shelby and the church already and we are going to hold a memorial service on Saturday. We will bury Papa next to Mama and James at the El Carmelo Cemetery in Pacific Grove. If possible, I would like it if you could be back in time for the service."

"Absolutely! I will definitely be back. We'll easily have the business issues here wrapped by then. The only other reason I was staying in Napa was, well, to give that video thing some time to blow over. But, we don't need to talk about that now."

"Thank you, Jacob. And, about the video, I believe your story. I watched it again, closely, and as painful as it was to re-watch, it is evident you were not engaged in any activity with that girl. She was the only one moving. I'm so sorry you have to deal with such an embarrassment."

"Ella, we really don't need to talk about that right now unless you want to, but I am grateful that you believe me. By the way, the lab tests came back positive for the date rape drug GHB. It wasn't 100% certain, but a high likelihood, so at least that explains the how. I'm just still curious about the who and why."

"You can probably get answers to those questions from Cassie Weston," Ella suggested, "but I'll leave that to you. I don't think I could be civil to that tramp.

"Please come back as soon as you can, Jacob. I need you. Goodbye."

Jacob's heart was torn. He was sorrowful for Ella's loss yet elated over her expression of faith in him and apparent forgiveness about the video. And the words, "I need you," lingered in his mind like a soothing salve.

"Shelby," Ella said, "where in the world is Parker? It's just like him to disappear at such a critical time."

"I don't know, Miss Ella. I haven't seen him since he sent me home early last night. I got to see my grandson's band concert at school. It was wonderful, and it was so kind of Mr. Parker to let me go."

"Wait … he let you go early?"

"Yes, and I didn't even ask. I would never think to ask Mr. Parker for such a favor. You know, he's always so negative and sometimes even mean to me. I wouldn't want to upset him."

"You didn't ask? He just sent you home out of the goodness of his heart?"

"Oh yes, he was most kind. Maybe you are rubbing off on him." Shelby said, smiling. "He also said I could come in late this morning. That is why I wasn't here when you needed me most. I'm so very sorry about that, Miss Ella. I loved your Papa like he was my own father."

"Thank you, Shelby, I know many people loved Papa, and I'm confident we'll see many of them on Saturday. But your story about Parker is curious; kindness is just so rare for him ... very curious indeed."

CHAPTER 13

"You can see him now," the nurse said to the Westons two hours later. "He is in room 3217. He is going to be fine. He's quite banged up, but he's alert and asking for you."

The three walked through the expansive atrium area in the hospital lobby and then took the elevator to the third floor. After a quick glance at the floor plan map in the hallway outside the elevator, they walked down two corridors and past a nurses' station before arriving at the assigned room.

"Cassie, why don't you go in alone first, your mother and I will wait out here for a minute."

"Thanks, Daddy," Cassie whispered.

It looked like Nate was bandaged from head to toe. He had multiple Steri-Strip bandages on his face and arms. His head was wrapped in a turban-like fashion, and his arm was in a sling apparatus. The vital sign machines were busy clicking and blinking, and ESPN was muted on the television.

When he saw Cassie, Nate smiled broadly and clicked the off button on the TV remote.

"Hey," she said quietly.

"Hey," he replied.

Cassie's eyes began to well and tears of sorrow for her transgression and joy over the fact that Nate was safe, intermingled on her cheeks.

"Nate, I don't know where to start. I'm just so glad you're okay," Cassie began. "Mom and dad are still here, too. They're outside in the hall. You have to know, Nate, that video was a setup. I was nearly incoherent. I think I might have even been drugged. I would never ...."

Nate held a finger to his lips to quiet his contrite friend.

"I kind of figured that, Cassie. It was just so far outside the character of the girl I've come to know and like. We'll get to the bottom of it eventually. I've got my investigator looking into it as does Jacob's family. Who do you think might have done such an ugly thing and why?"

"Believe me I've been racking my brain about those exact two questions. I was with Parker that night on that balcony, so naturally, I'm suspicious of him. But it's even a low thing for him to do. I mean, we dated for a while, and I can't think of anything I might have done to make him angry with me. Everyone knows he can be an egotistical jerk, but it's tough to imagine he'd be so evil."

"Maybe not so hard to imagine," Nate replied. "I'm sure he's pretty upset about losing the legal injunctions, and I can also imagine he's not too happy about Jacob and Ella."

"Jacob and Ella," Cassie asked, "are they together?"

"They've seen each other a few times, yes," Nate answered. "I think Jacob is genuinely interested in her. I understand he even made time to go over and meet her father.

"You know, this whole thing is just so unlike Jacob," Nate insisted. "So I'm pretty sure he was drugged for that video, and I suppose it's entirely possible you were too, especially since you can't remember anything."

Then, suddenly shifting gears, Nate asked, "Hey, different topic, but do you know anyone with a beat up old dark blue pickup. That's the kind of vehicle that hit me."

"Hit you … you think someone hit you on purpose?" she asked.

"It sure seemed deliberate at the time. I mean there were no other cars out there, so even though the road is narrow, there was just no reason in the world someone couldn't have scooted over to avoid taking me out."

"I don't know about any blue pickups, off hand. But I'll start keeping my eyes open. Maybe we'll get lucky and find them," Cassie said.

"So, how long are they saying you will have to stay in the hospital? You know, if you need some help to recover I'm sure my folks wouldn't mind if you stayed at our place. In fact, I'm pretty sure my mom would love it if you did. She really seems to like you, you know?"

"Thanks, Cassie," Nate replied gratefully. "The doctors haven't said yet when I'll be released, and I might just take you up on that offer of assistance. Let's just let things unfold and see where we end up. Say, I've got some work I need to attend to. Do you think you could stop by my office and bring me my laptop? Even though typing is going to be difficult in this sling, I should be able at least to manage some basic communications and emails."

"Sure, Nate, but I think you're just a little obsessed with work sometimes," Cassie said with a smile, "but that's one of the things I admire about you. And thanks for being understanding about the video. I am really sorry about all the trouble it seems to be causing. I hope you'll be able to forgive me at some point, and I hope we'll be able to figure out the who and the why behind the video and your accident."

***

News of Armand Gillette's passing spread through the California wine world like wildfire. Ella was inundated with hundreds of calls and sympathy cards and emails. With Parker away, she and Shelby were left to make all the arrangements for the service themselves. By the time Parker returned, three days after the death, Ella was furious at him.

"I'm so sorry, Ella, for being away. Who in the world would have ever thought Father would pass?" Parker said remorsefully. "He was seemingly doing so well. After the news about our loss in court, I was devastated and just had to get away. I drove down to Vegas to decompress for a few days. Then, when I heard about father in the news, I tried to call you. I tried several times but couldn't reach you. The phone machine said the message box was full. That made sense since I figured you were probably receiving a ton of calls. So I decided to drive home as quickly as I could. I know my timing couldn't have been worse in all of this. I feel just awful. Sister, can you forgive me?"

As usual, Parker was the master of political cover and deception. He had made the Vegas plans as a cover for the video release and assumed the fates were just smiling on him when the opportunity to usher his father into the next world arose the same night he was planning to leave.

Confronted with such a seemingly sincere confession of apology and reasonable explanation,

Ella's anger was overcome by her kind heart and desire for family during the time of crisis, so she accepted Parker's excuse, at least for the moment. There would be time for more in-depth discussion and probing later, but the here and now required all hands on deck to complete the funeral arrangements and to deal with the myriad business calls coming in about which she knew very little.

"You're right about the timing being awful, Parker. I don't know if I forgive you or not, but right now I need your help. We've got to put our differences aside and come together now, brother. Shelby and I are going to the funeral home this afternoon to sign all the papers and then we are meeting with the priest to walk through the service details. I really need you to manage all the business issues that are coming up. There is a list on the desk in the library of more than a dozen important calls that need to be returned. Would you do that please, and then we can talk more tonight."

"Yes, anything, Ella, again, I am so sorry. I'll handle all those calls and any others that come in. And I'll gladly help with any of the memorial service details, too. Sis, I'm so sad about father,"

Parker said as he embraced Ella and gave her a long hug.

He was impressed with himself for even mustering moist eyes and two tears.

Not bad, Parker, not bad. Maybe you have a future in acting. Hey, maybe you and Cassie could even pull off a reality show now that her modeling career is shot, he thought cynically to himself.

*****

After the two-hour memorial service at the Carmel Mission, a long string of vehicles, led by several black stretch limousines, made the drive to the El Carmelo Cemetery in neighboring Pacific Grove. The funeral procession took the coastal route along the winding shorelines of Carmel and Pebble Beach. El Carmelo was located near the Point Pinos Lighthouse. The resting place was founded in 1891 by the Methodist church at a time when the town was nothing more than a religious retreat. Tiny parcels of land, just large enough for family-sized tents, were sold off along the shoreline near a rocky outcrop currently called Lover's Point, but which was known at the turn of the previous century as Lovers of Jesus Point. The cemetery was developed about a mile to the west of the retreat grounds near the place where the Monterey Bay and the Pacific Ocean converged. Several generations of Gillettes were buried there in a family plot located in the old section of the grounds. Ella's great-grandfather Antonio had purchased the plot. He loved the cemetery for both its location near the lighthouse and its name reference to the place of God's miracle through the Old Testament prophet Elijah.

The old section was easily identifiable because it was where distinctive markers and stones were allowed to be placed and maintained above ground, whereas in the rest of the cemetery all markers were flat to the ground to enable modern day lawnmowers easier maintenance. A grove of ancient cypress trees created a nearly solid canopy cover over the Gillette plot at the far south end of the old section.

Parking was limited, so the nearly 70 cars in the procession spread out and parked along the residential streets near the cemetery. A cool fog, typical along the Pacific Grove shoreline in the summer, blanketed the area. The moisture in the air was so thick that some collected in the tree canopy and fell to earth as scattered droplets among the gathered crowd. Ella sat alongside her brother near the edge of the freshly dug grave as the priest offered a final eulogy for their father.

"Armand Gillette was beloved to all. First and foremost he was a loving husband and devoted father of three beautiful children, James, Parker, and Gabriella. He now goes to join his bride Maria and their eldest son James in heaven. We know they are having a great reunion there today and that all the angels are celebrating alongside them. Sadly, we do not celebrate in the same way today for we feel the departure rather than the arrival of our beloved friend. Armand was also beloved in the world of wine. I had the privilege of walking with him many times in his vineyards in Carmel Valley which he lovingly called the Pastures of Bounty. The bounty was indeed rich, not only in terms of grapes but in terms of love, generosity, and kindness. We can only hope that same bounty continues to bless our community through his two adoring children here today, Parker and Ella. They are what remain of the Gillette legacy, and we pray God's mercy and grace on them both. Let us now honor our departed friend with a moment of silence."

As the heads of all in the crowd were bowed, Parker took the opportunity to peruse the group and make mental notes of who he needed to be sure to connect with before they left. His ascension to the throne would require diligent pursuit of both old and new business partners, and he was determined not to allow such a spectacular opportunity as his father's funeral to escape him.

Ella wept quietly. During the priest's remarks, Jacob had politely made his way forward to stand directly behind Ella during the prayer. He placed his hand on her right shoulder, which startled her a bit. She glanced up and smiled through her tears. When she reached up to take his hand in hers, she accidentally bumped Parker who was seated to her immediate right. Parker shot a quick look at his sister, thinking she might be nudging him to ask something, but was surprised to see the reason for the bump was to take the hand of his nemesis Jacob Wingate.

What the ... he thought, *how can she still show affection to that loser after the video? Of course, she's already seen it. Half the world has by now. Doesn't she realize he's a two-timer who made out with Cassie Weston in prime time? My sister is either blind or stupid or both. Well, fortunately, it doesn't matter that much anymore since I'm now in control of the business. She can go off and live in some fantasy land with her besmirched Prince Charming if she wants to as long as she stays out of my way.*

The priest then said an audible "Amen" and invited the siblings to each place a rose on the top of the coffin as it was slowly lowered into the ground. After the two were again seated, others amongst the closest family and friends lined up to pass by the gravesite and offer their final blessings. Gradually, the group began to disperse. Parker disappeared to make business connections and schedule important meetings, while Ella shared consolation with all who were in need.

When only a handful of guests remained, Ella turned her attention to Jacob.

"I'm so glad you were able to be here, Jacob. Father liked you so much, as do I, you know. I have much to attend to, but I think it can wait until tomorrow. I'd love to spend the balance of the day with you if you're available."

"If you're sure, I'd love nothing more, Ella. Perhaps we should head back to your house so you can change and then we'll go out for an early dinner. We've got so much to talk about and catch up on."

"That's perfect," Ella said quietly. "I'm pretty sure Parker won't be back to the house until late tonight, he's doing a bunch of business schmoozing. I swear his timing and priorities are so skewed. Sometimes I really can't fathom that we're even related. Anyway, at least we won't risk a confrontation with him. I sense he is desperately jealous of our relationship. I'm not really sure why he would be other than the fact that he just can't stand for anyone to be happy."

"Oh, there's one other thing I'd like to do this afternoon, if it's alright with you," Jacob suggested. "I'd like to stop by the hospital for a few minutes. My friend and lawyer Nate Donohue is there. He was in a bicycle accident a few days ago and hurt his shoulder pretty severely. I just want to look in on him and say a quick hello. I don't think you've met him, but he is a real gem. You'll like him."

"You are right that I don't know him," Ella replied, "but I have, of course, heard of him. My brother has cursed his name many times. Any friend of yours will, I'm sure, become a friend of mine."

***

When Jacob and Ella arrived at the hospital, they checked in at the visitor's desk which in turn rang Nate's phone. Nate encouraged the visit, so the couple made their way up to his room.

"Nate!" Jacob burst out when he walked into the room, "you look far better than I thought you might. Man, I can't believe you got hit by a truck while riding. That must have been awfully scary. Any leads on who the culprit was?

"Oh, excuse me, I'm sorry, Nate, this is my friend Gabriella Gillette. Since you two hadn't met before, I thought I'd bring her along to say hello," Jacob said more calmly.

The three sat for several minutes exchanging news about the accident and the funeral. Their conversation was interrupted when the shift nurse came in to take Nate's vitals and ask what he wanted to order for dinner.

"Well, look, Nate, we should let you get some rest," Jacob said, wrapping things up. "I'm so relieved to see you healing so quickly. I really want to talk about things as soon as you're able. Maybe I'll give you a call on Monday. I need to bring you up to speed about our planting plans, and the brand launch, and, of course, we'll need to talk about how to address that accursed video and my test results, and how I might be able to help track down your assailant. We've got a lot to discuss; that's for sure."

"Monday should work just fine," Nate said. "I'll be home by then, or maybe staying at the Westons. They've offered to help me recover for a few days. Anyway, I'll have my cell phone on me, so use that number."

"The Westons ... as in Cassie Weston?" Jacob asked curiously.

"Yes, one and the same. I know it may seem a bit odd under the circumstances, but I'll explain when we talk more. I think Cassie may have been taken advantage of in a similar fashion to the way you were. Anyway, we'll discuss it. Thanks for stopping by, friend, and nice to meet you, Gabriella."

On their way out to the car, Ella said, "Cassie Weston is going to help during his recovery. That girl is like a chameleon isn't she? Sinner one minute and saint the next. I'm not so sure about her. She seems to be the source of so much trouble, and if she's collaborating with my brother, I can see no good coming from it."

"I have to agree it does sound strange, but I trust Nate's judgment, so we'll have to wait and see what he has to say on Monday. Meanwhile, let's you and I not focus so much on that tonight. Rather, let me treat you to some relaxation. And I'd really love to hear some stories about your dad and your family when you were growing up. If we're going to be dating, I want to learn everything about you."

CHAPTER 14

The following Monday morning Ella and Parker received a call from the family attorney wanting to schedule a meeting to read their father's final will and testament. The two scheduled a time to meet at the lawyer's Monterey office at 11 a.m. They drove over together in Parker's Lexus.

Even though she had been offended by the way Parker had launched into business mode almost before their father was in the ground, to get the day off on a positive note Ella offered, "Parker, thank you for handling the business affairs before the service and over the weekend. I know there was a lot to deal with."

"Sure, Ella, and you're right there was and still is a lot to deal with. Not to speak ill, but over the past year, our father didn't really pay much attention to the business. The books are a mess, and now this lawsuit is putting a crimp on our future plans. I tell you, Wingate is a serious thorn. He seems to have taken a fancy to you. I would hope maybe you can work your feminine charms to get him to back off. We both have a big stake in the company now."

"Parker, really, you think I'm seeing Jacob in an attempt to help our business? Do you really think I'd ever do such a thing? Do you know me at all, brother? I don't operate like you do. I don't scheme and manipulate, and I wish you wouldn't either. Papa was always open and honest about his business dealings, as was Grandfather, and I believe that's why the business has always been so successful. If you're going to change all that, then I think we, you and I, are going to have a real problem. I've tried to be nice to you, Parker. I've really tried, but you just make it so hard. My relationship with Jacob has absolutely nothing to do with 'business,' nor will it ever. Please keep that in mind if you ever suggest again that I help with any of your twisted machinations!"

"Ella, Ella," Parker responded condescendingly, "you are so naive, Sister. It's just a good thing father has entrusted the business to me and left you to attend to the social affairs. At least he understood that business should be left to the men. And as far as being 'nice,' as you put it, I don't frankly give a rip whether you're 'nice' to me or not. I only put up with you because we're blood. So if you and your boyfriend are smart, you'll both stay out of my way. I trust you can understand that. Wingate obviously doesn't, but he'll learn, sooner or later."

"Parker, are you threatening me?" Ella asked with disdain.

"Take my advice as you will little sister. Just be smart and don't ignore it."

Neither said anything to the other for the remainder of the thirty-minute drive to the lawyer's office. When they stepped off of the elevator, they were greeted with a panoramic view of downtown Monterey in the foreground and the harbor and bay in the distance. The family lawyer's office was in the penthouse suite of the oldest and tallest building in Monterey. The firm had been established in 1927 and was renowned as the best law firm in all of Monterey County. The lawyer they were meeting was the head of the estate planning department of the 23 lawyer firm. His name was Arnold Ames. The receptionist seated the siblings in the main conference room and served them coffee and croissants. Ames joined them a few minutes later.

"Good morning," the bespectacled, silver-haired man said. "Oh, don't get up, please make yourselves comfortable, we've got some important business to attend to. First, let me say how sorry I am for your loss. Armand was not only a wonderful client, but I counted him a close friend as well. The memorial service at the Mission was beautiful. I was impressed with the number of people who attended. Your father was loved by so many, including me. If there is anything I can do for the family to ease the transition of things, just let me know. We stand ready to do whatever we can, and speaking for the firm, we would love to continue representing the family."

Nice enough man, Ella thought, *but even he is pitching business. Why is it that people just can't seem to separate personal from professional?*

"Thank you, Arnold," Parker jumped in with his business mask on. "Of course we will continue to look to you and your firm to handle our local estate matters and occasionally other items. We respect and appreciate your loyalty and commitment to the Gillette family. And thank you for your condolences; they are much appreciated."

Ames closed the conference room door and sat at the head of the long table. Parker and Ella were sat across from each other, on either side of him. He poured himself a glass of water and set a thin manila folder down on the table. He then slowly opened it with a certain calculated drama and removed the single document inside. It was about a half inch thick. Solemnly placing his right hand on the document, the lawyer began.

"This is your father's will. He updated it about nine months ago, shortly after your brother, James' accident. We spent several days working through his plans for the future of Pastures of Bounty and ownership of Casa de Abundante. He was extremely lucid and clear during our meetings. Several other lawyers and paralegals were also involved in the series of meetings we had, and all would join me in testifying that he was absolutely of sound mind and possessed full testamentary capacity when this plan was put together. So, I can assure you, beyond any shadow of a doubt, that this document represents your father's will and intention.

"Before I continue, I should also note that he included a special provision at the end of the will.

It says if anyone mentioned in the will should elect to challenge it, they will thereafter be disinherited from the estate and all their share of the assets will go into a trust for the exclusive benefit of whatever children either of you may produce in the future. Your father was, as I'm sure you know, very interested in 'legacy,' and he cared very much about the land and the Casa, and he wanted to ensure it remains in the family for the next generations to enjoy as he did."

Both siblings listened intently to what the barrister was explaining. Ella did so with calm and peace in her heart as she contemplated the words and could almost envision Papa saying them himself. Parker, on the other hand, listened with a sense of foreboding.

Why would Ames make such a big deal of all of this? Why doesn't he get on with it and read the will? Worst case, Parker thought, *we'll end up sharing the estate equally and later I'll find some way to wrestle control away from her. After all, CPA or not, she doesn't know the first thing about the wine business and all but admitted as much during the drive over.*

Finally, Parker could no longer endure the suspense. "Fine, Arnold, we understand all of that. We already know what father probably said in the document, but let's go through the formality of reading it anyway. I've got several other appointments I need to prepare for this afternoon."

"Very well," Ames said. "Before I read all of the details, I prepared a brief synopsis to start. That way you can be thinking through and understanding the details in context as I read them to you. I find the summary to be a beneficial tool in meetings like this, especially when the pain of the loss is still fresh."

"Yes, yes, fine, fine," Parker pressed. "Now get on with it."

"Your father was very thorough and addressed all of his assets in the will. The first was the house, Casa de Abundante. He directed that ownership of the house, its furnishings and the immediately surrounding estate grounds, other than those comprising the vineyard and winery facilities, be shared equally by the two of you. He provided an inventory of the art in the house and designated various pieces to each of you. For each piece assigned to you, you will own that individually. His portfolio of cash and stocks will be liquidated, and the proceeds will be distributed equally. If you'd like, I can refer you to an investment adviser. Any questions so far?"

Both siblings shook their heads in the negative.

"Alright then, with regard to all the rights, land, facilities, equipment and vehicles related to the vineyard and wine operation, Pastures of Bounty, your father has given 51% ownership and control of everything up to and including the disposition of the assets entirely to Gabriella. Parker will still enjoy a 49% interest in so far as revenues are concerned, but absent express written consent from Ella, Parker is not to have any role in the management of the business or the properties."

Both siblings stopped taking notes and looked up in shock.

"I know this may come as somewhat of a surprise to you both, but I can assure you this is precisely what your father wanted and, of course, neither I nor either of you can change that fact. Gabriella, your father acknowledged that in the past you had not been very involved in the day to day operations of the business, but he expressed every confidence that you would be able to learn and/or enlist the assistance of capable advisors and consultants."

Parker's mind was swimming in confusion and anger. He jumped in, "Arnold, this can't be right. Father must have known such a decision would be suicide for the business. There must be some mistake."

"I'm afraid not, Parker," Ames responded. "Your father was exceedingly clear on this, and I suspect he knew you'd be upset and that is why he included the no-contest clause. Of course, I would be remiss if I didn't invite both of you to seek independent counsel to review the documents, and I will gladly participate in doing whatever I can to facilitate a smooth transition within your family."

Parker abruptly got up from his chair and left the room cursing. Ella stayed behind, and Ames dutifully explained the rest of the will's details. When the attorney was finished, he made a copy of everything for Ella, and she then left. In his fit-a-pique, Parker had driven away forgetting that he and Ella had come to the lawyer's office in the same car. She stood in the parking lot staring at the empty stall where their vehicle had been parked.

Ella's mind was also spinning, not so much about how to get home, but about what Arnold Ames had just reported to them. While on the one hand she was thrilled with her father's confidence in her, and his wisdom to protect the business from Parker's unchecked avarice, on the other hand, she was concerned about how she would, in the long term, shoulder the responsibility. In the near term, however, Ella was most worried about what Parker might do in response to their father's decision. She was well aware of his impulsiveness and that he had a mean streak that ran deep in his soul. Would he seek to undermine the business somehow since it wasn't his? No, that wouldn't make any sense since he still stood to benefit handsomely from its success. Might he come to see the wisdom of his father's choice, look past his own pride, and offer to partner with her to manage the winery? That wasn't very likely, because that would require a capital "M" miracle. Probably something in between, she thought to herself, or maybe something worse? But what could be worse? Her intuition was in overdrive and anxiety was starting to set in.

***

Romero leaned lazily against a hay bale sitting on the floor in the corner of the old barn located in the far northwest portion of the vineyard. He had just finished repainting the old, dark blue pickup. Parker wasn't taking any chances and, in an abundance of caution, had instructed him to repaint the vehicle lest it be inadvertently identified as the weapon that had been used in the attempted murder of Nate Donohue.

Even though the east facing barn door was wide open, the air was still, and only a minimal breeze was blowing through the building. The heat was becoming stifling, and the smell of the lacquer began to nauseate Calderon. He grabbed his two thirds empty bottle of grocery store bourbon and stood up. Brushing the straw from his jeans, he cursed for no reason other than his mind was always cursing, and then strolled outside. A red-tailed hawk was circling overhead, no doubt hunting a rodent for lunch. Romero squinted as he looked up into the noontime sun to watch the graceful creature soaring effortlessly on the wisp of breeze that was apparently blowing a hundred feet above the ground. He took another swig from the bottle and then his cell phone buzzed in his pocket. Cursing again, only to entertain his dark subconscious, he retrieved the device and grunted into it.

"Yeah, boss. What is it?"

"Romero, where are you right now?" Parker asked.

"Down at the back barn taking care of the truck like you said." The alcohol had combined with the paint fumes to give rise to an impertinent mood in Romero. "You're paranoid; you know that, Parker? Painting that thing was a royal pain, and the whole place reeks now and almost made me puke. I think I deserve some hazard pay or something."

"Hazard pay? Sure," Parker responded.

The unexpected agreement took Romero by surprise. "Boss, are you feeling alright? I was just joking; you know that, right?"

"Yeah, I know, but I think you're right. You've been doing some extraordinary things for me lately, and I think you deserve some recognition. I'll tell you what I'm going to do; I'm going to rent you a hotel room, no ... a suite, down in Big Sur tonight, near that restaurant we visited the other day, you know the one with the balcony. You can enjoy yourself down there, on me, for a couple of days. I'll be sure you're well stocked with Jack Daniels and food. I'll even send some T-bones down for you. And at night, well, let's just say you will definitely enjoy the dessert I plan to send your way."

"Gee boss. That's awfully nice of you. What gives?"

"Oh, nothing big, just a little extra job I want to talk with you about when you get back. Probably the last hazard pay task I'll be asking you to do for quite a while."

"I actually like that kind of work, if you know what I mean. So, sure, I'll look forward to it. And boss," he added in a guttural lascivious tone, "about that dessert you're going to send down, I think I'm in the mood for either a redhead or maybe a blonde."

"No sweat, Romero," Parker said, "I'll send you one of each."

***

Before releasing him from the hospital, the doctor advised Nate to do as little physical activity as possible for the next week, not so much due to the shoulder, but due to some curious hair-thin lines, they thought they saw in one of the follow-up x-rays they took of the cervical vertebrae area of his neck. No cause for alarm, they said, they just wanted him to lay low until they could run some more tests. The news seemed serious enough that Nate decided, despite the lack of noticeable pain in his neck, to take the Westons up on the offer to stay at their home. Cassie was thrilled but tried not to let on.

His shoulder pain subsided more and more each day, and four days post-release Nate was able to perform non-weight bearing activities at a somewhat normal level. Nevertheless, he had asked his assistant to inform his clients that he was going to be away for two weeks and most of them took it to heart, so he had plenty of free time on his hands to convalesce. Of course, there were always those few clients who considered themselves "special" and expected Nate to be available no matter what his personal circumstances might be, whether on vacation or injured. Deep down, Nate had to admit that he enjoyed the constant contact almost as much as his clients did.

"Hey, Nate, this is Jacob," the voice on the other end of the cell phone said. "Hope you're feeling better and that Cassie is taking good care of you. Listen, I've got a couple of questions. Have you got a few minutes?"

"Sure, I was actually hoping you'd call. The Westons are great, but to be honest, I'm going a little stir crazy here with all this free time on my hands. I have no idea how anyone could ever think about retiring."

"Glad to provide you with a mental break, my friend. So, I've got two questions. First, about the video thing, you know, some time has passed now, almost two weeks, and it seems the view tracker has slowed way down. The thing is only getting a handful of new views per day. I'm thinking the episode has almost blown over and will probably be forgotten as old news in another week. I know we talked about holding a press conference to explain everything and to point the finger at some mystery assailant, but I'm worried that we might reignite the whole sordid affair. It may just be best to leave sleeping dogs lie. What do you think?"

"There is a lot of wisdom in that approach," Nate concurred. "Most people would want to do everything in their power to vindicate themselves, but you're right, old news is no news. And if in the future, someone ever does ask you about it, you can tell them what we have learned at that time. Plus, we still haven't been able to trace the source of the upload definitively, and without solid proof implicating Gillette, we might risk drawing a defamation lawsuit if we said anything. I'm sure he'd love to find something to sue you for. So, I agree, I think I'd let it lie. What was your second question?"

"Well," Jacob continued, "it kind of relates to what you just said. This doesn't involve me, at least not directly. Last Monday the Gillette family lawyer called Ella and Parker in to read their father's will. As it turns out, Armand gave control over the vineyards and the wine business to Ella. She's good with all of that but is thinking she may need a local lawyer who can help her going forward. I recommended you, and she agreed. Do you think you can help her?"

"Well, thanks for the referral, Jacob. But you are technically suing them right now, and that would create a conflict of interest for me. So, at least until the lawsuit gets resolved, I'll have to decline. But if we can get past the lawsuit, then if you both consent, I could probably help her out, sure."

"I figured you'd say that, and of course, I understand. But I think we may actually be able to settle the lawsuit now that Ella is in charge. I think there is some court process that needs to be accomplished to formally document her authority to speak and act for the company, but their family lawyer, a guy downtown named Ames, says he will try to expedite that."

"Oh yeah," Nate followed, "I know Arnold Ames. He's a pretty decent guy. I'll give him a buzz and ask if there are any issues he foresees. I'll tell him I'm a friend of the family, would that be okay?"

"That would be perfect, Nate, thanks. Oh, and one last thing. Parker went ballistic when he heard the news about the will. He hasn't spoken to Ella since their Monday meeting with the lawyer. She's worried about him and what he might do. He hasn't made any direct threats or anything, Parker's too smart for that, so there would be no basis to seek a restraining order, but nonetheless, I think we should all be on guard. I don't trust him, and that henchman of his, Calderon, borders on crazy-dangerous. Anyway ... just FYI."

CHAPTER 15

Parker sat in the dark corner booth of a two-bit Moss Landing saloon near the seedy end of the harbor sipping on his fourth Jack and Coke. Though he wasn't partial to the sweetness, he figured he'd need the caffeine to get him home. The stench of stale beer and urine wafted in from the men's room and mixed oddly with the body odor of the salty sailor sitting two booths down. The old salt was seducing the platinum blonde he had picked up at the bar twenty minutes earlier. The late forties balding bartender was leaning on the bar and fixated on an ESPN special about NFL concussion victims. In his mind, he was trying to figure out how he might sue his high school for allowing him to engage in such a dangerous activity thirty years ago. The low key crowd was rounded out by a painfully obvious lady of the evening throwing darts in the opposite corner while munching on stale popcorn.

Romero slipped in through the back door and sat across from his boss grinning from ear to ear.

"Hey, boss. This is a new place for you. I kind of like it. Classy, you know. And man oh man, I have to thank you big time for that Big Sur pleasure. You really know how to pick'em, boss. Those girls wore me out something good. I think I'm gonna see the redhead again next weekend. She kind of took a special liking to me."

Parker hailed the barkeep and ordered a bowl of heavily salted nuts, an unopened bottle of Jameson, and two shot glasses. He overfilled both glasses and both men slammed them down and then a second and then a third. As Parker spoke, Romero stuffed his face with the salty morsels.

"So, are you still interested in some hazard pay work?" Parker began.

"Yeah, boss, you bet," Romero mumbled in response, almost choking on the handful of goobers he was munching.

Wanting him to focus, Parker slid the snack bowl out of reach from the glutton. Calderon's face saddened, but then immediately brightened again when Parker then slid the half-empty bottle to the spot the bowl had been. The big man poured himself another and chugged his fourth in five minutes. His gasp of satisfaction caught the ear of the lady of the evening who started making her way from the dart board to their table. Parker caught her eye and waved her off, mouthing the word "later" and flashing a C-note. She winked agreement, and adjusting herself in an intentionally conspicuous way, turned and took a seat at the bar pretending to become a temporary disciple of the science of football concussions.

"Romero, I'm glad you enjoyed your dessert, and I know you're looking forward to seconds, but I need you to focus with me right now, okay?"

"Yeah, boss, focused," the fast becoming soused giant said, as he pointed two fingers back and forth between his eyes and Parker's.

"We need to ratchet our little terror campaign up a notch," Parker said. "You did real good with the kid lawyer, but now I want to go after that schmuck Napa boy again. He's got his head in the clouds with this lawsuit, and now he's trying to take over my whole operation by seducing my stupid sister."

"Ella and the Napa boy -- you don't say," Romero's eyes wandered, "hmm, that would look interesting."

"Focus man, remember, focus. This is important!" Parker said in an angry whisper. "I want you to deal with both of them together, got it? And nothing polite this time. I want you to finish it. I need you to finish them."

"Ella, boss? Your sister? Finish? I'm confused," the behemoth said scratching the side of his head.

Parker cursed under his breath as he reached across the table and grabbed the drunk man by the collar. "Do I have to spell it out for you? I want them permanently out of the way. As in gone forever. Never to be seen or heard from again. In other words, give them a one-way ticket to go visit my father."

Romero paused and poured himself two more successive shots before speaking. "You mean kill them?"

"Yes, you cretin, kill them. Now lean in, I'm going to tell you how I want it done."

282

Jacob and Ella held hands while walking along the beach after dinner at the Cantina. The sunset was soft and ethereal, but the crescent moon rise was magnificent. The surf pounded so loudly up the steep sand shore that rose up from the depths of the sea that the ground literally shook. A "V" formation of brown pelicans floated effortlessly, just over the crest of the breaking waves, seemingly inches above the water, but never letting a drop of moisture touch their wings.

They walked south along the bluff trail which hovered precariously over the jagged shoreline below and occasionally stopped to watch and wait for a huge wave spray to dissipate in front of them. The string of gigantic mansions to their left loomed on the steep hillside above them almost as if waiting, wanting desperately to fall into the sea. The homes were, however, dark and silent as their owners lived elsewhere, only partaking in the joys of the venue two or three weeks a year. The horizon before them was harshly interrupted by the jagged crust of earth called Point Lobos, so named by Spanish conquistadors who mistook the barking of sea lions for wolves. As darkness fell, the two found themselves enveloped in a shroud of misty fog that was so thick it felt like Seattle in January.

"Jacob, I am so glad you met Papa before ..." her voice trailed off. "Before, he went to be with Mama and James. He never said it, exactly, but I think he loved you, Jacob. At least I felt he gave me permission, perhaps unspoken in words, but communicated nonetheless, to love you. And, I do, Jacob Wingate, I do love you."

Ella stopped walking and leaned into the chest of her man. She felt his heart beating strong and steady, and then, she felt hers in perfect syncopation. The two were beating as one. She shuddered slightly from the chill in the air, and he responded by hugging her just that much more tightly.

"I love you, too, Gabriella. I was certainly not looking for love. Not that I didn't hope to find it someday, but now just wasn't in my plan. Ha, 'my plan,' that is funny. I don't think 'my plan' has ever come to pass. I don't believe in the fates as your father did, but I do believe in Providence. I think our love is Providential, Ella. I am so hopeful for the future. We have come through much together already, and I think these trials have prepared us for what is to come. Whether adversity or blessing beyond our wildest dreams, the future we will confront will be manageable as long as we are together.

"Ella, I feel privileged to have met your father before he passed, but you have not met my family yet. Would you come to Napa with me this weekend to meet them? Of course, they know all about you already because I speak of nothing other than you these days. My father is actually concerned, thinking my mind is so preoccupied that I will be unable to focus on birthing BP - Carmel. But I assured him that without you by my side, Bountiful Pastures - Carmel will mean nothing to me. I know he remembers his early love for my mother, and he smiles inside to know his son is so happy."

"Yes, Jacob, yes, I would love to go to Napa. I would love to meet your family ... the family that I hope someday I may call my own."

***

"Are you sure you understand everything I've told you, Romero? And it must be done in such a way that no one can ever discover that you or I were involved. You must be absolutely clandestine, and you must not fail. We will only have one opportunity, and we must make it count. If you are successful, my friend, I promise that you will be rich beyond your wildest dreams. I will make you the manager over all of my kingdom. You will be lord over hundreds, and they will bow before you as they do me. Together we shall rule the Pastures; we shall rule Carmel Valley; we shall rule California. There will be no end on this earth to our glory for I shall be greater than Orion, greater even than Zeus himself!"

***

"Ariana ... Charles, I'm not entirely sure how to thank you for all of your kindness and hospitality," Nate began. "My folks passed away in an accident when I was younger, and so I haven't enjoyed the blessing of parents for a very long time. You two have taken me in, a relative stranger really, and treated me as a member of the family. I know it's only been two weeks, but still, it's meant the world to me. Thank you from the bottom of my heart."

286

"Nate, it has been our sincere pleasure," Charles returned. "You are a gentleman in every sense of the word, and we have enjoyed your company. This big house needs a little novelty and excitement now and then, and you have brought both to us. I know Cassie hasn't minded your being here either, have you, Cass?"

"Why Daddy, you're embarrassing me," Cassie replied with a wink. "Of course, I've enjoyed Nate being here. And Nate, I'm so glad you are feeling better and can go back to work. I will miss your cute face at the breakfast table every morning though," she said, feigning a pout.

"By the way, while we're all together I have a little announcement to make."

"What is it, Cassie?" Ariana asked. "I know you've been awfully busy on the computer in the study this past week. Are you writing a book or something?"

"Hardly that, Momma," Cassie chuckled, "but I have been researching about study programs to become a paralegal. In talking with Nate about what he does as a lawyer, and then also talking with a friend of mine from high school, you remember Jessica Blair, anyway, she's a paralegal in Phoenix now. She enjoys the work, and I thought maybe that could be something I might do. I'm looking for a more serious career path now, and, well, I think I might have found it."

"Cassie, I think that's a great path," Nate offered. "I know several local paralegals that I'd be happy to put you in touch with. I'm sure they'd be glad to talk with you and share their insights about the job and the study programs they attended. The work can be a little paper heavy sometimes, but if you work for an interesting lawyer, the work can be a lot of fun."

"Interesting like you?" Cassie said in a half teasing and half serious tone.

"Well, I don't know how interesting you'd find my practice, but I like it, so maybe, yes. Like me," Nate replied in the same teasing tone.

"Are you offering me a job, Nate Donohue? Well, I accept. Offer and acceptance, I think that makes for a binding contract, right?"

"Paralegal nothing, you already sound like a lawyer," Nate said, smiling. "Let's raise our glasses to toast Cassie's new path. I'm proud of you friend, and wish you, all the best ... and about that job ... we'll definitely talk more about it."

The four raised their lemonade glasses to the center of the table and clinking them together in unison the three said, "To Cassie!"

After the meal, Cassie and Nate wandered down to the creek. She sat on the edge soaking her toes while he skipped a few smooth stones upstream with his good arm. Both were nervous and neither wanted to start the conversation. Cassie was the first to succumb to the silence.

"Nate, I meant what I said about missing you when you leave. I know it sounded like a joke, about your cute face and all, but I am going to miss you. I can't tell you how much it means to me that you listened and understood and believed me about the video. So many people assume they know me, but few actually do. I know I have a reputation, and the video certainly didn't help me disabuse anyone of it, but, well, it's kind of the curse of being a pretty girl, I guess. And, to be honest, I never really fought it. That was probably my biggest mistake. But being popular and liked by everyone is kind of a nice place, you know? The reality is, though, when it comes down to it, all those friendships tend to be pretty shallow and surfacey. I can count on one hand the 'real' friends I've had in my life -- those who weren't interested in my looks or my money or my popularity. You're one of those friends, Nate, and for that, I'm very grateful.

"I hope when your life gets back to normal we can continue developing our friendship like we have been this past couple of weeks. I really mean that. I don't want to seem pushy or clingy; I'm just trying to express my heart here."

Nate tossed down the rest of the stones he had gathered and sat with Cassie at the edge of the stream. He removed his shoes and put his feet in the water next to hers.

"Ooh, that's cold to start," he involuntarily exclaimed. Then gathering himself, he continued. "Cassie, I, understand what you're saying. The primary reason I've avoided you for so long, and I'm sorry if I was overly obvious about that, is precisely because of all the things you just mentioned. Well, not so much the reputation part, but the pretty girl part and the popularity part. I'm just not like that, and I was, to be honest, kind of afraid of you. It's a classic guy thing to categorize girls as being in a 'league,' you know, either in or not in my league. That's very sexist, I admit, but I did that. I put you in a league that was far above what I might ever aspire to. I mean, even that day in church a while back, when you cornered me into coming here for lunch - and by the way, your parents were excellent co-conspirators that day - anyway, even then I was trying desperately to decline because I didn't want to embarrass myself with you.

"But, as you say, these past two weeks have been very eye-opening, and I do think I've gotten to know the real you beyond all the hype and glamour. And Cassie, I really like the real you.

"I may be going out on a limb here, and I may regret saying this because I don't want to mess up what we have, but if I'm honest, which I always try to be, I'd like to date you … you know, on a regular basis."

"That kind of honesty won't mess up anything," Cassie said. "I feel the same way. I think we've got something worth building on, and I'm excited to see where it might go. So, yes, let's go on a 'date!'" she said with a wink.

***

Romero wasn't particularly adept at Internet research, but he knew enough to be able to access a few tutorials on brake and steering wheel lines. He spent the next week studying everything he could find. He also drove all the way to Sacramento to have lunch with a mechanic friend he had met while in prison at Soledad. In the end, he discovered it wasn't all that difficult to tamper with brake and steering lines to make it look like an accident when they failed. The trick was the timing - how to cause them to fail at the right moment to ensure a fatal crash. That part was not going to be so easy. But he had a plan.

His access to cars on the Gillette property was far simpler than getting to Wingate's car, so he had to figure out a way to ensure Ella would be driving on d-day. Parker kept him closely apprised of Ella's comings and goings from the house. The following

Friday the moment finally arrived for step one of the plot when Jacob planned to pick Ella up to go to a movie in Monterey. Naturally, he drove, so Ella's BMW X6 was left in the garage. It was easy pickings for Calderon.

He waited until after Shelby left for the evening before sneaking into the four-car garage on the east side of the Casa. He drew the blinds on the only window so the light from inside would not alert anyone who might happen by. Using a simple tire jack, he lifted the car high enough to slip underneath. Employing the technique he had studied, Romero rigged tiny IEDs on the brake lines and the steering line that could be detonated remotely by a cell phone call. He was in and out in less than 15 minutes, and the scene was set. Now he need only wait for the right adventure scenario to arise for the two. Parker had promised to help with that detail.

***

Parker's friend, Jason Bingham, owed him a favor, a big one. Parker had bailed him out of a Texas Hold'em game at the Club a few months back and saved the man over $5,000 by enabling him to stay in the game just long enough to draw the one card he needed to pull an inside straight. Parker was not one to forget about favors owed, and Jason knew it.

"Hey, Jase, Parker Gillette here ... Remember that Hold'em loan I made to you last spring ... yeah, the inside straight, by the way, well-played man ... So, it's time for a little payback ... No, nothing big, I'm just trying to make good with my sister. We're having a little family spat. Anyway, I want to surprise her with a private invitation dinner the proceeds from which will benefit her pet charity ... the Foster Kids program ... yeah, the same group we held the big gala for a while back. ... What do I need you for? Well, that's simple, I need you to host the swanky dinner at your house ... yeah, at your Big Sur house. It'll be a beautiful venue for the high rollers I'm going to invite ... oh probably no more than seven couples, you can handle a dinner party for 14, right? ... Good, I thought so. I knew I could count on you, Jason. You're a good man ... yes, this will completely cover your favor, at least until the next time you need me to spot you a couple thousand bucks. I want to schedule this for next Saturday. Can you pull it together by then? ... Great, I'll have the caterers call you tomorrow. I'll handle all the invitations; all you have to do is be the dutiful host. Thanks, man … yeah, later."

After hanging up with Bingham, Parker next hit speed dial one on his cell phone.

"Romero, it's all set. They'll be driving down to Big Sur for a fancy dinner shindig I've arranged on Saturday. The dinner will be at seven, so they'll probably leave here around six. The sun will be setting, so it'll be dark right about then. You'll need to disable Wingate's car that afternoon … I don't know, maybe just arrange for a hole in his front tire, but nothing fancy. Remember, we want this to look normal at every step. Have you got everything else ready? … Good. I'll call you on Saturday as they're pulling out. You can follow them once they get out to the highway."

CHAPTER 16

As he backed out of the driveway on his way over to pick up Ella for the charity dinner, Jacob didn't notice the several point-up nails that had been scattered on the road. The resulting hole in his tire was just small enough to enable him to complete the drive to the Casa and just big enough to ensure his tire would be flat by the time he got there. Ella spotted the problem as they walked through the portico and out to the car.

"Oh no, Jacob, look at your tire. It's flat. That's too bad. We don't have time to change it."

"Ugh! You've got that right," Jacob replied as he knelt down and saw the nail buried in the rubber. "Of all nights, I'm so sorry, Ella."

"No worries, we can take my car. I had it washed just yesterday, so it is in prime shape. We can open the sunroof and enjoy the beautiful drive down the coast. I can't remember the last time I drove along the coast. This should be fun. That is, if you trust my driving skills," she joked.

For such short notice, everything had come together for the dinner amazingly well. Ella was still curious why Jason Bingham had volunteered to host the affair, and the one time she'd tried to reach him to ask, he'd been unavailable. But when she saw the guest RSVP list, she couldn't say no, especially when the dinner was being held for the Foster Kids program. The proceeds from the Grand Vista Hotel gala had fallen short of expectations, and this dinner would just about make up the difference. Surprisingly, her social calendar had also been clear. It was almost as if Providence had stepped in to do her and the program a good turn. Jacob had to cancel another engagement, but other than that, the timing couldn't have been more perfect.

As they pulled away from the Pastures, Ella opened the sunroof and rolled the windows down. A stiff breeze was blowing in from the north, so the air flowing through the vehicle was cool and refreshing. It almost felt like they were riding in a convertible. Jacob reached over and turned on the XM Radio. He dialed in an Indie station. They were both familiar with the tune that was playing and joined in singing along. Ella was able to pick out a harmony part with ease while Jacob stuck with the tried and true melody line. Between songs, Jacob turned the volume down a bit and spoke over the noise of the wind.

"I love being impromptu with you, Ella. You are just such a joy in all things and at all times. I hope tonight is a grand success and that you raise even more money than you are hoping for. I called my father and BP - Napa has agreed I can auction off a weekend at our Napa estate's guest cottage complete with a case of our 2012 Old Vine Zinfandel and a free wine club membership for a year. The value of that package is right around $3,000, so we ought to be able to make at least that much extra for the program."

"Wow! That is wonderful, Jacob. You are such a blessing. Please be sure and thank your father for me."

"You'll be able to thank him yourself. He and mom are coming down tomorrow for a short visit and to discuss decor for the tasting room. The interior remodel of the old barn is coming along nicely. We've decided to stay with the same green color on the outside — the more historic and authentic, the better. We're going to keep the inside loft too and use it as a party room for member events. It will be fantastic. I'm getting excited about the progress. You're going to love it!"

"I can't wait. When is the grand opening?" Ella beamed.

"We're hoping for mid-October to celebrate crush. Of course, we won't have any BP - Carmel product to sell, but we'll be able to share the vision and at the same time introduce people to Bountiful Pastures - Napa's wines. Actually, I was thinking … what would you say to maybe providing some of your Pastures of Bounty product alongside ours as a local offering? That way we might get people to start thinking of us as partners of a sort."

Between the cool breeze, the music and the excitement about the dinner, neither occupant of the BMW paid much attention to things outside the car and neither had any clue about the relatively nondescript Pontiac Grand Am following them two vehicles back. When they crossed over the Carmel River, the visible houses began to dwindle in number. When they got to the open beach area immediately adjacent to the Carmelite Monastery, Jacob asked Ella to pull over for a moment so they could watch the final throes of the evening's sunset.

When the couple pulled over unexpectedly, Romero panicked for a moment in the Pontiac behind them. Realizing he might be seen if he suddenly pulled over with them in the mostly vacant beach parking area, he opted instead to drive past them and then take a quick left onto the Monastery driveway. Seeing it was too narrow to turn around in, he was forced to follow the path up a hill to the front of the grand church building. He turned around there and stopped when he realized he could see the parked BMW from his vantage point near the church.

Well, isn't this perfect. I can see them just fine, and there's no way they'll spot me way up here. Ha, and the irony is thick, me at a church. Maybe I should pray for forgiveness in advance and say my Hail Marys now, the henchman laughed to himself.

The bell toll for half past the hour rang, and a distant but distinct chorus rose from behind the walls of the cloister. The sound was angelic, and for the briefest of moments, it triggered a memory in the deep caverns of Romero's mind. He was nine when he received his first holy communion. His mother was especially proud of her young son. He remembered the sense of peace and purpose he felt and recalled a song much like that being lifted up by the nuns behind him. He remembered loving God in that moment.

The man gritted his teeth and spat on the floorboard of the rented vehicle as he cursed aloud at the unwanted invasion of his mind. *God ... huh ... not for me ... the only ones who are going to need God tonight, besides those helpless nuns, are the two in that car on the beach. I always did like Ms. Ella. Sad she has to go. She's a real looker, too.*

As the sunset's afterglow faded, Jacob reached over and pressed the switch to close the sunroof. He then reached into the pocket of his sports coat and withdrew a small black velvet box. He held it out for Ella to see before speaking. She gasped audibly.

"Ella, as a token of where I hope our relationship will someday go, I want to give this necklace to you. It's not much, but it is very special.

Remember I mentioned my Grandmother? Well, she was from the Black Hills of South Dakota, and they produce a very special kind of jewelry there called Black Hills Gold. My grandma always wore a necklace that grandfather gave to her when they were dating. I swear, I never saw her without it hanging from her neck. This is as close to the same design as I could find, and I'd be honored if you would wear it."

Ella took the box and felt the smoothness of the velvet on her fingertips. After gazing into Jacob's eyes for a long moment, she smiled and opened the treasure.

"It's beautiful, it's perfect, and yes I'll wear it forever, just like your grandmother did. Thank you, Jacob. I couldn't be happier than I am at this very moment."

She gave the box back to him and turned her head away so he could help fasten the delicate symbol of emerging love around her neck. She gathered her shoulder-length hair into a temporary ponytail and lifted it out of his way. After securing the clasp, Jacob leaned in as Ella turned back around and the two shared a kiss as the dark gray of evening descended on them.

When Ella restarted the car, its headlights came on automatically. Romero saw the unintended signal and immediately began rolling the Pontiac down the monastery driveway. When he got to the highway, he waited until the BMW passed. He then pulled out slowly and rejoined his southward pursuit.

The highway between Carmel and Big Sur was narrow and full of twists and curves. Once they got beyond the Highlands, much of the road hugged cliffs on the west side that fell precipitously down to the crashing surf below. Romero had scouted out two places where a fall over the cliff would almost certainly be fatal. He had his cell phone preset to dial the number he had programmed to ignite the tiny IEDs he had strategically placed on the brake and steering lines of the Beemer in front of him. All he needed to do now was stay back far enough to avoid being noticed, yet close enough for the phone signal trigger to work.

Ella was basking in the moment. Everything, it seemed, had finally come to a place of harmony.

She was at peace with her father's passing. The shock of being given control over the Pastures of Bounty had subsided, and she had put together an excellent team of advisors. She was living in one of the most beautiful places on earth. She was finding success in her quest to help others and pursue a meaningful life. And, most importantly, she had met a man with whom she felt compatibility and who had just, in a unique and beautiful way, expressed his love for her. Without speaking, she reached over with her right hand and took hold of Jacob's left hand. He squeezed hers three times and smiled.

"What do three squeezes mean," Ella asked innocently.

"Three words ... I love you," Jacob replied.

An old pickup pulled onto the highway from the left as the BMW scooted by on a short straightaway segment of the road.

"I'm going to need my hand back, Jacob," Ella said politely. "We're coming to a pretty curvy section up ahead as we begin to climb."

Jacob released her hand and jested, "Yes, ma'am. Hold that wheel carefully; ten and two, you know."

Romero cursed the fates when he saw the old pickup ease out onto the road. There was no room to pass as they were quickly into the curves. The pickup didn't have the power to keep up with the vehicle ahead of it nor did the local driver have any interest in doing so. Romero fell farther and farther behind his quarry as he climbed up the mountainside behind the pickup. He could still see the Beemer's headlights ahead of him, and when he guesstimated the car to be at the predefined location for the crash, he pressed the send button on his phone. He waited, expecting to see the car swerve and then fall headlong 100 feet over the cliff and onto the rocky shore below, but nothing happened. He pushed the button again and still got nothing. He cursed a blue streak at the top of his lungs as he pounded his fists on the steering wheel. Seeing no oncoming lights, he floored the accelerator and raced around the old truck screaming obscenities as he flew by and then fishtailed back into the lane. Within a mile, he was comfortably back in range of the BMW and calmed down enough to try again at the second kill spot.

After climbing the hill and then descending it, the road once again straightened and calmed. The beacon from the Point Sur Lighthouse came into view off to the right.

"Have you ever been up to the lighthouse?" Ella asked.

"No, not yet, but it's on my shortlist regarding places to see. Maybe we should visit it on Sunday."

"That would be nice," Ella said. "Papa loved that old lighthouse. In fact, I remember when I was a little girl, he and Mama celebrated a wedding anniversary there by renewing their vows. They were so in love. I think I get my sense of romance from them."

"Well, I'm certainly grateful to both of them for that. How much farther is the house we're going to?" Jacob asked.

"Not too far, maybe another three or four miles is all."

The second target spot Romero had defined was coming up just around the next bend. The descending road became unusually narrow, and there was a sharp switchback curve to the left. A pullout area for tourists to enjoy the vista and snap photos existed on the right, but it was small and, if anything, Romero calculated it would act as a perfect launch pad for the vehicle's take off into space and oblivion below.

He pulled up closer than he had been all night to ensure sufficient phone signal strength for the IED trigger. Ella noticed him briefly in her rearview mirror, but before she could say anything, she was distracted by a car coming toward them from the south and drifting into their lane.

"Watch that guy close, Ella," Jacob said nervously. "It looks like he may have had a bit too much to drink."

Ella swerved slightly to the right to give the wandering vehicle a little extra space. Her headlights, however, served as a hypnotic magnet to the intoxicated driver who unintentionally allowed his car to follow the lights. He crossed the dividing line just as the BMW passed by.

"Whew, that was too close for comfort," Ella exclaimed.

She looked into her rearview mirror to see if the driver would correct his course and watched in horror as she saw the car behind them suddenly veer off the road and come to a skidding, gravel and dust billowing stop in the tourist pull-out they had just passed.

"Oh my gosh," she uttered breathlessly, "the guy behind us just barely avoided being run off the road by that drunk. Jacob, we should call 911 and report that driver. He's a menace."

While Jacob dialed the emergency operator, Romero tried to collect his thoughts sitting on the cliff edge in the pullout.

Unbelievable! That jerk almost caused me to go flying. I'd chase him down and beat him senseless if I didn't have this job to do. He then paused and took a deep focusing breath. *Now I'm going to have to get creative, and fast. They're already passed the two kill spots and getting close to the dinner house. I'm going to have to "improvise" to make those improvised explosive devices serve their purpose.*

Knowing that his time was extremely limited, hanging back to avoid detection became a far less important goal. Romero quickly accelerated out of the pullout, leaving a rooster tail of gravel behind him. He caught up with the Beemer in less than two minutes. Though acquainted with the highway they were traveling on, Romero didn't know it well enough to recall what was around every bend in the road. What he could determine, however, was that the further south they traveled the lower and closer to the water's edge they were getting. Losing the fall factor would reduce the odds of succeeding with the mission, so he figured he had better blow the lines sooner than later.

When he was right on their tail, he sped up and tapped their bumper in an effort to get them to speed up to try to get away. His plan worked as Ella hit the gas trying to put some distance between them and the mystery car suddenly behind them again.

"What in the world does that guy think he's doing!" Ella reacted to the bumper being nudged. "We're almost to the turnoff to the Bingham place -- another mile or so. I just need to keep some distance from this lunatic."

Romero fumbled for his phone and tried to open the dial function that would trigger the IEDs. At the speed he was going, every time he looked down to work the phone his vehicle drifted, and he then had to swerve it back into the lane. His driving was looking even more erratic than the drunk's had been moments before. Cursing aloud all the while, he finally got the phone open to the proper place and as he tapped Ella's bumper one final time he pushed the dial signal.

Ella and Jacob heard three dull thuds that sounded like they had come from underneath the car.

"Did you just run over something," Jacob asked. "I didn't feel any bumps, but it sure sounded like you hit something."

"I don't think so," Ella replied nervously, but I heard the sounds, too. There were three of them, right?"

"Yes, that's what I heard, but … wait … Ella, are you okay? You're starting to drift to the right," Jacob said, anxiously.

"Yes, but the steering wheel doesn't seem to be responding very well. This feels really strange. I think I should pull over, maybe whatever we hit got caught in the steering line."

When Ella went to slow the car down, she pressed on the brake as she usually would, but nothing happened. She then did so again, with the same result, nothing.

"Jacob, I don't have any brakes either," Ella said hysterically.

She grabbed the steering wheel with both hands trying desperately to maneuver the car around the curves in the road, but nothing was working. Jacob leaned over to try to help her with the wheel, but it was almost entirely unresponsive. He then quickly suggested she downshift, which she did, and the car lurched forward as the engine kicked into low gear and began to whine loudly. Jacob then pulled up on the emergency brake lever located between the two bucket seats. Again, the car lurched. It slowed a bit, but not enough. Ella screamed as they careened into and then off of the guardrail to the right. The car bounced and swerved harshly to the left and then glanced off the shear wall on the leeward side of the road. Jacob yelled to Ella involuntarily as fear rose and erupted in him. The car swerved back to the right, toward the guard rail, which was the only thing separating the hurtling juggernaut from the edge of the cliff and the water below. Ella pounded her foot to the floorboard and pumped the brake pedal over and over but to no avail. The car crashed once, and then a second time against the guardrail and then began scraping alongside it. Sparks started flying so high they could see them flaming up to the passenger-side window.

"Oh no, oh God, Ella, we're going to go over the edge!" Jacob practically screamed.

Ella cried out, "Jacob, oh Jacob, I love you. Oh God!"

They heard a horrible crack as the car finally broke through the guardrail and then ... nothing. The BMW took flight. Silence for what seemed an eternity filled the space the two sat in. The headlights streamed out into an abyss of dark and illuminated nothingness. The car's trajectory gradually leaned forward and then began to point down. Neither passenger said anything further before the nose of the vehicle lit with a crushing blow on the ground below, and then the car flipped, and they were then once again soaring, this time upside down. The last thing Jacob remembered as the car bounced and rolled down the hill was the realization that he was strangely thankful they had hit the ground instead of the water.

CHAPTER 17

Calderon doubled back to the break in the guard rail and pointed his car to shine its headlights out over the cliff. In the distance, he could make out the form of the crumpled vehicle lying on its roof. It had not made it to the water but appeared to have rolled several times before coming to a stop a good forty yards from the road edge. When he saw headlights approaching from the north, Calderon quickly re-entered the Pontiac and sped away to the south. Several miles later he pulled into a convenience store parking lot near the town of Big Sur to report in.

"Boss, Romero here, it's done. They're done. Mission accomplished," he grunted into the phone.

"Did they crash into the sea?"

"No, they didn't roll that far. But the car flipped several times and is flat as a pancake. There's no way either of them will walk away. You won't have to worry about Napa boy ever again."

"Excellent work, Romero," Parker said into the phone as he leaned back in his desk chair at the Casa and took a long toke on a cigar. "Now, I need you to lay low for a few days. I've rented a room for you at the Sea Haven motel about an hour further south in the little town of Cambria. Stay there for two nights and then head south to L.A. Drop the rental car at the LAX airport and then take a bus back home. Oh, and by the way, I ordered dessert for you again at the motel in Cambria. Enjoy."

***

The Bingham estate sat high on a hilltop looking down on the Pacific Ocean and the Big Sur coastline. Of course, it was dark, so the view wasn't nearly as spectacular as during the day, but you could still feel the sense of sitting in the clouds. The hint of moonlight on the water below shimmered, and the sound of the crashing surf carried up to the top of the mountain. The winding driveway climbed a mile and a half from the highway, and the dinner host sat on his cantilevered balcony deck under a heat lamp sipping a cocktail while he watched the headlights of the invited guests wind their way up the mountain.

The formal entry to the house was stunning. Where the road from the highway met the large circular driveway in front of the house, a twenty-foot tall gate made of ancient redwood logs greeted the arrivals. Hand carved into the wood at the top of the structure, lit by spotlights, cleverly concealed within the vertical tree trunks, was the name of the property "Castillo Grande." Though not necessary for the number of guests invited, each car was welcomed by a valet who assisted the occupants from their coaches and then parked the cars out of sight.

The mansion's motif was classic Big Sur in every respect. Gnarled wood and natural stone were everywhere. A small artificial stream meandered through the inside of the house with live plants along its banks. A redwood tree the house had been built around stood in the center of the living room and grew through the rough-hewn ceiling as it reached to the heavens. The furniture was rustic, and each piece was a work of art in and of itself. The guests were ushered through the living room to the dining area which commanded spectacular indoor-outdoor views of the coastline below.

By 7:30 all the invitees had arrived and were comfortably chatting over drinks and appetizers. Bingham excused himself to his private study and picked up the phone. He dialed Parker Gillette's number.

At Casa de Abundante Parker sat in his office, nursing his third bourbon and still working on his cigar. He was relishing his moment of anointing and ascendancy to the throne. He was also enjoying the satisfaction of his plan unfolding and the fact he was playing his part so perfectly.

The cell phone vibrated on the desk in front of him, and he saw the call was coming in from his friend, and patsy, Jason Bingham, just as he had expected. He sat patiently, almost salivating as it rang five times before going to voicemail. He then listened as the message was recorded.

"Parker, this is Jason. Hey man, all your guests have arrived. Quite the group, I must say. You really know all the heavy hitters, don't you? Anyway, I'm just calling to ask about your sister.

She is coming, right? She's not here yet. I would have expected her to arrive maybe even a little bit early. So, she's not here, and some of the people are beginning to ask about her. If you know where she is and what time we can expect her to arrive, give me a call. I want to hold dinner for her, of course, but I get the sense that these people are getting hungry and are going to want to sit down to eat fairly soon. So, call me ASAP and give me an update. Later."

Perfect, Parker thought to himself with satisfaction, as the voicemail stopped recording, *perfect. My script is playing out exactly as planned.*

The next morning Parker was awakened by another phone call. This one was from the California Highway Patrol. Again, as he had planned, he let it go to voicemail, too.

"Good morning. This call is for Mr. Parker Gillette. This is officer Borchard with the California Highway Patrol. Sir, we need to talk to you as soon as possible regarding a car accident last night in Big Sur. It appears an SUV registered to your company was run off the road by a drunk driver last night. It went over an embankment and crashed. There were two passengers in the vehicle. They haven't yet been identified, and we don't know the extent of their injuries at this time. We will attempt to extract them from the vehicle and then airlift them to the hospital in Monterey. Please call me back at this number as soon as you receive this message. Thank you. Goodbye."

As expected, Parker mused as he listened and noted the time. *Everything except the extent of injuries part -- they're supposed to be dead. If they survive, everything could be ruined. Unbelievable! Calderon can't ever get anything right,* he fumed.

Parker took a long shower and then fixed himself a Denver omelet for breakfast which he ate leisurely. After cleaning up, he went upstairs to call Bingham back.

"Bingham, good morning, hey, I just got your voicemail from last night. How did the dinner go? By the way, what time did my sister finally arrive? ... What? She never showed up? ... That's crazy. She wouldn't miss such an important affair -- especially not one raising money for her favorite pet charity ... Did anyone have any idea where she might be? ... Hmm, that is very strange. Look, I'm going to check her room and see if maybe she's here. If not then I'm going to call the sheriff. Maybe they'll know something. I sure hope she's alright ... Thanks, man. I'll let you know. Bye."

So the time stamps on the calls would be realistic if later compared, Parker went through the motions of checking on Ella's room, After confirming what he already knew, he went back to his study and picked up the phone again and called the Sheriff.

"Hello. My name is Parker Gillette. I'm calling to ask if you have any information about my sister, Gabriella Gillette. She was supposed to attend a dinner in Big Sur last night, but I was just informed by the host that she never made it to the event ... No, I haven't heard a word from her, and she's not here at our house which is the only other place I could think she would be. I'm concerned there may have been an accident or something. Would you please ask your men in the field down there to look into it and call me back as soon as possible. I'll stay right here by the phone. I'm very worried ... thank you. Goodbye."

Next, Parker pushed the play button on his message machine, and he listened to the recording from the Highway Patrol that he had already heard. He immediately returned the call and gave an Academy Award-winning performance of a distraught brother begging for information about his missing sister.

"Well done, Park. The timestamps on all those calls will tell the perfect story. I think a little celebration is in order, don't you?" he said to himself half out loud. "Huh, but it's only 8:30 in the morning … well, it's five o'clock in Barcelona, so why not." He laughed at his own inane joke as he poured himself a double from the whiskey bottle on his desk and grinned with wicked satisfaction.

***

The loud whirr of helicopter blades overhead jostled Jacob back to consciousness. He then heard what sounded like men yelling directions and trucks and equipment. His body was pinned, so that he couldn't turn to look at Ella. He tried to call out to her but winced at the pain in his chest when he took a breath. She didn't answer. He tried to call her name again and began to panic when there was no response. He tried to focus. Except for his left arm, his appendages were all constrained by the crushed exterior and roof of the vehicle. It was morning, but other than that he had no clue about day or time.

"Hey, I've got movement down here. The male is alive. Quick, send down the EMTs, and get the 'Jaws of Life' down here pronto!

"Hey, mister, can you hear me? My name is Officer Johnson. I'm with the Highway Patrol. Can you tell me what you're feeling, where you're hurt?"

Jacob was still trying to process the whole scene. His mind wandered back to the night before. The three successive sounds, the car running into their rear bumper, the sudden loss of steering and brakes, the vehicle bouncing between the guardrail and the mountainside, the scraping along and eventually breaking through the railing and then taking flight before the crash. It all replayed in his mind as if it had happened just moments before.

"Mister, can you hear me? We're here to help you. What's your name?" the voice continued to hound his consciousness.

"Uh, Jacob … Jacob Wingate, is Ella okay?" he muttered in response.

"Ella? Is that the name of the lady here in the car with you? Ella what?"

"Ella Gillette. Is she alright? I can't see her. I'm pinned in here."

"Honestly, sir, we can't tell. The EMTs will be here any minute. She is not conscious right now, and that is all I know at this time. She does have a pulse though, so that is some reason to be hopeful."

The Jaws of Life team finally made it down the cliff to where the car had stopped rolling. Another two rolls and it would have plummeted another fifty feet straight down to the jagged shoreline rocks below. The first order of business was to secure the car to prevent it from accidentally rolling any further. Next, the EMTs swarmed both sides of the vehicle to try to determine the injury status of each of the victims. They didn't learn much more than Officer Johnson had.

Within the hour, both Ella and Jacob were in a helicopter flying up the Big Sur coast to Monterey. Typically it would have been a breathtakingly beautiful ride, but not today. As the two were being admitted, Officer Johnson, who had remained with the victims during the medevac, completed his initial report and then began making calls. His first was to Parker Gillette who, he had been told, had called in earlier to report his sister missing.

"Hello, Mr. Gillette … yes, good morning … this is Officer Ken Johnson. I have news about your sister … We're not sure about her condition at this time. She was in a car accident and has been admitted to the hospital … Yes, down near Big Sur. It was a pretty bad accident, over a cliff. It's a miracle they survived … Uh, they? … Well, I'm not at liberty to discuss that at this time. I think it might be best for you to come to the hospital if you can. I'm sure the doctors will know more by the time you arrive … Yes, the hospital in Monterey, you're welcome, sir. Goodbye."

Parker cursed under his breath after hanging up the phone. *Alive, she's still alive. It will only be a matter of time before they find out the brake lines were tampered with and that spells risk. And who knows what they may have seen before the crash. They might even be able to identify Calderon. This is bad, very bad.*

He picked up his cell phone and hit speed dial one.

A groggy voice on the other end picked up after four rings.

"Boss? Do you know what time it is? I just got to sleep a few hours ago. I thought you were going to give me a few days off to enjoy my dessert."

"Romero, are you alone?" Parker asked in a whispered tone.

"Uh, no boss, dessert is laying right here, looking awfully good I might add."

"I need you to get somewhere private, now. We need to talk. We've got a big problem."

"Okay, hang on a minute. I'll throw some clothes on and slip outside," Romero said quietly.

A minute later Romero was in the Pontiac which was parked just outside the motel room. Parker told him what he knew.

"So, Romero, you need to keep driving south. You need to get across the border to Mexico. You remembered to bring your passport and the go bag I prepared for you, right?"

"Yeah, boss. The bag is in my trunk, along with my Winchester. But do you really think it's necessary to go all the way to Mexico? Seems kind of extreme. I know they didn't see me and there's no way they can link the IEDs to me, at least I don't think they can."

"But what if they do?" Parker's voice was now rising in anger. "If they connect you they might connect me and then we'll both be spending Christmas in Soledad prison. You have to disappear, at least until I can figure this out. Maybe we'll get lucky, and they won't make it, but we can't bank on luck.

"Once you get to Mexico I want you to hole up somewhere inconspicuous. Nothing fancy and no nightlife, you understand? Use the cash in the go bag. No credit cards. And stash the rental car somewhere it can't be found. I'll call you in a few days, and we'll make a plan. Got it?"

"Yeah, I got it," Romero said as he spat on the floorboard in disgust.

***

The battery of diagnostic tests they ran on Jacob showed that he was a very fortunate man. The way the vehicle had crushed around him had formed a kind of cocoon which, combined with the seat belt system and the front and side airbags, saved him from serious injury. He had several contusions, two broken ribs, and a fractured left arm, but showed no signs of concussion or internal organ damage. The word miracle was circulating among the ER staff.

Jacob called his parents who were already on their way to the Peninsula and gave them the Reader's Digest version of the story. They came straight to the hospital from the airport, and the three were together in Jacob's hospital room when Parker arrived.

"Hi, Jacob, I just came from Ella's room. Have you heard about her condition?" Parker asked.

"Hey, Parker, these are my parents, William and Mary Wingate."

Consistent with his charade as the caring brother, Parker thought it best to show some manners toward his arch enemy -- who would be dead but for Romero's bumbling -- so he extended a welcoming hand.

"Hello, Mr. and Mrs. Wingate, I'm Parker Gillette. My sister Ella was in the car with Jacob when they crashed last night."

"Yes, hello, Mr. Gillette," William said, shaking the man's hand. "Jacob has mentioned you."

Everything was friendly enough on the surface amongst the group, but they could all feel the tension in the room as Parker walked over to Jacob's bedside.

"Hey, sorry about your injuries, Jacob, but at least you were more fortunate than Ella. The doctor said that while she doesn't have any broken bones, she suffered a traumatic blow to the head. There is swelling on her brain so they had to induce a coma hoping the swelling will lessen and healing can take place. Even though that's very serious, the doctors are still saying you were both fortunate to walk away from that accident. Have you seen any of the photos of what's left of the SUV?"

"No, I haven't seen any pictures. Thank you for the report on Ella. With all the privacy rules these days, no one would talk with me because I'm not family," Jacob replied.

"I'll keep you updated on her progress. In fact, I'll ask them to make information available to you directly. You obviously have a vested interest."

Jacob was grateful for the offer and thought maybe he was finally seeing the side of Parker that Ella had prayed would appear. But he kept his guard up anyway just in case the chameleon decided to change colors.

"Are you feeling up to talking about what happened?" Parker asked caringly.

Jacob explained what he remembered. It was mostly the same rendition he had already told the Highway Patrol, the Sheriff, and the doctors.

"So," Parker casually probed, "some car came up behind you and hit your rear bumper? Did you get a look at the car or the driver?"

The answer Parker hoped to hear was delivered.

"No, it was dark, and he came out of nowhere," Jacob relayed.

"He? You saw the driver then?"

"Well, actually I suppose it could have been a she. I didn't see anything one way or the other," Jacob confirmed and then continued. "I know the police will do their best, but in my experience sometimes they overlook things, so I've asked Nate Donohue's investigator to do some independent analysis of the vehicle. I'll let you know if we learn anything helpful. Thanks for dropping by, Parker. Much appreciated, especially the report on Ella."

Following obligatory niceties with the elder Wingates, Parker left. In the parking lot of the hospital, he hit speed dial one.

"Listen up," Parker barked into his phone. "Wingate has hired a private detective to comb over the SUV. I'm sure they'll find your fingerprints. To explain those I need you to access the computer records at the house and dummy up some maintenance work you did on Ella's Beemer within the past week. Got it? And stay down in Tijuana until I tell you otherwise. And remember, no nightlife. I want you ordering delivered pizza and drinking sodas only. No booze or pills, man. You need to be sharp at all times. I'm working overtime on things here, but it's not going to be easy.

"You didn't tell anyone where you were going did you?"

"Uh," Romero hesitated, "I might have mentioned it to the dessert. I mean, hey man, I needed to explain why I was running out on her. She was beautiful, so she'd have known it wasn't my choice to leave."

Parker cursed at his henchman before asking, "Did you tell her your name?"

"Uh, actually no, I didn't, boss, at least not my real name. I called her Wonder Woman, and she called me Superman, so I guess that's good, huh?"

"Yeah, good enough for now," Parker said. "We'll talk more later."

As he clicked off the phone, he cursed again and wondered *why is it that I had to go and hire a hit man with only a sixth-grade education? He's never going to be able to pull this off. Romero my friend, I'm afraid you may have to become a casualty of war. The combination of your fingerprints and the fake maintenance log you're going to create, which will be time stamped today in the embedded metadata, are going to send you away for a long, long time.*

***

As expected, the following day the Sheriff asked Parker to come down to the station for an interview. Parker was well rehearsed and ready to continue his Oscar-worthy performance.

"Thank you for coming in, Mr. Gillette. Hopefully, this won't take too long. We're just trying to piece the puzzle together," the deputy began.

"Puzzle?" Parker acted intrigued. "Was this more than just an accident? What do you think happened? Do you have clues? Do you have a suspect?"

His rapid-fire delivery was all part of the script. Feign ignorance, then show surprise, then show interest and even a modicum of anger; they were buying his act hook, line, and sinker.

"It looks like the brake and steering lines were deliberately tampered with. Pretty ingenious, really. Traces of explosives, probably from an IED, were found under the car chassis. We've also identified some fingerprints on the underside of the car. They belong to a friend of yours, Mr. Gillette."

The tone of the deputy's last sentence differed from the preceding ones. It subtly shifted to quasi-accusatory. Parker was shaken inside, but maintained his character role on the outside.

"A friend, what friend would want to hurt my sister? Who is it?" he asked incredulously.

"Your ranch manager, Romero Calderon, would you happen to know where he is, Mr. Gillette?"

"Romero? No way. He's worked for our family for fifteen years. He'd never hurt Ella. There must be some explanation," Parker said, feigning defense of the man he was about to betray.

Even Judas could take a lesson or two from me, Parker thought to himself.

CHAPTER 18

The interview continued for another several minutes while Parker continued to deflect questions about his friend, knowing full well that eventually, when he thought they would be convinced of his desire to protect his man, he would finally allow them to believe they cracked him.

"Mr. Gillette, your man Romero, he did have access to the car, did he not."

"Well, yes, he did. He did the maintenance on all of our vehicles. We even keep a computer log of the work done. You can check that if you'd like. So, it's not all that surprising Romero's fingerprints might be on the SUV."

"Perhaps," the interrogator acknowledged, "but on the brake lines?"

"Well, that I can't really say. I'm not a mechanic myself. Isn't the oil pan down near there somewhere?" Parker asked, playing dumb.

"Mr. Gillette, can you think of any reason Mr. Calderon might want to hurt your sister? You know … would he have any motive or stand to gain anything by her death?"

Well, it took you long enough to get to the right question you idiot, Parker chuckled to himself. *Boy, do you ever need to go back to detective school. It's no wonder criminals are running wild and free in this County. You guys are worthless. Okay, time to pour it on thick for the audience.*

"Well, as I said, Romero has been working for our family for a long time, and he has always been a hard worker and loyal. But, since you ask, and I don't really know if this is relevant at all …." Parker stopped himself mid-sentence for effect.

"What might be relevant, Mr. Gillette," the questioner asked with widening interest.

"Well, Romero might have been jealous of my sister and her new boyfriend, Jacob Wingate. You see Romero is kind of juvenile when it comes to, you know, women. I always thought it strange that he would tell me, her brother, and I always

338

chastised him for it. I even threatened to fire him if he didn't stop."

"Stop what, Mr. Gillette?"

After a heavy, embarrassed sigh, Parker continued, "Stop fantasizing about my sister. He has been obsessing over her for almost a year. It got kind of creepy, the things he would say. Inappropriate things, and like I said, I threatened to fire him. He apologized and said he'd stop, and I never saw any further evidence until Ella started dating Wingate. Romero seemed agitated about their relationship. I noticed he started watching them when they were together at the house. At first I thought he was just being protective, but now that I think about it, he might have been acting out of jealousy. He's always been a bit of a loose cannon. Frankly, his mean disposition and threatening demeanor are part of what makes him so good at his job protecting our ranch. I suppose if he channeled all that aggression toward my sister, he might ... no, I really can't see him going that far. I mean he can be one tough hombre, but a killer? I don't see it."

Parker could tell he'd set the bait, and he watched with sinister pleasure as the officer furiously scribbled notes on his pad. He could almost see the man's brain calculating and realizing he had just scored a critical win in the investigation, and with a little luck, might be able to collar a murder suspect.

Following the interview, the sheriff asked for, and Parker provided, the computer records of vehicle maintenance he had mentioned. The computer forensics expert for the sheriff made quick work of reviewing the log entries and the accompanying metadata that lurked in the depths of the system and which contained a trove of hidden information including when each log entry was made. When they learned the maintenance entry for a week ago, had been made the day after the accident, they put two and two together, smelled a cover-up, and issued a warrant for Romero Calderon's arrest.

Among the other facts they investigated, the sheriff's office traced Romero's credit card history. They found he had rented a car in Santa Cruz the day before the accident and that the vehicle was still unaccounted for. They also learned his card had been used in a liquor store near Cambria the day after the accident. Things were beginning to add up. Since they had the make, model and license plate number of the rental car, they decided to review street cams along the freeway system in L.A. Finding nothing they looked further south, theorizing that the man might be on the run. Seeing nothing in San Diego, they decided to check the camera records at the border to Mexico. There they struck pay dirt. At 3:13 p.m. two days after the accident, the rented Pontiac crossed the border into Mexico. Close-ups showed the occupant matched the description of Calderon, and there was a noticeable dent on the right front fender of the vehicle. High fives circulated through the local sheriff's office as they celebrated having found their man.

Because he had crossed over into Mexico, the Mexican Policia Federales had to be contacted. Extradition treaties between the U.S. and Mexico made for reasonably smooth transition and cooperation when it came to fleeing felons. Romero, for better or worse, hadn't understood that.

Despite Parker's explicit instructions not to use his credit card, Romero had done so. He had plenty of cash in the go bag to pay for gas, food, and lodging, but the adult channel on the motel TV wouldn't take cash to allow a viewer to sign on, so Romero had used his credit card, not thinking about the possible consequences.

The Mexican authorities arrived on the scene at dusk. After identifying the car, they asked the front desk clerk for a key to Romero's room. The clerk complied and then, after locking the lobby door, slunk back into his apartment and turned all the lights out. The sheriff had earlier obtained a warrant to search Romero's house, and they found a cache of drugs and weapons, but they noticed that the rifle Parker had mentioned he carried with him during his rounds in the vineyard was missing. That coupled with the fact that Romero was wanted for attempted murder and had fled the country, resulted in his being characterized as armed and dangerous. The Federales were taking no chances and had twelve armed officers on the scene. They surrounded the ground floor unit the desk clerk had told them contained Calderon.

They peered into the room through the ragged curtains and saw Romero sprawled out on the bed drinking and watching a soccer game on TV. A variety of hand signals were flashed to all the officers so that everyone understood the plan of attack. Banging loudly on the door, the Federales announced themselves and demanded Romero come out with his hands raised.

Romero's eyes widened as soon as he heard the police. He immediately rolled off the bed away from the door and made a move to the closet next to the bathroom. He grabbed his aught-six and crouched down low. He pumped the lever action to load the chamber and waited. Another bang on the door and another demand to surrender filled the room. Romero's mind raced, and the cocktail of liquor and pills was screaming at him. Flashes from the past few days pierced his consciousness in rewind: the last call from Parker; crossing the border; dessert; hitting the rear end of the SUV to propel it forward; nearly being driven off the cliff by the drunk driver; the two failed attempts to trigger the IEDs; following his targets from the beach to Big Sur; laying in wait on the hill at the entrance to the monastery; listening to the nuns singing ... that song. The backtracking stopped, and the song flooded his mind, both as the cloistered sisters had sung it, and as he remembered it during his first holy communion. He remembered again, his family's pride in their boy and the sense of fulfillment and joy he felt. How did he end up here, alone in a foreign country, crouching in the small closet of a dingy motel room with nothing to comfort him but the cold steel of a killing machine?

The police banged on the door for the third time and announced they would break the door down if he did not respond. Romero crouched lower and aimed his rifle at the door. His mind then went to the movie scenes he remembered where the star went down in a blaze of glory: Butch Cassidy and the Sundance Kid; Bonnie and Clyde; and Scarface. He wondered if his story would be written and a movie made so that his final moments would be etched in glory. He fired his rifle at the door, and the next moment the room was a hail of bullets ... and then smoky silence.

***

The following morning Jacob was allowed to get up and walk around the hospital corridors. After being assured he would fully recover, his and his parents' prayers focused exclusively on Ella. She remained in the medically induced coma, but progress regarding the brain swelling was being seen. The doctors were optimistic and scheduled the procedure to bring her back to consciousness for later that afternoon. Nate and Cassie came to the hospital to share lunch with the Wingate family. Afterward, the five waited nervously outside Ella's room as the doctors went in.

***

News of the gunfight in Mexico had not yet reached those gathered at the hospital, but the Sheriff's office had informed Parker. He was told Romero had suffered multiple gunshot wounds and had been admitted to a local hospital, but was not expected to live. Parker found himself actually feeling a twitch of sadness and remorse over the loss of his longtime friend, but was resigned to the fact that it had been a necessary evil. He would honor Romero privately as a hero of the cause and send money to his family if he could find them. But he still needed to figure out a way to deal with Ella and spent the rest of the day plotting and planning his next move.

***

Charles and Ariana Weston joined the group at the hospital just after 2 p.m. Jacob told the story of their accident for the umpteenth time and the group, including Jacob himself, continued to marvel at the good fortune both he and Ella had been the recipients of to have survived the crash. At half past three, the doctor walked into the waiting room.

"We have good news. Ms. Gillette is going to recover," he announced rather matter-of-factly. "The swelling on her brain is gone, and she is conscious again. We do not expect there to be any lingering complications from either the accident or the procedure. She is an extremely fortunate young lady. You may go in to see her in small groups of two or three. Please stay for no longer than a few minutes. She is tired and needs rest."

"Thank you, doctor!" Jacob said standing to shake the man's hand. "You and your staff here have been amazing. We are fortunate, not only to have survived the accident but to have such a wonderful hospital here in our town."

346

Then, turning back to the group, he asked, "Would you all mind if I went in alone first? And then I'd like to introduce Ella to my parents. She and I were talking about her meeting them the night of the accident."

Everyone nodded their concurrence and Jacob stepped into the room alone.

Other than severe bruising and a nasty cut near her left temple, Ella looked surprisingly whole. She smiled at Jacob as he approached her bedside and his eyes welled. He leaned over and gently kissed her forehead and then sat in the small chair next to the bed and took her hand in his. The necklace he had given her at the beach was lying on the bedside table. When she saw his eyes look at it, she spoke.

"I know I said I'd wear it forever, and look, it's only day three, and already I've broken my promise. Would you help me put it back on?"

They laughed softly together as Jacob fumbled with his casted arm and she struggled to lift her head.

"I don't think this is going to work right now. Maybe we should do this tomorrow," Jacob finally suggested, with a grin. "For today we both know our intentions and can rest on those. Ella, you have no idea how afraid we have all been. We didn't know if you were going to make it, but, well, God has seen fit to bring you back to us. We are blessed -- you and I -- and I plan to make the most of that blessing for the rest of our lives."

"How are you, Jacob? Obviously, you broke your arm, but do you have any other injuries?" Ella asked.

The two chatted privately for several minutes before Jacob interrupted their conversation. "Oh, I almost forgot, I have a little surprise for you. Wait just a minute, while I go get them?"

"Them?" Ella asked curiously.

Jacob poked his head out the door and whispered. He then held the door open for his parents to enter.

"Ella, these are my folks, William and Mary. See, I told you you'd get to meet them. I just never imagined it would be in a hospital."

Mary stepped forward first, "Ella, we are so glad to meet you and grateful to know that you will recover from this horrible accident. Jacob has told us so much about you and your beautiful ranch." Then winking she added, "And I think he might be just a bit sweet on you, my girl, and we couldn't be happier about that."

"Yes, Ella," William added, "it is a genuine pleasure to meet you finally, the girl our son just can't seem to stop talking about. I had begun to wonder how he could possibly be distracted from his mission here in Carmel, but now, seeing you, well, it's no wonder at all. You are a true beauty and according to Jacob even more so on the inside. We will continue to pray for your speedy recovery and return to health."

Even though the doctor had limited the number of visitors, Jacob called the Westons and Nate to join them, and the seven stood around Ella's bed, and they all talked together for ten minutes. Charles and William stepped away briefly into the hall to find chairs for their wives. While outside the room they saw Parker down the hall walking toward them. Gillette waved casually and forced a smile. Charles stepped forward to greet him while William ducked back into the room.

"Jacob, Parker Gillette is here. He's just outside, talking with Charles. What do you want to do?"

"I don't know; this is awkward. He certainly has a right to see his sister. I guess I'll go out and ask him if he wouldn't mind waiting a few minutes. I'll tell him what the doctor said about visitors and that we'll be done soon. I don't think it would be a good idea for him to join us at this point."

Jacob stepped out into the hallway and approached the two men speaking near the nurse's station. After Jacob explained the circumstances to Parker, he agreed to wait for the room to clear.

"I'm so relieved to hear that Ella is going to be okay and that you are as well," Parker said. "I know we have had our differences, but blood is thicker than water, as they say. And sometimes it can even be thicker than wine. Look, I know you and Ella are developing a relationship, and if I'm honest, I wasn't too happy about it, to begin with. But I am coming around to accepting it and well, with our father's passing, I've been reevaluating some things. Jacob, I'd like to talk with you about settling the lawsuit and moving forward. What do you say?"

Jacob's initial reaction was cautious. Everyone had warned him about Parker's deceitfulness, but death and near death experiences can change a man. And besides, this is what Ella had been praying for. Maybe her prayer was being answered.

"I'm certainly open to talking, and I've always been open to finding peace. This lawsuit isn't really my style, but I felt forced into it. So, yes, let's meet and talk. How about later this week? And I'd like to have my attorney join us if you don't mind. If we make progress, someone will need to write it up, and it would be good for him to hear our discussion first hand to understand any subtleties we agree upon."

"Good. Let's meet at my house on Wednesday," Parker said. "And bring Mr. Donohue along if you'd like. Moncrief will send him an email consenting to his meeting with me directly. Let's shoot for noon. I'll have lunch ready."

The two men shook hands and parted.

Before he left Ella's side, Jacob shared with her about his conversation in the hall with Parker. Her reaction was the same as his, cautiously optimistic, and they interpreted that since they both felt the same way it made sense to proceed, carefully.

***

The Wednesday morning newspaper contained a front-page story about the accident and Romero's capture in Mexico. Attempted murder and ensuing shootouts didn't happen every day in Monterey County, so the news spread quickly. The two local news stations called to request interviews, and a message was left on Ella's phone by the nationally syndicated TV news program called, "Hotline."

Parker had anonymously called the hospital in Tijuana and was unhappy to learn that Romero was still in critical condition and barely hanging on by a thread. If he regained enough strength to speak with any of the press that would now almost certainly be camped outside his room, things could go very bad. All the more reason, he calculated, to try to reach an agreement with Wingate as soon as possible.

***

The three sat down to lunch on the back balcony overlooking the vineyard to the north. Moncrief was not present but had sent Nate the consenting email. Shelby served a bottle of the Reserve Cabernet to pair with delicious New York steak sandwiches and savory potato salad.

"How is my sister?" Parker asked as the three began eating. "I wasn't able to make it over to the hospital yesterday."

"She is getting stronger each day," Jacob reported with a big smile. "They are talking about sending her home on Friday."

"That is the best news," Parker exclaimed. "And how about your arm. Has the pain lessened at all?"

"It's a bit better, thanks. What's hurting the most are these broken ribs. They obviously can't cast those, so I just have to live with the pain for six weeks. It's pretty intense."

"I can imagine," Parker continued. "I bruised a rib once playing high school football. And that was only a bruise. I was in agony for a month."

Nate listened and carefully observed the conversation between the two enemies. Even through his skepticism, he had to admit that Gillette appeared to have turned a page and was seemingly being genuine.

Eventually, Nate joined the conversation, "So, Parker, I know my role here is mostly just to listen, but I'm curious about the settlement idea you mentioned to Jacob. Can you tell us something about it?"

"Sure Mr. Donohue. You may know that when my father passed away, God rest his soul, he willed 51% of Pastures of Bounty to my sister. Financially I have no problem with that, but I remain concerned, no disrespect intended, about Ella's ability to, and frankly, her interest in running a full-fledged wine operation. She is great with numbers and books, of course, but there is much, much more to it than that, as I'm sure, Jacob, you can attest.

"So, I think it would be in the best interest of my family's estate, the business, and our future, that I should be the managing partner of Pastures of Bounty. That would mean I would have to purchase two percent of Ella's interest.

"As consideration, I would offer two things. First, I would give all the art and furnishings in Casa de Abundante to Ella. Father split those between us and the total value easily exceeds two million dollars. I know Ella shares my father's fondness for art and, well, I really don't. Not to be crass, but I look at art as an asset and would be likely to liquidate my items anyway.

"The second thing I would offer, and this is perhaps a bit more attenuated, but still I think it would be of value to Ella and eventually to all of us in the Pastures, I would offer to settle the lawsuit. We will, as you have suggested, share the water, and as long as you change your label art, I will drop the claim regarding the name."

"Well," Jacob responded, "I think that is pretty clear, and I saw Nate taking good notes. Obviously, this will involve Ella even more than me, but I do appreciate the connection you've made between us, and I think there is a future link there. Let me talk with Ella tonight, and if she's amenable, I'll have Nate draft up a memorandum of understanding. We'll send something to you and Moncrief to review and see where things go from there. Agreed?"

"I couldn't ask for anything more at this juncture," Parker concurred. "So yes, let's go down that path and see where it leads. Now, let me tell you the story behind this fabulous Cabernet."

CHAPTER 19

That night Jacob joined Ella for dinner at the hospital. She was able to move around the facility with ease. The only reason she was staying was so they could continue to monitor her brain for a few more days, but all the signs were very positive for a full recovery.

"Jacob, I never really said how much I enjoyed meeting your parents," Ella noted. "Since I don't really have a family anymore, except for Parker that is, I hope I can develop a relationship with yours. I don't want us to get ahead of ourselves or put any pressure whatsoever on us taking it slowly as we discussed, but I am grateful how things seem to be unfolding. I mean, obviously I'm thankful that we both survived the accident, but the timing of everything else just seems so perfect. I know Papa would have seen the hand of Providence in all of this. Although, I suppose he might have referred to it as fate. He always seemed a bit confused between the two, you know, fate and God. He kind of faded from the church after Mama passed away. Anyway, whatever one chooses to call it, it is wonderful, and I'm very optimistic about the future … our future."

"Ella, speaking of your brother, I met with him earlier today. Actually, Nate and I both met with him. He wanted to talk about settling the lawsuit."

"Oh, that would be great, Jacob. No one wants that lawsuit to continue, and I know you, and I, have been trying to find a way to resolve it. Knowing my brother though, I'm sure there will be a catch, or maybe even two. What exactly did he propose?"

"To start with, he said we could share the water and the Pastures name as long as I changed the label art. As you know, I've been willing to do that all along, so that's not a problem," Jacob explained.

"That sounds pretty positive but, okay, so what's the catch?" Ella probed suspiciously. "Nothing is ever that simple with my brother. He's always angling for something that works to his advantage. He is so very shrewd that way -- shrewd as a serpent."

"You're right; there was one more thing. It involves you, actually. It's a pretty big ask, and, of course, I'll support whatever you decide."

"Me? How could I possibly be involved in settling the lawsuit?"

"Please hear me out before you go jumping to any conclusions, okay. I'm not advocating anything, but I think he may have some legitimate thoughts here." Jacob took a deep breath before continuing. "Parker wants to buy two percent of your interest in Pastures of Bounty, so he can manage and control the business. Now, I've talked it through with Nate, and we think there is a way we can structure things so you can both share in the control of the business at a macro level, but allow him to make the day to day decisions regarding the vineyard and the wine. He explained how he has always had a hand in the business and that you haven't really been directly involved. As I recall, you even expressed some hesitation to me about managing things when you first learned about your father's will.

"In exchange for your two percent, he will give all of the art and furnishings in the house to you. He estimates the value of his share of the art at over a million dollars. You might want to get a formal appraisal to confirm that number, but it sounds like that amount is probably in the ballpark based on what you've told me.

"So that's pretty much it in a nutshell. To be honest, Ella, it does make some sense, at least to me, and we'd be able to put the lawsuit behind us and move forward together, both personally and in business. And if this satisfies and calms Parker down, then it really could be the best of all worlds."

Ella looked deep into Jacob's eyes for any sign of reservation but saw none. "I hear what you're saying, and I understand it. I'll have to think about it for a while though. My biggest hesitation is the conflict with my father's will. He was very specific about me carrying the business forward. I don't think he trusted my brother, and honestly, I'm not sure I do yet either. I know it seems like he is coming around, but I've seen changes like this before, and they've always been short-lived. He usually has a secret agenda of some kind. As long as things go his way, everything is fine, but as soon as something goes sideways on him, even a little bit, he reverts to his old conniving self. I want to believe the best, really I do, but I've just been burned by him so many times in the past. We need to be very circumspect. But that said, I will think hard about it, Jacob. And your opinion is very important to me, perhaps more important than even my own. Thanks for meeting with Parker and working through the details of this with Nate. I am truly grateful.

"Now onto other, more important, things, did you notice I have your necklace back on?" Ella said lovingly. "It makes me feel special knowing the story behind it. You make me feel special. I think when I am released we should throw a party to celebrate our health and to celebrate our relationship. I can host an event at the Casa, and I'll invite my closest friends, many of whom you haven't even met yet. If we're going to be together, you may as well get to know my friends. I've lived here for a long time, so there will be many of them for you to meet. I know you'll love them, Jacob, and I know they'll love you!"

***

Romero's condition stabilized sufficiently to allow him to be transferred from the hospital in Tijuana to a more secure facility on the U.S. side of the border. He remained in intensive care but was slowly gaining enough strength to be able to speak with detectives. They quickly realized that Calderon was not smart enough to have planned the entire operation himself and the local sheriff had advised that he didn't completely buy into the jealousy theory they had been operating on.

"I think there has to be something more to this," lead investigator Jim Briggs suggested to his partner Pete August. "The whole murder attempt was pretty sophisticated, what with the micro IEDs and then the planning and forethought to have that go bag ready in the trunk with all that cash. A jealous lover acts more out of passion than premeditation, and this smells like premeditation to me."

"Yeah, I can see that," August responded, "but how are we going to get Calderon to snitch on whoever is behind this, assuming there is someone else? Do you have any theories or other leads we might pursue to develop a path we might take him down?"

"Maybe," Briggs replied. "I've been talking with the local Sheriff, and he's been nosing around back at the estate the girl was from and where Calderon worked. Her brother, Parker Gillette, was the fellow who tipped us off to Calderon in the first place. The Sheriff said he acted real cool about it and was very believable at the time. But the more I thought about it, the more I began to wonder. So I kept digging, and I think the brother had plenty of motive himself, even more than Calderon. The senior Gillette, their old man, died about a month ago and word is he left the controlling interest in the family wine business to the girl. She also recently started seeing the guy who was in the car with her that night, Jacob Wingate. The Wingate family is a big player in Napa, and this Jacob fellow recently moved to Carmel with the intent of making his own name in wine there. In other words, he would be a direct and major competitor of Parker Gillette."

"Hmm, sounds interesting." August said, rubbing the stubble on his chin, "go on."

"Well, then about a month ago Wingate filed a lawsuit against Gillette over some water right and trademark issues having to do with his winery.

363

He won the first battle in court, and Gillette got spanked pretty hard by the judge. That would make anybody angry and vengeful, and the word is that Parker Gillette has quite a temper. So, I think we should consider Gillette a person of interest and see what we might be able to coax out of Calderon."

"I like it. I'm in," said August. "Let's do it."

Six bullets had hit Romero during the firefight at the motel, two of them nearly fatal. If the Federales had not had an ambulance already on the scene, he would have bled out within minutes. Despite their less than stellar reputation, the Mexican hospital team did an admirable job patching Calderon up after the shooting and then keeping him alive for the next several days. The fates, as Armand Gillette would have called them, smiled on Romero Calderon, but in so doing, dealt a bad hand to his boss, Parker Gillette.

As soon as he regained consciousness, Romero asked to speak with the authorities. He was perplexed about how they found him so quickly and was suspicious that someone must have ratted on him. After racking his brain for hours, he concluded that the only person who could have possibly betrayed him was his friend and longtime employer. The dagger of that realization cut viciously, and the wounded man's anger seethed. Betrayal is what had landed him in prison the first time, and in that case, he never found out who was to blame. This time, however, he was sure he knew who the Judas was, and he was determined to make sure Gillette would never be able to spend any of his thirty pieces of silver. By the time Briggs and August arrived, Romero was ready to confess everything to exact retribution on his betrayer.

"So, yeah, my boss Parker Gillette, he's the one who ordered the hit on his sister. The fact that Wingate was in the car was kind of icing on the cake. A twofer, if you know what I mean," Romero said as he relayed the details of the story to the investigators.

"Parker suggested the IEDs and helped me get access to the SUV to plant them. He then helped me rent the Pontiac, he set up the dinner they were driving to in Big Sur, he prepared the go bag in the trunk, he ordered me to run to Mexico and lay low. He was behind everything. I was just the fall guy. We also did some other nasty stuff. About a month ago I killed Wingate's dog. Gillette then told me to drug Wingate and help shoot a racy video of Wingate with Gillette's own girlfriend, so that he could embarrass Wingate on the Internet. I've gotta hand it to him, Parker has a real mean streak, and he's good at exercising it. I sure wouldn't want to be on his bad side, but I guess I won't need to worry much about that now since I'll be going back to prison. Hey, if I'm lucky, maybe we'll be in the same cell block, and I can thank him personally ... real slowly."

Although not the most reliable witness, Briggs and August felt the information was sufficiently detailed and consistent with the time sequences that it warranted an arrest of Parker Gillette. They called the authorities in Monterey and began planning the takedown.

***

The following day Ella called Jacob and asked if he and Nate could meet her at the hospital. The two arrived late morning.

"Jacob, I've decided on the settlement proposal," Ella began. "Even though it makes sense on the surface and even seems fair, I just can't agree to it. I can't overrule my father's will in this. He and his forefathers have worked for over 70 years to make Pastures of Bounty what it is today. Papa was a brilliant man, even if he was a bit eccentric, and I always trusted his judgment completely. I know he loved me and would never give the instruction that Parker not run the business if he didn't have a very good reason to do so.

"I'm sorry, Jacob. I know this means the lawsuit will continue to drag on, but once the court papers are finalized regarding the estate, I should be the one you'll be dealing with on the legal issues relating to the business, and at that point, I will settle. We will share the water. We don't need Parker to resolve this. He won't have any control unless I give it to him and that I just can't do.

"I'm most sad to think that if my brother really has changed his heart, my decision may set that back, you know, cause him to revert to the old Parker again. That would be horrible, and I will hate myself, but I must honor Papa's wishes in this, even if it hurts my brother. I'm torn, I really am. I hope you can understand my decision."

"I do, Ella," Jacob responded. "I actually came to the same conclusion about eventually being able to settle with you at the helm. I trust your judgment in this. I'll have Nate call Parker later today and relay the news to him. I'm sure he'll be upset, but we'll hope he doesn't go off the deep end."

***

Parker had spent the evening and the better part of the morning honing his plan to gradually manipulate the business to marginalize Ella's interest even more and to eventually convince her to give up and leave. If he couldn't stop Wingate, he figured maybe he could at least dump his sister on him and make her his burden.

He toasted himself, in the privacy of his study at the Casa, for his performance over the past several days.

You know, Park, after you parlay your formidable skills into becoming a famous actor in Hollywood, maybe you should think seriously about going into politics.

The phone interrupted his private revelry.

"Parker, this is Nate Donohue."

"Donohue, I've been looking forward to your call. I've been conferring with Moncrief, and we have some finer points to add to the deal that I think you're going to like. We are hoping we can perhaps skip the MOU exercise and go straight to drafting the agreement. I'd like to get things in place soon, so I can begin planning for next year."

"Parker, uh, I'm sorry to be the bearer of bad news, but, well, Ella has decided to decline your proposal. She's not willing to part with control of the business. I think she may be open to defining some management role for you in the day to day operations, but concerning ultimate authority, she's not going to relinquish that."

A long pause ensued while Nate waited for a response. Finally, he spoke into the receiver, "Parker, are you still there?"

Nate had dealt with plenty of disappointed people before, it came with the territory, and he was fully prepared to engage in as much conversation as might be necessary to smooth over the news. Ella and Jacob had even authorized him to go into detail about possible alternative arrangements, and he had several pages of notes on his desk in front of him. But the response he received surprised even him.

In a voice that sounded more demonic than human Parker Gillette screamed a vulgar two-word curse at Nate and then abruptly hung up.

Nate called Jacob to relay the news.

"It went far worse than we thought it might," Nate reported. "He sounded possessed, Jacob, actually kind of scary … Yeah, he just swore at me and hung up. Not a single word other than the curse … I don't know what to think other than you should probably stay with Ella tonight, and the two of you should be on guard for a few days. I think the guy may be deranged. I mean, compared to the courteous manner we saw at lunch yesterday, he was like Stevenson's Dr. Jekyll and Mr. Hyde today. I'd be cautious. And if he does anything dangerous let me know, and we'll go straight to court and get a restraining order."

Back at the Casa, Parker raged. He took his anger out on the art pieces in the room that his father had given to Ella and began smashing them on the floor. He screamed and bellowed and ranted at the top of his lungs. He cursed the fates with every profanity he knew and then, raising his hands in the air as if praying, Parker called out audibly to Zeus to bestow upon him the power of Orion, the mighty huntsman that he might track down, and this time kill his prey.

***

With the additional information provided by Calderon, the police were able to trace the video upload he had mentioned back to a known associate of Parker Gillette's. It didn't take much persuasion to turn the lurid video distributor, and he confessed to the entire affair in return for a promise of leniency. Using Romero's phone data, they were also able to confirm calls made to him by Gillette at critical times including the evening before and then just after the accident in Big Sur and just before the SUV maintenance records had been remotely doctored to make it look like Romero's handling of the vehicle had been routine. Everything was coming together for the case against Gillette, and the authorities were confident they would be able to convict him of assault, fraud, and conspiracy to commit murder.

They had been monitoring the Casa for the past two days and knew Parker was inside when they called in the arrest team. They labeled Gillette both a flight risk and considered him armed and dangerous, so they took every precaution in preparing the raid.

They waited until the staff left and darkness had fallen to provide them with cover for the approach. The only light visible in the house was coming from a second-floor window on the east end of the building. Two officers covered the back door, one was positioned at the garage, and three were distributed about the portico area. Briggs, August, and the Sheriff comprised the final grouping, and they approached the front door together.

Briggs knocked loudly on the door.

An intercom voice calmly answered. "Yes?"

"This is special agent Briggs, and I'm here with the Sheriff. We are here to see Parker Gillette."

The intercom went silent. Parker quickly hurried to the window and peered out into the night. The moonlight gave away the positions of several of the officers as well as three vehicles parked on the driveway that didn't belong there. He next ran across the hall and snuck out onto the back balcony. Looking over the railing, he saw the team covering the back door. He returned to the study and pressed the intercom button for the second time.

"This is Parker Gillette; what can I do for you?"

"Mr. Gillette, we'd like to talk with you about your sister and your friend Romero Calderon. May we come in?"

Calderon! Parker thought to himself as panic began to rise. *Calderon is still alive. He must have spilled his guts to the cops.*

His mind went on another rampage of cursing, and he struggled mightily to regain his composure.

"I'll tear his heart out with my bare hands," he said aloud to himself.

Then speaking into the intercom, Parker said, "Uh, give me a minute Mr. Briggs. My staff is gone for the evening, and I just stepped out of the shower. I'll throw some clothes on and be right down. I hope everything is alright with my sister."

Parker used the time he bought with the shower excuse to open his gun safe and extract and load an automatic machine gun and a handgun. With the front and back doors covered, Parker realized he was trapped. Like the Tower of London, he was a prisoner in his own castle. His only chance to survive would be to hide and hope they would give up and conclude he had escaped through some secret passage. He had two choices, the attic or the wine cellar in the basement. In his state of panic the thought of being surrounded by wine was somehow comforting, so he headed downstairs.

After the second request for entry went unanswered, Briggs ordered the entry team to break down the door. Six men stormed the house interior as Briggs called out their entry and demanded the surrender of Parker Gillette.

The wine cellar was accessed via a secret passageway behind a hidden door that was cleverly concealed next to the fireplace in the main ground level living room. Parker sat quietly at the bottom of the secret staircase in the back corner of the wine cellar. The cellar was hewn out of the solid granite that underlay the Casa. Hundreds of bottles of Pastures of Bounty library wine as well as expensive bottles from other famous vineyards throughout the world lined the shelves. As he crouched down and waited in the darkest corner of the room Parker's idol curiosity got the best of him and, using the flashlight feature on his phone, he started reading the labels nearest him. The third bottle he pulled from the rack struck him as strangely, almost poetically, ironic. It was a 2006 Cabernet Sauvignon, and the label on the bottle read "Bountiful Pastures - Napa."

CHAPTER 20

The police swarmed the mansion, cleared every room on the ground floor level and then did the same on the second floor.

"The entire building is empty, Mr. Briggs," said the field officer in charge. "I don't know how, but somehow the perp must have escaped. Perhaps he had access to a secret passage or something. I don't understand it. Maybe we should get the blueprints of the building and come back."

"No, that will take too long, and this guy is a serious flight risk. Go through each room again, this time not to clear it but to look specifically for any kind of passage or door we might not have seen the first time. He has to be in here somewhere. Call for more backup, too, The more eyes we have to search this place the better," Briggs ordered.

The police combed through the house for an hour, examining each room for an access or closet that the suspect might be hiding in. Frustrated,

Briggs, August, and the team gathered in the main living room to consider their options.

"Alright, think! Come on; we have to be smarter than he is. If you lived in a giant mansion like this where would you hide?" August asked.

"Maybe an attic or a cellar?" one of the officers answered.

"Good. Jones, take two men with you and go upstairs and look for an attic access. Look for a pull-down door and check all the closets for possible ladder access. Matthews, you take a team and do the same here on the ground floor. Look for a cellar door, or maybe even a secret closet access. Knowing this guy, I wouldn't be surprised if they had some kind of moving panel door. Hey, wait they're wine people, right? Well, I haven't seen a wine cellar. They have to have a wine cellar somewhere. That has to be it! Go, go!"

Parker could hear the discussion at the top of the cellar stairs and knew it would only be a matter of time before they stumbled onto the panel door he was hiding behind. Resignation began to set in. What would happen if they captured him?

If Calderon told them everything they will certainly have enough evidence to convict me of several crimes and even with the best legal representation money can buy, I'm not going to get out of this. Maybe we can delay things with appeals. Maybe I can post bail and run to South America. But what if they freeze my assets? Maybe I can get rid of Romero before he can testify. But if I can't then I'll end up in prison. I'm not cut out for prison. I'm supposed to be the king of California wine not making license plates in Soledad.

His resignation gradually turned to depression and then finally to desperation. He continued to wait and listen. His hand began to ache from gripping the gun he was holding so tightly. His body tensed when he heard a voice call out from above, "Over here, look at this!"

Knocks on the wall began, and even he could hear the different tones between the solid walls and the false-wall door. The knocking became more focused on the door and then stopped. Parker strained his ears to hear the whispered conversation above him but couldn't make out the substance of what was being said.

"So this is it," he said to himself. He lifted the pistol and cocked the trigger. "Orion, I'm coming. Make a place for me, oh great huntsman."

"Here it is, I found it!" August called out. "Is everyone ready? I'm going to open it. He is probably armed so be careful."

The secret panel door slid open into a clever pocket in the wall. The granite steps leading down into the darkness were steep. August felt around for a light switch just inside the door and found one to the right. He crouched down with his service revolver drawn and ready. He reached up and flicked the switch. A dim overhead light flickered on. August pointed his handheld flashlight down into the cellar. At the bottom, he could make out racks of wine along the back wall and a small bistro table with two chairs. Still in a crouching position, he signaled the officers to follow behind him as he slowly moved down the steps. He felt his trigger finger itching as fear rose up within him.

August then called out, "Parker Gillette, we know you are down here. Please don't do anything foolish; there is no way out. We have more than a dozen armed officers surrounding the house. Drop whatever weapon you may have and come out into the light, slowly, hands first, palms up and open."

August paused and listened for a response, but heard nothing.

"Gillette, come out, or we'll be forced to come down and get you. Make this easy on yourself, man. We know what you've done. Calderon told us everything. Don't make things worse than they already are. I'll give you, to the count of five and then we're coming down."

August counted slowly and deliberately, "One, two, three ..."

A single shot rang out causing everyone to jump back. The echo filled the room.

***

The doctors at the hospital decided to release Ella a day early. Jacob drove over to assist her during the checkout procedure, and they then went out to a light dinner on the wharf in Monterey.

The crowd on the wharf was thick for a Thursday night. Many things on the Peninsula were still new to Jacob, and he was enjoying the energy and the hustle and bustle of all the tourists. As they walked about, he couldn't help but think of the business opportunities he might explore in the City when it came time to introduce his new wine label. Carmel was pretty saturated with tasting rooms, but oddly the tourist mecca of Monterey didn't seem to be. He had been told it was because the kind of tourist that visited Monterey didn't spend the kind of money the average visitor to Carmel did, but as he observed the people milling around the wharf, he had a hard time seeing the difference.

"Ella, did your father ever think about establishing a tasting room in Monterey, maybe down here on the wharf or somewhere nearby?" Jacob asked casually as they walked.

"Funny, you know, I asked him that same question about a year ago. He seemed excited by the idea, and I thought, for a while, he might give me the green light to pursue it. I thought it would be fun to go through the process of finding a space and then remodeling it and decorating it -- kind of like what you're going through planning your barn tasting room. I even spoke with a realtor, who started doing some research, but then the news of James' accident came. Papa's interest in everything came to a screeching halt. Then Parker started taking things over and, well, my idea kind of got pushed aside. I was too busy taking care of Papa to say anything, and so I just let it go."

"I wonder if perhaps we might think about a joint effort down here," Jacob continued. "You know, Pastures of Bounty and Bountiful Pastures - Carmel teaming up in a new tasting room. Maybe just call it Pastures. I think our wines complement each other, and we'd both stand to gain from some cross-marketing. It's the kind of idea I had wanted to talk to Parker about in the beginning, but he was never interested in anything I had to say. He was always just about him and how big a deal he thought he was in the wine world. I told him the secret of Napa's success was collaboration and that I thought the same could be true here, but he wouldn't listen. Maybe such an idea could be our first endeavor together ... anyway, just a thought. We can talk more about it later."

They tasted a few clam chowder samples as they strolled and eventually arrived at a restaurant near the end of the wharf that caught their eye. They sat outside waiting for a seat as the sun set over the bay. The squid boats began pulling out of the harbor for their nightly vigil on the sea and gradually the dark settled in. After dinner, during the walk back to the car, their conversation evolved to more immediate concerns.

"Do you think it's wise to spend the night at your house tonight? I mean, in light of what Nate said about Parker's reaction to your decision?" Jacob asked as they dropped a dollar in the open guitar case of the musician serenading the passers-by. "I don't think we need to be paranoid, just careful. You could always stay at my place. I've got a pullout couch that I can sleep on, and you could have the bedroom. Or, if you'd rather, I bet the Westons would be willing to put you up for a night or two."

"I appreciate your concern, Jacob, but I really don't think Parker would do anything rash. He might be belligerent toward me, but I'm sure it's safe to go home. If you want, you can stay in our guest room if you'd feel better about being around to protect me. Why don't we just go to the Casa and see where things stand. Parker may not even be home for all we know."

The couple held hands as they left the wharf and headed toward Jacob's car. Jacob opened the passenger door for Ella, but before she slipped into the car, he caught her up and held her close. The two stood together beside the car for a minute without speaking. Suddenly overcome by the moment, Jacob finally broke the silence.

"Ella, I've been … I've been holding everything in since the accident. I just need you to know how scared I was for you, and how glad I am that you are okay. I constantly prayed for your healing. I know this may sound a bit dramatic, but I can't imagine my life without you. Ella, I love you." Jacob's voice broke as the emotions he'd been holding back finally flooded to the surface.

"I love you, too," Ella responded quietly. "God has been gracious to us both, and I have great hope for our future together. It is so amazing how much life can change in such a short time. I could never have imagined two months ago that I would be standing here in the arms of a man I'd never met. You know, I'm convinced my father was wrong."

"Wrong, about what?"

"About the fates. All that has happened to us has not been fate. Only God could have brought this to pass."

***

As they slowed to pull off the highway and turn onto the country road leading into the Pastures, Jacob heard a siren. He looked into his rearview mirror and then veered over onto the right shoulder to let an ambulance race by.

"That's odd," Ella remarked. "I hope it's nobody we know."

Another mile down the road, when they rounded the final curve before the Casa, Ella exclaimed, "Jacob, look!" Ella pointed toward the house on the hill up to the left. "That ambulance was going to my house! Hurry, something must be terribly wrong."

As they turned off the road and began climbing the driveway up to the entrance gate, they were met by a sheriff's deputy waving a flashlight.

"Sorry, sir, but you'll have to turn around. This property has been sealed off as a crime scene."

"A what!" Ella protested as she leaned over from the passenger seat. "Officer, this is my house. I live here. My name is Gabriella Gillette. Please let us pass."

The man stepped back from the car and spoke into his handheld radio to relay the information he had just received. He listened intently and then returned to the vehicle.

"Okay, you folks can go on up, sorry for the trouble."

As they passed through the gate and got closer to the house, they were greeted by four patrol cars, two unmarked vehicles with portable lights on the top, a fire engine and two ambulances.

"Jacob, it looks like something dire has happened. But I don't see any smoke, and at this time of night the staff would all have gone home. The only person that could be here would be," she paused, "Parker! Oh no, Parker must be hurt!"

They both jumped out of the car as soon as it stopped and ran toward the house. Once inside the portico, they were again intercepted by a deputy.

"Ma'am, uh, Ms. Gillette, we need to ask you to stay out here for the time being. The officers in charge, Briggs and August, will be out shortly to talk with you."

"But what is wrong, just tell me! Is my brother alright?"

"Ma'am, please sit down, we'll have information in just a …"

"Thank you, deputy; we'll take it from here," Officer August interrupted. "Ms. Gillette, my name is Pete August, and this is my partner, Jim Briggs." Extending his hand to acknowledge Jacob's presence, Briggs offered, "And you must be Jacob Wingate."

"Yes, officer, uh, Briggs. That's right. Can you tell us what is going on here? This is Ms. Gillette's home."

"Yes, well, Ms. Gillette, we came to arrest your brother."

"Arrest him? For what?" Ella said her voice quickening.

"We had reason to believe he was ... I'm sorry, but this may come as quite a shock, maybe we should sit down here next to the fountain."

"No, officer, please tell me what you think my brother did!" Ella demanded.

"We believe he conspired with a man named Romero Calderon to ... to cause the car accident you two had in Big Sur last week."

"What? Parker was the one who tried to run us off the road? That's impossible. He would never do that. He's my brother."

"He didn't do it himself, ma'am; he hired Calderon to do it. We caught Calderon in Mexico, and he confessed to everything. We came here tonight to talk to your brother about it, but, well, he didn't cooperate. He barricaded himself with weapons in the wine cellar and when we ordered him to surrender, he ...," Briggs paused.

"He what!" Ella yelled. "He what! Where is my brother? I want to see him right now."

"Ms. Gillette, I'm sorry, but ...."

Before Briggs could finish his sentence, Ella's attention was diverted to the main door of the house. A medical team was rolling a stretcher out. The body on top of the apparatus was covered from head to toe with a blanket. Ella began to cry, and she fell into Jacob's arms.

"He shot himself, ma'am. I'm afraid your brother committed suicide. We are sorry for your loss."

***

For the second time in less than two months, Ella found herself standing beneath the ancient Cypress canopy at the El Carmelo Cemetery. The weather was not so cooperative this time, and a heavy drizzle was falling. Unlike her father's funeral, today less than two dozen people were in attendance. The news had spread, and most of Parker's shallow friends were quick to abandon him and his memory as soon as they learned the details of his passing.

In the weeks following his death, the police shared with Ella all the information they had gathered about the conspiracies and Parker's role in everything. As troubling as it all was, the report was strangely satisfying in the way it answered so many of the questions Ella, Jacob, and the others had been struggling with.

Despite learning all the details, Ella had decided Parker should still be laid to rest in the family plot. Deep down she hoped that perhaps, somehow, he might still find peace and reconciliation in the next world. She instructed, however, that his marker be a small, plain stone. On it, she had inscribed the minimum information: name and the dates of birth and death. The only other marking, on the upper right-hand corner of the grayish stone, was a simple representation of her brother's favorite constellation ... Orion the Huntsman.

Jacob held an umbrella over Ella with his right hand and awkwardly draped his casted left arm over her shoulder. Nate and Cassie were also among those in attendance. The four huddled close together against the stiff breeze that was blowing. Following the priest's final words, which in truth offered little comfort, the foursome withdrew to the black limousine that awaited them and returned directly to Casa de Abundante. During the drive home, the drizzle progressed to a full-fledged rain.

Once inside the house, Shelby served the group tea and pastries in the library. Ella walked over to the balcony window and stared blankly into the drab, cloud-filled sky. The others gathered together to share the warmth of the crackling fire in the fireplace and allowed her to have a quiet moment alone with her thoughts.

Papa, I'm so sorry about Parker, Ella prayed silently. *I know how excited you were to see James again, but I'm sure you didn't expect Parker to join you so soon, if he is even in heaven? I honestly don't understand what possessed our brother to do the things he did. I'm sure it was no reflection on you or Mama. I promise, with time, I will find it in my heart to forgive him. I hope you will, too. He was a troubled soul. He condemned himself, declared his sentence and carried out his own execution. I don't think he needs any further condemnation; now I think he needs love.*

Papa, I am alone now to care for your legacy. Please pray for me, will you? I know you believed in me, and I promise I will do my best to fulfill your dreams. I think I may have the right partner in Jacob. He will be a partner in business and hopefully one in life as well. I love him very much, Papa. I'm so glad you were able to meet him and approve. He is a wonderful man, and I feel blessed to have him in my life.

Say hello to Mama and James for me ... and to Parker, if you see him.

Ella stopped, closed her eyes and stood quietly. She opened the sliding door and let the cold wind blow through her and into the room. She spread her arms and took a deep breath. Refreshed, she then opened her eyes and smiled as she surveyed the gray ensconced Pastures before her.

***

The sun shone gently on the vineyards of the Pastures. The ladybugs released the week before were flitting from vine to vine doing their work to protect the emerging fruit from pests. The roots of the plants were enjoying refreshment from the fresh spring water that soaked down into the earth to give them respite from the dryness of summer, and the rose bushes at the end of each vine row were in brilliant bloom. The barbed wire fence that had once separated the Pastures of Bounty and the Bountiful Pastures was gone. The fully restored Granger farmhouse was now the residence of Mr. and Mrs. Nate and Cassie Donohue and the fully restored old green barn was a successful tasting room that thrived with visitors coming to enjoy the renaissance of Carmel Valley. The locals in the valley were all abuzz with excitement over the nuptials planned for the afternoon.

"Nate, I can't believe today is finally here," Jacob sighed aloud to his best man. It seems like forever ago that we all sat in this very room and talked about what the future might hold for us. Can you remember that afternoon? It was cold and raining, and we had just buried Parker. So much has transpired this past year, yet so much remains in front of us. Your role in bringing us to this place has been critical, my friend. Thank you, again, and thank you for standing up for me today. I know I have no reason to be nervous, but I am."

"Jacob, truthfully I should be thanking you," Nate responded. "Never in a million years would I have expected to be married right now, let alone to Cassie. And the fact that she is now working with me as a paralegal, and we are living in the Pastures is just, well, it is more than my wildest dream. And our friendship is the best. But, you know, mostly I'm happiest for you and Ella.

"We should probably be leaving pretty soon. It's a long drive to the ceremony venue at Point Sur, and we certainly don't want to be late to your wedding!"

***

The morning marine layer had lifted, and the breeze was uncommonly calm. The surf below crashed rhythmically as it rolled up and back on the beach and the sea in the distance glimmered in the afternoon sun. Twelve rows of white wooden folding chairs anointed the northern end of the bluff just below the grand lighthouse beacon. Jacob and Ella stood together underneath an arbor draped in freshly cut wisteria.

"Welcome friends and family to this wonderful celebration of love and covenant," the pastor said. "Please be seated. Jacob and Ella selected this unique venue for their wedding because this place is where Ella's parents celebrated a renewing of their vows on their 15th anniversary. As I have spent time with these two, I have come to learn that they are both hopeless romantics. Ella tells me that her love of romance and poetry comes from her father, Armand, and I think Jacob's comes from, well, I think his inspiration must come from Ella. I mean, who wouldn't be inspired by such a beautiful bride -- both inside and out.

"In addition to the uniting of these two wonderful people today, we are also witnessing the union of two families who represent the best of California wine. The bible is full of imagery regarding vineyards and wine. Jesus' first miracle was, of course, to turn water into wine at, of all places, a wedding. He also taught many lessons using the vineyard as his example. As we all know, the vineyard, like life, is not without its difficult times.

The soil can sometimes be rocky, and drought can cause the vines to struggle. Pruning must take place and sometimes there is loss, but it is that process of struggle which leads to character in the fruit and makes the vines grow deep and strong. Jacob and Ella have seen their share of adverse days, but through them, they have emerged stronger together. As a result, today they, and we, can have great hope for their future. Indeed, it is fitting that today they should become one flesh as they have already become one in winemaking by merging their vineyards. Their endeavor will undoubtedly bless our community for many years to come.

"Please join with me in a prayer for these two beautiful souls who are today becoming one."

Following the prayer and vows, the pastor stepped away, and Jacob and Ella moved through the arbor to a small table that had been set up behind it and shared a quiet moment of reflection and promise. The two then took communion together following which Jacob held up a crystal goblet of dark red wine and Ella held up one filled with white wine. They kissed and poured their goblets into a single larger one on the table to symbolize the merging of their lives into oneness. Following the private moment, the two stepped back through the arbor and faced the small group that had come to celebrate with them. Jacob held the unity cup up to let the sunshine through the dramatic pink colored liquid they had created.

"Ella and I want to thank you all for joining us today," Jacob began. "Our journey to this place has been, well, let's just say, interesting, and maybe a little miraculous," he paused and smiled at Ella. "We know going forward we're going to need each and every one of you by our sides. Your friendship and support has been and will continue to be what keeps us strong. Please, beneath each of your seats you will find a small bottle of wine and a glass. Fill your glasses and join us in a toast."

The two waited for a moment as each guest did as instructed and then everyone stood holding their glasses up against the pure blue of the Pacific sky. The wine had a soft pinkish hue and smelled of plumeria and pear. Whispers of praise circulated as the guests sniffed at the offering.

"Ella, why don't you do the honors," Jacob said.

"Friends and family, this toast is to you -- for being here for us and for loving us. The blush wine in our unity cup is intended to represent the blending of our two lives and our two families' legacies. We thought it fitting to celebrate our wedding with wine, as Jesus did at Cana. The wine you are about to drink is from the first barrel of our future flagship Rosé from our newly established Carmel Valley winery which we are going to call 'Pastures.' In honor of how we came to this place today, the wine will be called, Providence."

As the outdoor reception was winding down, Ella sought out a private moment with Jacob, Nate, and Cassie. "You three, you are my future now," she began. "The past has been so incredibly painful, but all of that is behind us now. You have all been like a moonrise to me. I remember the first thing Jacob ever said to me was that a moonrise is a promise of light in the darkness. Thank you for helping me through the darkness, and now, together, we can look forward to the sunrise of a new dawn.

"Ha," she stopped herself and laughed mid-sentence, "listen to me, I'm beginning to sound a lot like my father, the old romantic poet. I guess the apple never falls too far from the tree." Then, winking at Jacob, she quipped, "Well ... maybe, in this case, it's the grape that didn't fall too far from the vine."

THE END

I hope you enjoyed reading my story as much as I did writing it! If you did enjoy the story, I would appreciate it if you would please take a moment to leave a review/rating on Amazon.com to let others know.

search: johnsterlingbridges

Thank you and God bless!

A little about the author -- John lives in the Monterey Bay area of California's central coast. He is a retired attorney who has been writing novels since 2018, and, to date, has published a dozen-plus books. Writers are often counseled to "write about what they know," so John's books weave together themes revolving around adventure, suspense, mystery, the law, romance, faith, and always "place." When not writing and publishing his books, John is busy traveling and adventuring with his wife, Lorrie, hunting lighthouses (and volunteering as a docent at the one near his home), tending to his rose garden, walking his dog along the Pacific coastline, and enjoying his "Grands" (a.k.a his seven grandkids). You can chat with him at sterling.granddad@gmail.com

OTHER BOOKS BY JOHN STERLING BRIDGES

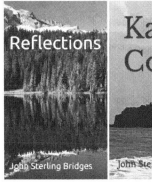

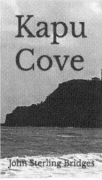

403

Made in the USA
Columbia, SC
15 February 2024

31695378R00220